Alois Essigmann
Sagen und Märchen Altindiens

SEVERUS Verlag

ISBN: 978-3-95801-695-8
Druck: SEVERUS Verlag, 2017

Satz und Lektorat: Christine Frieling

Der SEVERUS Verlag ist ein Imprint der Diplomica Verlag GmbH.
Bibliografische Information der Deutschen Nationalbibliothek:
Die Deutsche Nationalbibliothek verzeichnet diese Publikation in der
Deutschen Nationalbibliografie; detaillierte bibliografische Daten
sind im Internet über http://dnb.d-nb.de abrufbar.

Amy's Choice

A More Perfect Union Series Book 2

Betty Bolté

Chapter One

Charles Town, South Carolina – 1782

"I must say, I hope we can relax and enjoy the festivities." Samantha McAlester tried but failed to release the tension building between her shoulders. As night descended upon the garden, she cringed as barks of laughter interspersed the hum of the party guests' conversation, increasing in volume along with the flow of wine and ales. Before long, Trent would arrive, and then what would she do? How could she tolerate his presence after his disdain the last time?

"I find it hard to fathom the danger you and Amy faced last week." Emily Sullivan tugged her shawl around her shoulders to ward off the late November chill. She swiveled to look at Samantha, her long skirts rustling with the movement. "If Benjamin hadn't caught up with you, and then Walter hadn't stepped in to sacrifice his own life to save all of us, I don't know what we'd have done."

"That's all in the past, Em. Do not dwell on the matter." The horrifying sound of gun shots around the manor house

1

surely would echo in her mind in a similar manner as to other shots and shouts she'd experienced over the past several years. Walter had vowed to die defending his home, and he kept his word. Emily's cousin, Evelyn, had lost her husband but gained her freedom from his overbearing nature. "No good can come from reliving that awful day. Let us close the book on those events."

Emily shrugged and let her gaze drift over the garden. "You're probably right, but it's hard to ignore the sobs from poor Evelyn up in your spare room. Besides, planning a double wedding with such sadness hanging in the air might be considered disrespectful. What do you think?"

"I think you and Amy have the right to marry your betrotheds. And moreover, this town needs the happy event after the terror and uncertainty we've endured under the British occupation." Standing beneath the peaked roof of the white-washed gazebo, which was draped in dormant climbing rose vines, Samantha hesitated to follow two of her closest friends as they made their way toward the cluster of guests.

Emily's white teeth flashed as she chuckled. "I never thought I could be as happy as I am in preparing to marry Frank."

"The idea of holding the wedding at the end of the holidays is brilliant." Samantha couldn't prevent a smile from easing onto her lips. "Everyone will already be in a festive mood and gathered in town to be with family and friends."

Emily bobbed her head and then indicated the pair moving away from them. "They appear to be as besotted with each other as Frank and I."

Amy Abernathy and Benjamin Hanson ambled away from her, arm in arm down the crushed seashell and pea gravel path toward tables laden with a variety of meats and sweets. So much had happened over the past year, month,

Also by Betty Bolté

Becoming Lady Washington: A Novel
Notes of Love and War

FURY FALLS INN
The Haunting of Fury Falls Inn
Under Lock and Key

A MORE PERFECT UNION SERIES
Elizabeth's Hope
Emily's Vow
Amy's Choice
Samantha's Secret
Evelyn's Promise

SECRETS OF ROSEVILLE SERIES
Undying Love
Haunted Melody
The Touchstone of Raven Hollow
Veiled Visions of Love
Charmed Against All Odds

Preface

Emily's Vow is the first historical romance I ever published and as such it was written many years ago as I was a new author. It's amazing how much my storytelling skills have improved over the past six to eight years. The core of the story remains the same, but hopefully with more skilled telling. This edition is a revised and expanded version of the first book in the A More Perfect union historical romance series. I have added some new scenes and corrected and revised the text throughout the story.

Thanks for reading!

Chapter One

Charles Town, South Carolina – 1782

"Why must Frank be coming back to town now?" Emily Sullivan shivered. If asked, she would blame the autumn evening breeze blowing inland across the Charles Town harbor for her reaction. How dare he even show his face? Why was he pretending to be a loyalist? For his own profit or was he a spy? Either way, she'd have naught to do with the man. "Father's plan may solve one problem but it will cause more for me."

"I'm sure he thinks he is doing what is best for you." Samantha McAlester matched her stride for stride as they continued down the street.

"Perhaps, but I don't agree that marriage is necessary." Emily's long skirts swirled about her hurried steps. "I'm glad you wanted to walk with me, Samantha. It's nicer than traversing the distance home from Aunt Lucille's house with my servants."

"Together we'll be safe enough for such a short walk," Samantha McAlester replied, "though I doubt your father will agree, given his recent demand that you remain at home."

"It's my fault we left the sewing circle later than I intended, but I miss St. Michael's bells chiming the hour. What shall we do without them? The British should pay dearly for stripping our treasured bells from the steeple."

"Come, let's get you home and off the streets." Samantha quickened her pace.

Emily hurried down the sandy road beside her friend, noting the waning sunshine draping shadows across the street. The slap of the waves at the distant convergence of the Cooper and Ashley Rivers beat a syncopated rhythm against the array of ship hulls, large and small, in the protected harbor. Many of the masts bobbing against the darkening sky sported the hated British flag. The losing army had resorted to sanctioned looting of the beautiful homes—those still standing after two years of British occupation as well as fires and bombardments—as booty for the officers and soldiers before they withdrew.

The British officers sought retaliation for the threat posed by the patriots, who had hidden their true allegiance, against the loyalists living in the city. The officers encouraged harassment of the Americans, which translated into her father, a leading merchant in town, fearing for her safety. She'd walked alone throughout the occupation, so why did he suddenly want her to stay at home?

Dragging in a deep breath, unease settled over Emily's frayed nerves at the thought of Frank's return. "I cannot believe Father insists I marry him after all that man has done. Surely Americans have matured enough they wouldn't force a woman to marry. I'm not a child. Why doesn't he understand?"

A seagull glided past, its laughing call bringing a smile to her face. Her enjoyment didn't last long, though. The occupation of the town created fear and disquiet throughout the citizenry. Add in the horror of her sister Elizabeth's fiancé Jedediah dying, leaving her pregnant and in need of a husband. Then Jedediah's brother Frank, the man Emily had always cared for, married her sister to keep the child from being a bastard. Emily survived the misery of watching Frank marry Elizabeth, struggling to understand as her heart broke. Only to suffer much more when Elizabeth died in childbirth with Frank away at war. Emily had come to terms with the prospect of raising her nephew, but being forced into marriage with Frank, too? After he'd betrayed her by marrying her sister. Life turned and twisted with disregard for her future goals and plans.

Frank's imminent arrival now distressed her as much as the three hundred British ships crowding the harbor. The rumor about town suggested the ships stood poised to carry away the defeated enemy troops along with any loyalists wanting to flee the town. Many slaves would likely take the chance on freedom offered by the British, despite the American protests.

"Have you told your father how you feel?" Samantha matched Emily's stride easily despite her slight limp and the basket she carried.

Sharing her feelings with her father had once enjoyed an easy place in Emily's heart. Now his demands for her to cloister within the theoretic safety of the town house, joined with his desire that she marry to secure her future, made confiding in him difficult. His concern stemmed from her advancing age and the few prospects for marriage with able-bodied men away fighting an overbearing mother country. She longed for those carefree days, years before, filled with friendly banter and heartfelt discussions with her father.

Emily wrinkled her nose. "I haven't spoken with him, not that I think he'll care. He's more concerned with my supposed need for a protector while he's away." What a pickle. Did he have to choose Frank to serve as both bodyguard and suitor?

The thought created ripples of fear along her spine. Marrying a man, any man, meant losing her individuality, a fate she dreaded. The vows included obeying and honoring him, which translated into having his children. She shivered, recalling her twin sister on her deathbed mere days after delivering her son. Emily had held her hand as Elizabeth's life departed, her fingers falling limp within Emily's clutching grasp. Just like their mother before.

So many young women across the country feared pregnancy and being brought to bed for that very reason. Elizabeth, like many of those women, had written out her will when she discovered she carried a child. At least the document detailed her wishes for her son. And her surrogate husband, Frank Thomson. Elizabeth was to wed Jedediah, the betrothal announced and celebrated, before Elizabeth revealed she was with child. If Jedediah hadn't been killed, Frank would not have felt obligated to do his duty as Jedediah's brother to wed Elizabeth and give the unborn child a father.

Emily used to think of him as *her* Frank, until he told her his decision to wed Elizabeth. Her heart had hurt for months as she tried to accept the reality that she could never have him. But once Elizabeth died in similar circumstances as their mother, Emily's fear of dying as a result of childbirth eclipsed any naive desire to marry.

No, better to pursue her dreams of opening her ladies' accessories shop. She squared her shoulders, ready to face the astonishment of the ladies in town as well as plan a strategy for the battle when her father voiced his objections.

Lost in thought, Emily slowed involuntarily as Samantha paused in front of the empty bakery, its door shut tight. Next door, the printing office boasted the glow of lanterns through the windows, signaling someone working to prepare the British broadside for the morrow. Emily turned her attention back to the vacant bakery. She loved the little building so full of wonderful memories. Signs posted in the two plate-glass windows flanking the front door vainly tempted passersby with blueberry or cranberry muffins, apple pie, or pumpkin bread. She inhaled expectantly. Tears smarted her eyes when she smelled only sea salt and wood fires.

"I cannot believe they actually hanged the poor Widow Murray." A gust of wind snagged a few strands of Samantha's ink-black hair, tugging them free from the casually wound bun nestled inside her bonnet. She tucked the strays behind one ear and glanced at Emily.

"It is not surprising, when you consider her penchant for gossip, now is it?" Emily stopped also. The stooped woman had delighted in sharing titillating chitchat while Emily selected her two loaves of bread. Mischievous, she was, cackling over another's indiscretion. The woman refused to be circumspect, saying more than acceptable once too many times. But to be hanged as a spy? The foul Britons had no respect for American ladies.

The darkened shop sat cold and lonely compared to the once-bustling business. A chill skated down Emily's spine. She hugged herself. The Widow Murray had survived the death of her husband at the fight for Stono Ferry in June of 1779, and her bakery served as a popular early morning and late afternoon stop for the townspeople, until the British invaded Charles Town in May 1780. Then everything changed.

Sadness mixed with anger settled in the pit of her stomach. She missed her brothers, off fighting with the militia, but at least their efforts yielded the nearing peace. "And to think, she stopped three deadly attacks on our boys just by sharing with my father what she heard."

Samantha shrugged. "Yes, but it still makes me sad."

"Her little shop feels so abandoned." Emily squinted at the store, assessing its size and features.

The quaint store sat along a normally busy thoroughfare that would provide plenty of customers after peace returned. But first, she had to find the right moment to share her intentions, starting with her cousin Amy Abernathy and Samantha. Amy was her strongest ally and thus the perfect person to stand with her.

Second, find a way to tell her father. After all, her new resolve to take care of herself unfortunately still required his assistance to secure the shop, given contracts were men's domain. Convincing her father she meant to conduct business on her own presented a nearly insurmountable challenge, but she would find a way to do so. Then she'd have to share her plans with the ladies in the sewing circle in order to garner their support of her efforts.

She envisioned mannequins within the cool dimness behind

the glass panes, displaying embroidered dresses, shoes, slippers, and gloves. She pictured herself waiting on customers, sweeping up scraps of floss and fabric from her sewing, keeping the windows shiny clean.

Peering at the empty building, she sighed. The stone and wood-plank structure invited passersby through its half-glass door. Large glass windows would allow the sunlight to filter inside, illuminating the interior in a way that made Emily smile with pleasure. She wanted to set up shop immediately. Her father would resist allowing her to do such a daring thing, citing society's expectations of women. Marriage, children, housework. No mention of a proper education nor avenues to personal achievement in the merchant world. Her father's stature in the community dictated her options, limited such as they were. She wanted more than a clean house and a productive garden from life. Somehow, she must persuade him to see reason.

With a long last look, Emily turned away from the temptation of the store. "We must go. I don't want my father to catch me here, and we're very late as it is."

Few other people ventured onto the street as darkness crept closer and the stars began to wink above. A lone wagon lumbered by, pulled by a dapple-gray draft horse, its ribs clearly visible in the evening light. Emily's heart went out to the beast. Even the horses suffered from want of adequate food, much like the townspeople. The prices of food and wares had increased a thousand percent since the onset of the war. The Continental Congress embargoed staples such as rice, indigo, corn, beef, and pork to ensure the American armies had provisions. If it weren't for her father ignoring those embargoes and continuing to export rice and indigo to the West Indies and France, they too would suffer financial distress. He also imported goods for sale in town, enabling them to continue to purchase food despite the exorbitant cost.

In years past, Charles Town had bustled at this time of day. The town's women would have been chatting together while strolling to the marketplace, once replete with a variety of foods and wares. The men engaged in heated discussions on their way to McCrady's Tavern for a pint after a day spent at the Exchange conducting business. Wagons and carriages rumbled along to the steady rhythm of horses' hooves, creating puffs of dust to drift up and settle on the long skirts and pants of those on the street. All under the watchful eyes of the seagulls soaring overhead.

Danger patrolled the streets in the form of British soldiers searching for anyone who dared be a patriot within the town limits. Those who had not signed the loyalty oath to King George's dictatorial ways were either run out of town, their property confiscated, or imprisoned on the ships at anchor in the harbor.

Samantha gripped the basket's arched handle with both hands and shrugged. "Your father will chastise us no matter, so what's the point?"

"At least I can honor his request by being home before night completely falls. He objects to me being on the street, but my skills are needed. The cloth and shirts we're sewing will make our soldiers' lives a little more bearable. Perhaps even one of my brothers will receive comfort, wherever they are now." A seagull swooped onto the street in front of Emily, and she shooed it away with her skirts. Looking down the shadowy lane, she tensed. "Fiddlesticks, I'd hoped to avoid this."

Two British soldiers, replete in crimson coats boasting dark blue facings and white breeches, ambled up the street, their rifles slung over their shoulders, bayonets sheathed. The two men saluted a third—a loyalist officer, by the hated dark blue coat faced with white and the crossed white straps—as they neared him on the opposite side of the road. To her mind, loyalists were worse than the British regulars because they chose a distant, controlling king over their friends and, in many cases, their own families.

"Quick, while they are busy." Samantha pulled her bonnet closer around her face, though she kept an eye on the men. "Perhaps they won't notice."

Emily's heart sank. She'd gone and done it now. Her father would skin her like a rabbit if she landed in trouble. Again. Try as much as she did, she seemed to invite mischief. She furtively watched the men engage in a brief exchange. Solidly built, they stood as tall as young saplings, their broadcloth uniforms stretched taut over massive chests. One soldier winked at her with a slow, hungry leer as they approached. She lowered her head so the bonnet shaded her face but still allowed her to watch their actions. "I fear it's too late."

She glanced at the men, the lanterns they carried casting wavering light across their features, alarm sparking inside her at the hungry amusement on their faces. She grabbed Samantha's arm and started down the sandy road. Her heart beat a staccato rhythm when the men neared, intercepting the two women on the nearly deserted street. As the soldiers drew to a halt in front of them, a low, menacing chuckle from the taller of the men sent terror snaking down her back.

"Now, now, ladies, don't be in such a hurry," the first soldier said, blocking her path.

He reached out to tug loose a string from her tea-colored bonnet, her last decent one. She'd pulled it from her mother's trunk, forced to use even those last remaining articles of clothing. The filth. Bad enough they were British. Emily recoiled, gagging at the odor of sweat and tobacco. She swatted his hand away. The major—from the insignia she could now see far too closely—approached them. Something in his eyes, glittering beneath his hat, tugged at her memory. She dared not investigate more for fear he'd misinterpret her look as one of interest. She glanced away but kept an ear on the soldiers' movements.

"They just want to have some fun," he said, his voice sharp as he stepped closer. "Where is your father, Miss Sullivan? Surely he didn't allow you to venture out alone?"

"He's awaiting my return, if you'll permit me to pass." Emily made to continue on her way, but the officer raised a hand, stilling her movement.

even week, she couldn't imagine what more awaited in the near future as the fight for America's independence from British rule finally ended in victory. One thing remained certain: all the dueling and fighting, the anxiety and terror, her friends had endured since the beginning of the occupation had been relegated to the past. As the Britons prepared to evacuate, she and her compatriots could all look to the future and plan for a better world. Mostly, in the event. Her heart sunk at the thought of Trent's imminent arrival and his disdain of her methods.

From where Samantha stood at the very back corner of the property, she could see over the heads of her guests as they wandered through the unusually large and diverse garden. Winding paths crisscrossed the area, providing easy access to the variety of flowers, vegetable and herbal plants, and bushes. Several tall oaks and cypress lent shade in the summer heat as well as ingredients for her simples and poultices. She drew in a deep breath of crisp fall air along with the sense of peace only this space evoked. As long as her parents owned the sizeable property, she'd be content with life.

They'd spent years designing and creating the perfect medicinal garden, containing every kind of beneficial plant that would grow in the hot and humid southern climate. Surely they'd never move. Not after all their hard work and expense. But with the tensions in town targeted at those who sympathized with the British, the future for her family remained unclear, like the harbor on a foggy morning. What if they were forced out by the British? Or someone else? The South Carolina government had initiated a list of known loyalists whose property was subject to confiscation as the British withdrew. Had her father's loyalties become too flagrant in recent months? She pressed a hand to her waist, trying to quell the turmoil within. What would she do without her garden and charming home? Indeed, without her loving yet stubborn parents?

The gazebo had provided a shady space for numerous tea parties with her dear friends over the last year. Of course, the tea came from plants within the garden or from other countries. As long as it was not imported from Britain or any of its territories she'd consume it. They'd shared many a strong opinion on the war and the depredations on both sides. The soldiers took advantage of the women, children, and property in the absence of husbands, brothers, and fathers. With peace on the horizon, the fog of the future could begin to lift the uncertainties of life in the past.

Now, while she and Emily watched in quiet happiness, Benjamin escorted Amy down the path, newly betrothed to each other as of mere minutes ago, his hand possessing hers where it lay on his arm. On top of Benjamin's skirmish with renegade loyalists a week before that had resulted in his right arm in a sling from a gunshot wound to his shoulder, his slightly bowed carriage hinted at the pain which plagued him. She'd mix up some more simples for him to take home after the feast. And definitely she'd keep a close watch on his condition. Not only would she do all within her power to heal her friend, but her reputation as a healer remained at stake, especially since young and ambitious Dr. Trent Cunningham had arrived in town.

"They're so perfect for each other." Emily smoothed a wrinkle from one elbow-length white glove. "Who could have guessed she and I would be betrothed to such handsome men so soon after our joint vow."

"Who indeed." Samantha tossed her head, her ebony locks settling between her shoulders.

So much had changed in such a short period of time. Last month, the three friends had made a vow to remain unmarried. Each woman choosing their own independence rather than rely upon the whim and largess of a man. They'd agreed the vows could be broken only if the woman desired to do so, not by force or compulsion. Now, both Amy and Emily chose to follow their hearts and were making wedding plans for the biggest event of the holiday season, a joint affair on Twelfth Night.

"At least you have managed to stay faithful to your promise." Emily's porcelain cheeks reflected the soft light from the many hanging lamps decorating the edges of the gazebo. "And if Frank hadn't protected my reputation in that scary duel, I'd never have let him persuade me of his affection."

"I won't mention such an act in my comments later. He might have died for you, you understand, right?" Samantha sniffled. Pondering Frank's close call reminded her of other similarly dangerous situations. Ones so painful to recall she hadn't shared them with anyone and probably never would. She slipped the perfumed kerchief from her sleeve to dab at her nose, and relished the scent of lavender floating on the night air. The crowd mingled in the open spaces between the variously colored bushes and plants and strolled the many winding paths through the garden. "Frank truly loves you and will always protect you. Speaking of whom, someone appears to be seeking you out."

Emily's smile widened when she spotted Frank Thomson walking toward her. "It's about time for your speech, so I'll go and…"

"Right. You two should find a good place to watch." Samantha chortled and shooed her friend toward the tall blond striding purposefully toward where the ladies conversed.

Frank reached Emily's side, taking her hand in his with a smile, a nod of greeting to Samantha. Emily had once vehemently declared she would never marry. Samantha permitted her lips to curve into a smile, having anticipated the two cousins would succumb to the desires of the men accompanying them. She may not know everything, but she did know how to interpret a woman's behavior and thus descry their next actions. In the event, her friends would succumb to the attentions and intentions of Benjamin and Frank.

The guests mingling about the garden included all of her family and her friends, the new lawyer, George Manning and his wife Catherine, as well as a few artisans she'd not been introduced to yet. The invitation list had not changed much over the years, adhering to her parents' desire to include a balanced mix of political views. Her father's attempt to appease both camps; one she feared may have failed. Her parents had held a harvest feast each November for the past ten years, war or no war. This garden, packed with medicinal herbs and flowers, soothed her chaotic thoughts and emotions. Mingled scents of jasmine and rosemary tickled the noses of the throng of guests. Her father had bowed to her midwife mother's demands to forego the typical decorative garden most residents had surrounding their two-story homes and open piazzas. Instead, they created an extravagant oasis of flowers, bushes, and trees. She pulled her silver shawl around her shoulders, her midnight blue skirts swishing against the wooden floor of the gazebo when she pivoted to peruse the happy group milling amongst the multitude of plants she could identify by name and purpose. Her mother had ensured Samantha would be well prepared to follow in her calling as a healer and midwife. A purpose her father also endorsed and supported in every way within his significant means.

Her friends had chosen to marry, leaving her to carry on alone in this vow of staying unmarried. Her decision rested upon her desire to never again subject her heart to the anguish of watching a loved one die. The cries and groans. The blood. The agony. Once was definitely more than enough for her to bear. A sigh wiggled from her pressed lips before she could subdue it. She squared her shoulders, her gown soft against her skin. The past had no bearing on her plans for the future.

Points of light emerged overhead to surround the crescent moon hanging in the sky. The heavenly stars beckoned, guiding her healing endeavors as much as her day-to-day activities. She glanced to the dark bedroom window, imagining Amy's sister, Evelyn, sequestered and tearful over the death of her little boy's father. The horrific images flashed across her mind, but she pushed them aside. Just as she'd shoved aside the memory of the bloody field of battle the year before. One day at a time. How else could she cope with everything? Her focus must stay on helping her patients, her friends, as best she could. Tomorrow would be soon enough to discuss the widow's plans.

Tonight, Samantha intended to enjoy a respite from the tension and horror of the occupied town and the rampant violence across the countryside. Fortunately, no recent tar-and-feathering patients had landed at her door. The vengeance of the patriots against the loyalists continued, maybe even increased, with each passing day. For one night, she hoped the townspeople would join together. Her neighbors, her friends, fellow citizens all without regard to political leaning, had gathered to celebrate as they did every year, even though the repast was meager compared to what they enjoyed before the war and the British occupation of Charles Town. She shook off the weight of sadness, determined to focus on the approaching evacuation by the Britons, as soon as the unusually active hurricane season ended and they could safely navigate out of the treacherous harbor.

A strange blend of horror and hope pervaded both days and nights. Only a week ago, the three friends barely escaped with their lives when renegade loyalists attacked Evelyn's home. Tonight, a celebration of the culmination of the harvest. She would not perjure herself and say she'd miss Walter, not after his abuse and, she suspected, attempted poisoning of Evelyn. The stomach cramps and pangs Evelyn had agonized through completely vanished as soon as Emily assumed responsibility for the cooking at the country manor. Walter only reluctantly permitted the three ladies to invade his dwelling to provide care for his wife during her travails and lying in. He had declared he would die protecting his property. And so he did. Dying in such a manner did not equate to making him a hero in her eyes. Again, that chapter had ended and the book closed on the past events.

It was time to move on. She eased down the steps, bracing herself on the hand rail to prevent her injured leg from failing her. Despite her best efforts, the limb was not as strong as she'd like. She had to maintain her dignity, which did not include falling down among her guests. The puncture wound where a thorny stick had pierced through her thigh would eventually heal, no thanks to the tumble she had taken followed by the forced march by the renegades. Thank goodness they'd all made it safely back to town. A shiver worked her shoulders at the thought of what might have happened to the two women had they not escaped. Mentally, she closed the book, intent on writing a new beginning for both her and her town.

"Samantha, we're ready for the toast." Amy's grin shone in the subdued light. "Hurry, now."

"Coming." Samantha increased her pace, rehearsing her short speech as she limped along the seashell path reflecting the moonlight.

"Don't be in such a hurry."

"Let us pass." Samantha planted her feet and gripped the basket with both hands, glaring at the men. "Or I shall be forced to defend our right to."

She would, too. Samantha proved the strongest of her friends. Emily often wished for Samantha's fortitude. Where had she learned to confront an adversary with such confidence?

The officer chuckled, a rough unnerving sound. "And you'd both perhaps be injured, but in fact arrested for your actions. Perhaps then, Miss Sullivan, your father will mind his business ventures with more care."

What did he mean? Her father was a highly regarded man.

Samantha's eyes narrowed at his comment, but she held her ground. "We are late, sirs. Please, let us pass."

"We'll not detain you for long. I only want to kiss an American lady before I board one of those ships for England," the first soldier said, leaning closer to Emily and laying a hand on her arm to restrain her. He snatched the lace-trimmed bonnet from her head." You're such a pretty little blonde, too."

She gritted her teeth when he mauled her mother's delicate bonnet. "That's mine!" Emily grasped at it, clutching air until finding purchase on the hat, and pulled it from his filthy fingers. With shaking hands, she straightened the lace-edged brim as the man chortled. She inhaled to calm her roiling stomach. "Gentlemen, please."

Seething, she inspected her hat. At a minimum, he fouled it by his touch. Her hands trembled, but she steeled herself to face the loathsome men. "If you'll step aside, we'll continue on our way home."

The second soldier yanked the bonnet from her hands and lifted it to his nose. "Love the smell of a fine woman."

He rubbed her bonnet on his face, inhaling deeply each time it swiped across his nose. She swallowed the bile rising in her throat. Suddenly footsteps echoed behind her, but she dared not tear her eyes from her assailants to turn to see who approached. Might it be yet another foul British soldier attacking from the rear? The apprehension pounding in her ears along with her pulse prodded her into action.

If Samantha could defend herself, then so could Emily. Gripping the strings of her purse tightly, she swung it in a large arc at the closest soldier, hitting him on the elbow with a loud crack. Good, the tin of snuff she'd purchased for her father had earned its worth this day.

"Gramercy, woman, watch what you do there." The soldier rubbed the injured joint, scowling. "I just wanted a little kiss or two. No need to get angry."

"Let us pass unharmed like gentlemen should, or I'll hit you again." Breathing hard, she pulled back to deliver another blow when a hand gripped her upper arm and stayed her movement. The heat from the gloved hand seared her where it lay, the grip nearly hurting her but not quite.

"I'll thank you to leave the ladies alone, *gentlemen*. And I use that word loosely." The deep, familiar voice sounded above her head, sparking nearly dead embers of feeling in her core.

She knew that voice even with the new hardness in it. She heard it in her dreams on too many nights and had dreaded hearing it again in person. Its timbre reverberated against her chest, a physical caress as he stepped close enough his heat warmed her back. Relief mixed with despair as a jolt of awareness flowed into her body, tempting her to lean against his powerful frame.

Emily glanced over her shoulder at the tall blond. Her pulse quickened. Light from the open printing shop door pooled onto the ground behind Frank. Her lips parted, remembering the long ago fleeting touch which had started a feeling like a bubbling creek in her veins, a longing in her heart and inner core she did not fully comprehend.

She snapped her mouth closed, afraid she might reveal too much of the intense physical response she experienced when he touched her. She braced herself against the onslaught of emotions he stirred within her, attempting a frown to show her displeasure.

His dove-gray eyes enthralled her. She could lose herself in their tantalizing depths. When he winked at her, her breath hitched. She broke eye contact and turned to face forward.

"I believe you have something of the lady's." Frank held out a hand to the soldier, snapping his fingers, demanding the garment.

His steady gaze made the soldier shove the bonnet toward Frank before hastily stepping back several yards, well out of range of any physical response. Did everyone jump when he snapped his fingers? He may be surprised when she did not.

Frank handed the bonnet to her with a grim expression and a nod. Although still heavenly to look at, with lush, sandy-blond hair, chiseled jaw, and steely gray eyes, now a determination filled those eyes, his firm mouth. He seemed taller, broader, more dangerous than nine months earlier, before he left town after his swift marriage to Elizabeth.

She folded the offending garment and glared at the circle of men dwarfing her. Why must he show up now? After all this time away from home. Her heart skipped a beat, then restarted wildly with a crazy mix of joy and resentment. Where had he been when her home life fell apart?

Still, he was protecting her from these buffoons. And her father's subsequent anger, should aught go awry. She'd sacrifice her pride *this* time. She sidled behind him, placing his bulk between her and the aggressors.

The major evaluated Frank's height and size, his look changing from antagonistic to resigned when he noted the insignia on his uniform.

"What right do you have to interfere?" the first soldier asked Frank, seeing the change in the major's demeanor.

"General Alexander Leslie himself requested my presence. And this lady's father is my father-in-law, who charged me with ensuring the ladies' safe passage."

Frank knew the hated general? On top of that, Frank admitted he had already talked with her father. She had wanted more time. Time to face her father's unrealistic dreams for her.

Time to take the steps necessary to open her own shop and determine how she would proceed with her plans. If she were to be truly independent, then she must insist on being treated as such. Frank's officious behavior stoked her irritation.

"We'll see about that." The soldier surged forward and pointed his rifle at Frank.

Emily gasped, gripping Frank's cloak involuntarily. He set her from him then stepped forward, drawing the man's attention and the path of his aim away from her.

Frank braced his feet as he faced the frustrated soldier. "Be sensible, man."

Trembles rocked her core at the tableau playing out before her. Motion slowed to a crawl as she attempted to make sense of the scene. Her breath caught in her throat when the seriousness of the situation sank into her rattled brain.

The man stalked toward Frank, his finger on the trigger of the weapon. His thick fingers curled around the dark wood stock and supported the long metal barrel. Stubble shadowed his jaw and surrounded his yellow smile. He aimed the rifle at Frank's abdomen. "I'll have what I came for, and you cannot stop me."

At this close range, even if he tried, he couldn't miss. She fixed her eyes on Frank, saw when his eyes turned to mirrors, focused on settling the challenge. He appeared capable of killing her assailant then and there. Cold fear lodged in her chest. Frank came home, only to be shot? Over a bonnet? No. She wouldn't allow it. She made to take a step to intervene, stop the madness, but Samantha grabbed her arm with a fierce grip all while shaking her head. Emily tried to ignore her, but her friend held fast.

"I believe the lady has a say in the matter." Frank whipped a pistol from some hidden place, cocked the hammer with a deadly *click*, and leveled it at the man. "I'd think again about your intentions, sir."

Emily tugged on Samantha's hold. "Frank, no!"

Frank locked eyes with his opponent, his thumb ready to release the lethal ball. His eyes narrowed, hard and deadly.

"Stand down, soldier," the major cut in. "This has gone far enough. Next thing you'll be challenging him to a bloody duel over nothing more than a thwarted buss."

"Put your gun away," Frank said to the soldier, "or face charges of assaulting an officer."

The soldier reluctantly cradled his gun, glaring at Frank.

"Are you Captain Thomson?" the major asked, scrutinizing him.

"Yes, sir." Frank lowered his pistol, keeping it handy.

"General Leslie mentioned you were taking over the printing press and the broadside." The major considered Frank and the lethal weapon, his internal debate evident in his expression. "But your point is well-made. This is neither the place nor the time." He turned to address the soldiers. "All right, men, return to your duties."

"But sir—" The man's voice held a barely concealed whine.

"You heard him. Move along now." Frank replaced his pistol, though he did not relax his demeanor. Fortunately, the officer quelled the whiner's eagerness with a severe look before tipping his hat to Emily and Samantha.

"Ladies, my apologies," the officer said slowly. "You may be on your way."

"Thank you for your assistance." Frank studied the officer as the disgruntled soldiers stalked away. Still, he remained ready to defend himself even as the officer followed the men down the street.

The fear that had bolstered Emily's strength fled, leaving her weak at the knees. That was close. Taking a deep breath, Emily faced Frank.

Frank's dark gray eyes turned stormy, his hands on his hips as he studied her.

"Pray tell what you two are doing on the street alone?"

The next morning, Emily endured Frank escorting her to the sewing circle, acquiescing to her father's outraged insistence. He argued with her about the necessity of her attending, and she'd finally convinced him to permit her to go, but only if Frank walked with her to prevent any further attempts on her virtue. They stopped to pick up Samantha from her home on the way, which made the walk bearable.

Emily paused at the edge of the street and scanned the facade of Aunt Lucille's three-story brick house, shading her eyes from the sun. The lovely home stood in the middle of the block, with its courtyard of flowers and bushes below the upper piazzas. Two of her father's servants, Richard and Solomon, had lugged the necessary equipment and supplies from home to her aunt's house on Meeting Street, a double dwelling similar to the Sullivan home overlooking the wharfs and harbor on Bay Street. Fortunately, the men were among the few who did not take the chance when tempted with freedom as long as they fought for the British. Rumors abounded that the slaves who did so only ended up slaves elsewhere afterward.

Emily and Samantha, along with a brooding Frank, entered through the street door to the first-floor porch. The young men's strength had apparently made quick work of the assembly of the loom. Emily greeted her personal slave, Jasmine. She had tasked the young woman with carrying the spindles of flax thread used to weave the cloth and also with directing Richard and Solomon in their chore. Now the loom stood ready for Emily to take her seat and start the shuttle flying back and forth to weave the linen fabric. The men's immediate labor completed, they retired to the cooking kitchen to "assist" the women with preparing the midafternoon meal for the ladies, while Jasmine helped with the sewing. The sound of the women singing as they worked in the kitchen behind the house complemented the whir and chatter in the parlor.

Emily settled on the small seat of the loom, and placed her feet on the treadles, pressing them in a steady rhythm. She sent the shuttle's smooth wood sliding easily between the vertical threads, weaving the flax into cloth. With each toss of the shuttle, left, then right, then left, Emily thought of her three brothers and the other men still fighting. Small skirmishes continued to erupt whenever the militia happened upon scavenging British troops confiscating whatever provisions they deemed necessary from the surrounding plantations and homes.

Whirring spinning wheels hummed a tune to accompany the conversations in the large upstairs parlor of Aunt Lucille's home. The requisite fire kept the cool October air at bay. Emily passed the shuttle to and fro, glancing over to where Samantha now sat by the cozy fire stitching a sleeve onto a shirt. The room overflowed with women, white and black, free and slaves, working together.

"I imagine Frank's temper showed after you and Samantha behaved so boldly yesterday." Amy paused in her passage across the room to stand beside Emily. Cousin Amy's dark copper tresses cascaded down her back, catching the firelight, while her emerald eyes sparkled with mirth.

"A tad, but he soon recovered, I daresay. His displeasure increased when he realized Samantha and I had walked together through town." Emily paused to pat her kerchief across her damp brow. The memory of Frank's dark scowl and iron grip as he hustled them down the street the night before flitted in her thoughts. He'd been angrier than she'd ever seen him. More like outraged. "He's gone to McCrady's Tavern to meet Father on some business or other."

"I'm pleased that you arrived safe." Amy hugged her briefly before stepping back to gauge her condition. "The British and loyalists are desperate enough to seek vengeance on anyone who crosses them."

Emily could only nod. The chasm of fear that had opened within her when the soldiers accosted them would forever remain her secret. And when Frank had faced certain death, her heart nearly stopped beating. Those few minutes of uncertainty she and Samantha agreed to keep to themselves, given no good could arise from telling anyone about the men's inappropriate actions. It was bad enough her father had to be told. Frank's lecture all the way home had done nothing but vex her and spoil the evening.

Amy's mother, Lucille Abernathy, glided in to join them, making a path through the organized chaos inherent with the sewing apparatuses and materials strewn about the large room. Her mud-brown day gown sported a flowered apron with two pockets filled with thread, needles, and lace. Her gray-streaked black hair was swept up in a bun with a white cap perched on top. The years of war had imprinted worry lines radiating from the corners of her mouth in contrast to the sparkle of her eyes.

"It is dangerous for two young women to be alone in town, especially now," Aunt Lucille said. "You should have walked with Richard and Solomon from here to your house."

"I'm sure Father would agree with you." Emily surveyed the room, taking a few moments to stifle the annoyance bubbling within her. It all sounded so easy to rely upon some man being with her in order for her to do anything. But it rankled deep inside her soul to be forced to wait for an escort. To learn Frank served as the new printer, and thus working next door to where she planned to rent a shop, made matters even more upsetting. "Next time, mayhap I will let them escort me."

"Next time Frank shall escort you, now that he's back in town. After all, he is a nice man, honest and fair." Aunt Lucille slipped her hands into her apron pockets. "And able to look after those he cares about."

"I suppose."

She refused to think of Frank as more than her sister's husband—or widower now. Then why did her heart race so at the thought of Frank being nearby again? She mentally shrugged away the question. Likely she experienced indigestion at his unwanted presence. Whether attracted to him—an absurdity—or not, she no longer desired to encourage relations with a man. Her own plans did not include marriage, no matter how handsome or smart the man might be. Not any longer.

Jasmine crossed the room and waited for Emily to acknowledge her. "Your tea is waiting downstairs as requested, miss."

After thanking Jasmine, Emily beamed at Amy. Time to

reveal her plans to her confidantes. "Aunt Lucille kindly allowed me to arrange a private tea for us. I have a surprise I'd like to share with you and Samantha."

"Now?" Amy pinned her gaze on Emily. "We have much to finish."

"I cannot wait any longer." Her determination wavered as she contemplated the enormous task before her. She needed to know that both her cousin and friend supported this most weighty decision.

"You've always liked a good mystery." Amy's eyes lit with curiosity as she followed Emily across the room. Upon Emily's invitation, Samantha quickly agreed to the clandestine tea party.

They adjourned to the downstairs library at the front of her aunt's house. The tall, shuttered windows protected the inhabitants both against the dust rising from the sandy street beyond and from prying British eyes. A wood fire crackled and hissed in the fireplace.

Emily poured chamomile tea into flowered cups and set the china pot down before gazing at Amy and Samantha, who waited for her to speak. What to say? She'd longed for the courage to broach this topic for a week, hesitating to reveal her innermost desires even to her closest friends for fear of their reaction. Lifting the porcelain cup to her mouth, she sipped, debating how best to share her news. On a sigh, she set the cup and saucer on the table.

"I've decided to open a shop." The words tumbled from her mouth. Amy and Samantha stared, mouths dropping open at the announcement. Emily suppressed the nervous laugh that threatened. She twisted the tiny gold mourning ring on her right hand, silently asking Elizabeth for her support. She took a deep breath and let it out in a rush. "I do not want to be a wife and mother. Rather, I'll support myself and live the way I wish."

Closing her mouth, Amy eased her cup onto the saucer and gazed at Emily before laughing. "You cannot be serious, Em. A spinster? You? You've always wanted a large family and a loving husband. You mustn't tease us this way."

"I'm not joking. I do not wish to be owned by a man." Emily clenched her hands until they turned white at the knuckles. Not even by Frank, the man she once loved with all her heart. A quiver of remorse fluttered within her chest as she blinked back gathering tears.

"Owned?" Samantha gazed steadily at her. "Come now, you do not believe such folly, surely. A husband is not a slave driver."

"Pshaw. I've seen how men treat their wives." Emily dabbed her kerchief at the corner of her eyes. "How fathers give away their daughters with their dowry and little more than a kiss good-bye and good riddance. I'll not do it, I tell you."

"I cannot believe what I'm hearing." Amy rose to pace past the carved mahogany bookcase filling one long wall. She stopped by a round table with its cut-glass decanters of maroon port and amber sherry and four glasses. "You cannot believe your father would allow you to forgo marriage and children. You know he won't support you forever."

"He won't have to. For once, Father must understand my position."

"But Em, this is simply not done. You know this is impossible."

"It should not be impossible. Can't you see? I cannot risk having children." Emily's heart contracted in disappointment. She fiddled with the gold band, recalling her childhood dreams of robust sons and lovely, precocious daughters to help her and love her in her dotage. But no more.

"All because of Elizabeth's death?" Samantha moved to stand near Emily and peered into her eyes. "Is that what you're afraid of?"

"First my mother and then my sister perished after birthing children." Emily searched Samantha's eyes, willing her to understand. A tremor coursed through her. "Samantha, you, as a midwife, know even better than I do how many women die in childbirth. I dare not risk it."

Amy paced the lavishly furnished room. Her homespun skirts brushed her ankles as she turned at each corner of the oriental carpet, avoiding the cushioned sofas and side chairs.

"But, my dear, it's simply not permissible for ladies of our station to be shopkeepers. If I know Uncle Joshua, he will be furious once he hears of this ridiculous notion of yours."

"Why is it ridiculous?" Emily drew herself up to her full height. "Other women have shops in town. The Widow Murray's bakery was one. Mrs. Dunwoody has that lovely fashion store over on Market. And, and…"

She racked her brain for other examples, but few women desired to be independent. The coverture laws provided for wives to be supported throughout their lives. Unmarried women were merely a burden on the family, and thus encouraged to marry to remove the burden and be a useful member of society. Indeed, most women wanted to be homemakers and care for their families. They only worked in shops when forced to take over their husband's business upon his death or face starvation. Raised with the expectation of marriage, children, and household responsibilities, many looked on spinsters as neglecting their duty to marry and perpetuate mankind. With a wry smile, Emily realized she used to be one of them. With the passing of Elizabeth, her opinion had changed.

She snapped her fingers as more female merchants came to mind. "Mrs. Johnson sells candles and scented sachets over on Broad. Surely I can open a shop, a millinery, and sell decorated hats and gloves. My embroidery and weaving skills are both respected in town, so I shall make clothes and embellish handkerchiefs, satin shoes, dresses. I don't believe there is anything wrong with having a shop. Women should have as much right as men to earn a living."

"I don't entirely disagree with you, Emily. However, while women can help in the shops, only widows can inherit the shop from their husbands, not maidens. We cannot even own property unless we're widows." Samantha laid a hand on Emily's rigid arm. "Relax, my dear. We're not criticizing."

"No?" Withdrawing from Samantha's touch, she strode to the fireplace. Thoughts tumbled with rampant emotions, creating an intricate knot that settled in the pit of her stomach.

Amy and Samantha wanted the best for her and spoke the truth about the difficult path ahead. The challenges and sacrifices she faced made her more determined to succeed.

Amy crossed the room and sank gracefully onto the settee facing the fireplace. She arranged her skirts around her. The thump of Amy's hand on the cushion invited Emily to join her. "Em, please, come sit and let us discuss this rationally."

Emily did not move. A *pop* and *hiss* from the fire echoed through the silence. She could not move. She needed them to understand, not oppose her choice. If they couldn't accept and support her decision, she despaired of ever convincing the ladies sewing circle and even less her father. Her heart beat in her ears as she took two slow breaths.

Amy patted the cushion once more. "Em, please. Sit here with me."

"I don't see how it will do me any good, but if you insist." Emily sank onto the seat beside her cousin.

"Talk to me." Amy laid a hand on top of Emily's clenched ones. "What is truly happening?"

Emily stared into the fire for a moment before addressing Amy's question. Her hands trembled in her lap, and she pressed them together. "If I marry, I will be expected to have children, lots of them, no less, to support our young country. I understand what's expected, but I would jeopardize my very life."

"And?" Amy asked gently. "There's more to this story, I believe."

Her heart sank. Emily regretted confiding in her cousin. Frank's touch on her fingers, coupled with the light kiss on the back of one lucky hand, had created a sizzling sensation throughout her body, leaving her hungry and longing when he'd stepped away. She squared her shoulders and searched Amy's eyes silently, trying to convey her feelings without having to put voice to them. "I don't know what you mean."

Amy's hand tightened on hers, and her lips curved slightly. Emily closed her eyes and sighed, a tear crawling down her cheek. She brushed it away.

No tears. No more.

"I understand," Amy said. "I, too, do not wish to marry. I'm not afraid of having children, mind. But to give up what I want to do to be subservient to a man who has all the rights and privileges of this new country while I sit by and have nothing to my name?" Winding the long auburn curl hanging beside her jaw around her index finger, Amy stared thoughtfully into the fire. "I see your point. Perhaps it is best to be a spinster by choice and suffer the townspeople's insults than to be forced to remain at home, subject to the vagaries of men."

"What did you say?" Emily peered at Amy. Her cousin, who loved to flirt and dance, would willingly be a spinster? "Does this have anything to do with Benjamin Hanson's sudden disappearance a few years ago?"

Amy shook her head, but her action lacked conviction. Amy had sulked for months after the man's departure to serve in the Continental Army. Emily suspected Amy's heart underwent the same splitting in two her own had endured over Frank, yet she refused to admit such even to herself.

"What will Evelyn say?" Emily redirected the conversation away from the touchy subject.

"I believe my sister will understand and perhaps even applaud my choice. Her own marriage has not been, shall we say, what she expected." Amy cast a sideways glance at Emily. "Indeed, the abuse she suffers informs my desire as much as… Gramercy, it makes no difference now. I shall join you in your vow."

"Amy, my dear, surely you jest," Samantha said. "You'll break the heart of every bachelor in town."

"That is none of my affair." Amy chuckled. "After all, flirtation and marriage are very different activities."

Emily hugged her, the inner coil of tension relaxing as she grasped the fact she may not have to walk this path alone.

Samantha glided to sit on a side chair, her shimmery green dress pooled around her, reflecting the flames in the fireplace. She leaned back in the chair, her right hand resting on her leg.

"Am I correct in that you both wish to remain unwed? To forgo the pleasures of having a husband?"

Samantha's reference to the physical relations between husbands and wives in this setting surprised Emily for several reasons. She had not known her friend possessed such intimate knowledge of sexual relations. Indeed, having only become friends with Samantha the year before, surely there was much to discover about her past. Emily found herself practically holding her breath, waiting to hear what Amy prepared to say.

"Pleasures?" Amy leaned forward, one eyebrow lifted in question. "I cannot think of any pleasures associated with being married. From what little I've heard, the event is short and no fun. At least not for the woman."

"It's not always weighted in the man's favor," Samantha said. "But are you both sure of this vow of remaining unmarried?"

"Without any doubt." Emily considered her friend for a long moment, realizing Samantha had adroitly changed the subject. Sadness shaded her friend's eyes, dimming their sparkle like clouds on a starry night.

"Yes, we shall be true unto ourselves," Amy added with a theatrical flourish of her hand, "and follow our heart's desires rather than submit to the whimsical will of a man. Are you with us?"

Samantha contemplated the fire, dancing with red, orange, and blue licks of flame. Lost in thought, she lightly massaged the outside of her thigh. Shouts of laughter came through the window. A dog barked in response.

Samantha blinked and then regarded them. "I honestly never considered not marrying. The idea has its benefits, however."

Agitation mingled with hope forced Emily to her feet. She paced the room. When her father desired something, he didn't back down. He'd never give up until he had coerced her into the one act she longed to avoid. That was the problem. He wanted her to marry, and soon, for her protection, he said. His demand coupled with her sister's recent death solidified the idea percolating in the back of her mind. The vacant shop wouldn't be vacant for long, no matter the obstacles placed in her way.

"So you are with us, Samantha?" Amy asked.

"Yes, but we must keep it between us, to avoid open scorn whenever possible." Samantha grinned. "After all, we've reached the upper end of marriageable age. We may as well."

Emily crossed to the center of the room, her hands outstretched. The first steps of a journey often proved the hardest. "Come, then, let us take a vow together to keep this choice our secret."

Amy and Samantha rose and clasped hands with Emily, forming a triangle of friendship.

"How binding is this vow?" Samantha asked. At the startled response from Amy and Emily, she added, "I mean, should one or the other of us change our minds, is that allowed as well?"

The image of Frank's blond good looks and gray eyes floated before Emily. No matter how handsome and fine Frank or any man might be, the vow must, for her own peace of mind, be made. An inner voice cried out in anguish when she pushed the handsome face aside, locking it away in her heart. However, she did not want to force the restriction, or the pain, on anyone else. "As long as it is not coerced upon us, but is of our own choosing, I see no need for this to be forever binding."

"Then so be it," Samantha said. "I choose to remain unwed."

Amy cocked her head and smiled at Samantha. "But you have not stated your reason. What prompts you to this decision?"

A dour smile flickered across Samantha's lips. "Let us say, I have loved and lost and will not endure such pain again."

"Indeed?" Amy raised an eyebrow, glancing at Emily.

Samantha bobbed her head once as a tiny smile formed. The woman contained many secrets, secrets Emily hoped to one day learn more about so she better understood her friend. For now, Emily's relief that her confidantes stood with her swept aside her earlier uncertainty.

Emily broke away from the triangle and poured three glasses of sweet sherry. "Then we shall celebrate our agreement with a toast." Handing the glasses around, she raised hers.

"What shall we toast to?" Samantha asked.

"To life, liberty and the pursuit of happiness for *all* in America." Emily flashed a smile at her comrades.

"And a more perfect union for women," Amy added, her eyes sober.

Emily tapped her glass against the others, happy yet fearing the consequences of their vow as the ring of crystal quivered into silence.

Chapter Two

The view of the amassed fleet of British ships in the harbor through the grimy window of McCrady's Tavern did little to assuage Frank's distress. What should he do now? He was only vaguely aware of the activity along the wharfs reaching out from Bay Street to the turbulent confluence of the Ashley and Cooper beyond, the mixing point of the two rivers. Seagulls and terns swooped and dived over the churning water. Dark gray clouds scudded across the pale blue sky. The war ships mingled with merchant vessels, their furled masts tugged by the wind. Hammer blows and curses carried through the open door of the tavern as coopers built barrels for shipping the products from the colony to overseas markets.

Downing half of the ale from a heavy blue glass bottle, he tried to fathom what possessed the two maids to walk alone to the ladies' gathering rather than under the protective watch of the two strong slaves. Shaking his head, he cursed aloud at the absurdity and the damned danger they placed themselves in. Were they fools?

Naive and foolhardy. No wonder Captain Sullivan requested him to protect her from the threat of the enemy. His privateering against the British could indeed land him in trouble. That would leave Emily vulnerable. The fact that she possessed a wild side meant that someone needed to tame that out of her before she harmed herself. Or Tommy. He would speak to her father once more when he arrived. Emily had challenged the lusty men, showing her courage in the face of their threat. In the event, if any harm befell her Frank stood to answer to Captain Sullivan. Not an encounter he need ever experience, to his mind, as long as Emily behaved herself. He'd have to make sure she did.

The front door opened and abruptly filled with the bulk of the man in question, as if summoned by Frank's musing. Captain Sullivan acknowledged Frank's wave and stomped across the wooden floor to join him at the bar.

Sullivan settled onto the wooden stool. Flagging the barkeeper, he ordered an ale and eyed Frank. "Did you see Emily safely to my sister's house?"

"Yes, right before I found out I no longer have a home." Frank stared at the shiny surface of the bottle. Anger simmered to a boil at the actions the British had inflicted on him. "It was seized by some British officer for his office and quarters."

"I recall hearing something about your family's house a few months ago but didn't think more on it seeing as you weren't needing it at the time." Sullivan swigged his ale and glanced at Frank. "Damn shame. Where will you stay if not your family home?"

The captain's fatherly appraisal made Frank aware of how much this war had cost him. First his little brother, then Elizabeth. Now his home confiscated as well. He flung a prayer to heaven that the rumors of imminent peace came true.

"I know not, having learned of the theft only an hour ago." If he hadn't seen for himself that the enemy occupied it, he'd still be in the dark. They apparently did not feel the need to inform the previous owner of the outrage. Then to see the blasted loyalist, Major John Bradley, the buffoon responsible for the ill treatment of Emily and Samantha, emerge from the three-story brick mansion only darkened his mood.

After he met with the ill-tempered General Leslie, it proved short work to discover the facts behind the fate of his home.

He learned that only days after Jedediah departed town to join the militia for his year of promised service, the British swarmed the property, confiscating everything. Frank had not spent more than a day at a time in Charles Town since he signed up to fight.

The facts endured as facts. The bastard had stolen his property, and Frank planned to steal it right back. Next, he had to determine how.

"We have an extra room you can stay in until you find your feet." One thick eyebrow rose as Sullivan glanced at him. "One that will suit you perfectly."

"Thank you, sir. If it's not inconvenient, I'd appreciate that." The invitation allowed him to abide under the same roof as Emily and Tommy, very convenient on many counts. He tapped his bottle against Sullivan's, returning the grin.

"Not so fast. There's a catch." Captain Sullivan smirked at him. "You must keep an eye on my daughter."

He could live with such a condition. He longed to keep both eyes on that woman, with or without her father's request. Emily glowed with life and joy, and he became a better person when he drew near her. He'd allowed himself the thrill of kissing her hand and experiencing the electric awareness flowing between them. A pang of regret surged when he considered the time lost with Emily as a result of his sense of duty to claim his brother's child as a son. He swallowed the emotion filling his throat. "Any particular reason you wish me to watch over her?"

Joshua lowered his voice, his eyes intensely peering at Frank. "I've some business I need to work through over the next few weeks, which will take me out of town for a day or two, possibly longer." The captain glanced around before continuing. "Privateering business but don't tell Emily. It's best she not know for her own safety. Emily can be headstrong and temperamental as well as impetuous. I need someone with a firm hand on the reins. Especially given the questions being asked by certain loyalists. Understand?"

"Yes, sir, I do." He tapped his bottle against the captain's again. "You have my word."

"There's an empty stall for your horse, as well."

"Much appreciated. I'd prefer to trust the care of Mr. Abernathy's fine thorough bred horse to your groom instead of the boys at the livery."

"Indeed, as you should. Abernathy would have my hide if I let anything happen to his horse," Sullivan said on a chuckle. "After all the time he's put into developing the line, he may never speak to me again."

"I'll do my best to not let you down, sir." Frank raised his bottle.

Returning the salute, Captain Sullivan drained his ale. "I must go. I'll leave her in your hands while I handle a shipment arriving today. I'll see you for supper this evening."

After Sullivan left, Frank ordered another drink while he thought through his next steps. Living in the same house as Emily changed things in ways he needed to contemplate. Working through her resistance to him would take time, but he could do it. No issues there.

He returned to his ale, contemplating the bar surface. Despite the evidence of previous fights and scuffles, the mahogany gleamed darkly from the daily scrubbing the barkeeper insisted on. The floor did not receive the same attention, so he was thankful for the sturdy leather overshoes he'd purchased from the cobbler to protect his deerskin boots. Between the mud and sand and horse manure, the floor was little better than the dirt-packed road called Bay Street. Perhaps when the war ended and America was free—God willing— Governor John Mathews would see to using the pile of ballast stones from the British ships to pave the streets. For now they were a sore reminder of the lingering parliamentary tax on even the blasted stones, a tax the colonists refused to pay. He longed for cobblestones to replace the sand, dust, and mud that served as streets almost as much as he dreamed of the day this charade ended.

His earlier studies at Oxford taught him about the wealth of knowledge waiting for one who traveled the world. He channeled his thirst for adventure into supporting the creation and now rebuilding of the Charles Town Natural Museum. The specimens that arrived recently on one of Sullivan's ships gave him encouragement as they rebuilt the fire-gutted museum collection. He and the others working with him had stored the precious items in a rented warehouse until after the war ended, hoping the bombs and fires, as well as prying British eyes, steered clear of the new items.

He understood how to balance between the knowledge needed to accomplish a difficult task and the ability to manage others' actions. Working as a spy for the patriot cause while posing as a loyalist broadside printer and officer meant walking a thread that could break at any moment. Although he had never contemplated taking over his brother's business, it did provide a means for encoding troop movements and other military status for the forces waiting outside the town limits. Although the foraging-related clashes across the countryside were sporadic, innocent folks still ended up hurt and killed. He would do anything in his power to stop unnecessary abuses. Even stay in an office all day when he longed to see the wonders of far-off lands.

He quaffed the remainder of his ale. Time to go. Laying a few coins on the bar, he bade the rotund and sweaty barkeeper good day and strode out into the windy afternoon. The scent of rain filled the air. Whether the ladies wanted his escort or no, they would have one. He glanced at the building thunderclouds and quickened his stride.

Once more at the loom after their private tea, Emily relished the sense of purpose and freedom her decision yielded. Fortunately, her friends stood with her. Now to take the steps necessary to fulfill her dream.

"Emily? Dear, are you well?" Aunt Lucille waved a hand before Emily's eyes, drawing her focus back to the present.

"What? Oh, I'm sorry, Aunt." Heat crept up her chest and neck, finally warming her cheeks. The whir of the spinning wheels and the chatter of the other women in the upper parlor reminded her of the task at hand. "What were you saying?"

"I asked, what of Tommy? How does he fare?" A light frown etched miniature crevices between hazel eyes. Aunt Lucille's threadbare day gown stood silent witness to the sacrifices she and most of the ladies had endured throughout the course of the war.

"Tommy is well, at home with the wet nurse overseeing his needs. He's been a bit off with colic, but Samantha offered to bring a tonic for him. He'll be a fine, strapping man if he keeps eating as he does."

"'Tis good for him to eat so. That proves he is healthy and thriving. His mother would be happy." A shadow passed over Aunt Lucille's eyes and vanished. She looked away briefly, then beamed at Emily. "Tell me about Captain Frank. It surprised me to hear he returned yesterday."

"Father warned me his return was imminent." Emily shook her head as a reflex to her confusion. "I do not understand why he came back now. It's been almost eight months since Elizabeth died. He couldn't be bothered with coming to the funeral even though we sent word."

Aunt Lucille patted her hand where it rested on the loom frame. "The war changes everyone's priorities, my dear. He put duty to his country ahead of family during this crisis. It is to be lauded, not vilified."

"Yet now he hovers like a father goose, honking and snapping his mouth. Stalking around all self-important and righteous, preaching his demands. I won't tolerate it." Irritation simmered in the pit of her stomach.

Aunt Lucille laughed, wiping away tears. "Such an imagination you have. Just like Amy with her fiction."

"I make a point to stick to the facts as much as possible; that's the difference." Emily slid the shuttle along the loom threads, expertly tamping the new thread in place before sliding the shuttle back and repeating the motion. The rhythmic *whoosh* and *thump* of the loom reflected her feelings. "I enjoy her tales, but I don't encourage the telling of lies."

"Naturally. Will Frank escort you home this afternoon?" Aunt Lucille asked after a moment.

"Unfortunately yes, but I'd prefer he did not. I'm not a child in need of a governess."

Aunt Lucille's mirth sobered. "My dear, we live in dangerous times in town, nay in this country. The British soldiers as well as the loyalists all fear they have lost this war. They rightly fear the retaliation patriots will exact when that officially happens. Indeed, the list of known loyalists who will be forced to leave South Carolina when the British embark for London grows daily. Do not discount the tension surrounding us now."

"But must it be Frank to escort me?" Emily tried to quell the whine from her voice. "He has claimed to be loyal to the king. Even if that's untrue, I cannot tolerate the thought he would attempt to deceive us so."

"He cares about his family in this town—his son, his father-in-law, and you—and thus he made that claim so he can continue to do his duty and protect all of you. He is not like some who turned on their families when they switched sides."

"Family duty fiddlesticks. How can you be so sure this time is like any other time? We are at war."

"I've known Frank since he was a lad, dear. I know his sense of duty led to him returning from battle to marry your dear sister."

"Hmm, right noble of Frank to step in for Jedediah."

"Yes, it was," Aunt Lucille replied. "Quite a sacrifice for him."

Sacrifice indeed. Emily recalled the hurried private ceremony held in the front parlor. No flowers adorned the room due to the haste of the marriage. Emily had contributed an embroidered pale yellow gown with seed pearls along the scooped neckline and in rays down the full skirts. The same dress she had held aside for her own hoped-for wedding. The rector, apprised of the urgency of the situation, read an abbreviated set of vows and pronounced them man and wife. Then, within days Frank departed to return to his unit.

Emily had tried to forget she loved Frank. The only way she could imagine living with her sister as her little family began was to forget her feelings for him and guard her heart from further pain. She'd succeeded in large part. Yet a tiny piece of her heart waited to be his. A futile longing.

No tears, she swore silently, swallowing hard. Marriage and motherhood once seemed her destiny. Her sister's marriage and then demise had killed any possibility of ever achieving her dream.

Times certainly changed with the onset of the war and the necessary shift in women's roles. She inspected the weave before her, then bit off a thread. Hopefully Father would understand even if he did not agree with the new goals for her life. She wound the shuttle with more thread and replaced it on the loom with a satisfying *thump*.

Hadn't the tavern keeper's widow taken over the tavern when he died at Cowpens early last year? And the grocer's widow had run the store even while he was away fighting. In addition to doing her own domestic duties, of course. Even without the benefit of a formal education, the widows learned to manage the funds and accounts. Time and again women proved equal to the challenges brought on by this interminable fighting and fear.

"Lucille, darling!"

Emily looked up from her work as a boisterous woman hurried over to hug her aunt.

Catherine Manning was the town's most visible new matron. Her cornflower-blue gown with white eyelet apron and matching kerchief distinguished her amid the more somber colors of the other women's dresses. Emily scowled at her brown gown and sighed. Several patriot women in town wore mourning for their beloved Charles Town's occupation. Emily's array of gem-colored gowns had dwindled as the war progressed, leaving her with only the most durable ones decent enough to wear outside of the house. Those she had resisted wearing due to their dismal tones. Catherine represented the future of the new aristocracy of the town, and she dressed the part.

Her husband, George Manning, was a well-respected young lawyer who had made a name for himself in the local government. He had been responsible for the safety of the shipping lanes from pirates prior to the enemy occupation. Now the British ships were continually pestered and robbed by privateer ships. Once-honest merchants pillaged enemy ships at the bidding of the fledgling American government.

Fortunately her father eschewed becoming involved with the dangerous activity. His ships imported only those goods allowed by the strict regulations. His shop, located a few buildings south of their home and closer to the wharfs, boasted a wide variety of objects, furniture, and other household furnishings he'd imported from distant countries. He did so although the restrictions chafed, but he maintained his lucrative business despite the lack of trade permitted by Britain.

Routinely he asked her to update the books, assuring the sums balanced, and then overseeing the cleaning and arranging of the items. She enjoyed working alongside him and contributing to his business efforts, as well as gaining the education she needed to run a successful enterprise of her own. After the war ended, maybe he would even import the silks and satins and furnishings she would need for her shop, at a discount, of course.

"Mrs. Manning, how delightful to see you again." Samantha rose to receive the woman's affectionate embrace. "Please join us. Tell us, what is the latest?"

"I cannot wait to share what I have learned." The plump woman seated herself on a ladder-backed chair and arranged her skirts.

Her blue satin shoes were delicately embroidered with gold and silver flowers. How long would it take to embroider such dainty designs on the shoes, Emily wondered. Could she sew them fast enough to sell them profitably?

Aunt Lucille poured a cup of mint tea and presented it to Mrs. Manning. "I'm sure you could use a bit of refreshment."

Sipping gratefully, the young woman nodded her thanks. "Wonderful to have tea again, of any kind. I have drunk coffee along with the rest of our town since the Tea Parties, but it isn't quite the same, is it? Though it shan't be long before, I dare say, with good fortune we should have our town to ourselves again." She took another sip, her eyes twinkling as she watched her audience.

Emily stopped weaving to listen. The whir of the spinning wheels ceased as the other women stilled and activity quieted around her. Hope swelled her chest as she held her breath, waiting for Mrs. Manning's next words.

"What has happened?" Samantha laid her hands in her lap and leaned forward, waiting for a response. Her long, tapered fingers intertwined into one fist.

A grin teased the corners of Mrs. Manning's mouth. "Peace talks are occurring in France as we speak. The treaty is expected to be signed and all the fighting to end." She glanced around the room, a pleased smile emerging. "I see I bring welcome news."

Emily clasped the wide beam of the batten tightly in her hands, joy and fear washing through her. Her brothers would come home. Her own plans could truly begin. "Peace? But who will claim our noble city in the end?"

She dare not voice her hope that the Americans would win the war. To do so might jinx everything. The fighting had tapered off, so her father said, yet the frequent foraging parties by the desperate British and even the American army continued to strip the food and supplies from the neighboring plantations and terrified everyone in their wake. As a result he discouraged her from accompanying Amy to the plantation, saying the danger loomed greater beyond the town limits. She could not fathom why she couldn't but Amy could. Why was it more dangerous for Emily to escape the confines of the occupied town? Indeed, it was also supposedly dangerous in town for her. But her alone. Why?

Efforts to curtail the plundering had failed. He eased her worry by reminding her imports continued via his returning ships so all was not lost. How much longer could they survive this way, though? Food supplies had dwindled alarmingly over the two years of the besiegement of the town. Shortages of beef had even forced many loyalists to defect to the American army in hopes of finding more to eat. She and Jasmine had harvested all the victuals her little kitchen garden could supply. The berries and vegetables nestled in pickling jars in the cellar awaiting the coming winter months. Meat, however, was scarce due to limited availability, unless of course one had access to a plantation that had not been raided. No luck for them on that front, unfortunately.

"From what I've heard," Mrs. Manning said, leaning forward in her chair, the cup wobbling in its saucer, "the British only hold Charles Town and New York now and are desperate for soldiers and supplies as well. They are anxious to withdraw with what little honor they have left."

"Yes, they wait only for the weather to clear before they shall leave," Samantha said. "Or so I'm told."

Now where would she have heard that? Emily gazed at her friend's sublime expression. Perhaps while assisting her mother with the healing arts, she had overheard such conversation. Emily felt cut off from the happenings of town by the restrictions her father placed upon her. She must talk to him posthaste about her plans.

"Let us pray to God that this comes to pass quickly," Aunt Lucille said firmly.

"Perhaps we'll have something to celebrate at Captain Sullivan's Allhallows Eve dinner in a couple of weeks," Samantha said, her eyes sparkling.

A general murmur of agreement swelled across the room as all eyes gravitated toward Emily. She'd nearly forgotten the dinner that remained an annual social event despite the deprivations and uncertainty. Everyone attending brought some food to share with the others, whether a loaf of bread, a bowl of nuts, a pound of smoked venison, or merely some mint leaves to make tea. The coming together of the people and the ensuing chatter as they shared food, ghost stories, and singing created a happy occasion in the midst of the sorrow and worry hanging over the town. Elizabeth's haunted forest stories had been the high point last year. This year's party would not be the same without her.

Aunt Lucille clapped her hands to call for silence. "Ladies, please resume your work. When Amy and I return to the plantation on the morrow, we will carry your fine contributions with us to give to General Greene. The cold weather is fast approaching, and even if the treaty were signed today, it could be months before word reaches us from France. In the meanspace, our men will need the warmth of the fabric as well as the warmth of our support."

Emily caught Amy's eye. "*You're leaving?*" she mouthed.

Amy nodded with raised eyebrows and a slight shrug. Obviously she had not known until then of her imminent departure, though the trips were never entirely unexpected, as they made them frequently. The timing depended on obtaining a pass and arranging to discreetly meet the appropriate people to make the exchange. Indeed, Aunt Lucille instructed Amy on how to effectively "liberate" key items, such as boots and caps and epaulets, needed by the patriot soldiers so that the sentries were none the wiser. Emily frowned on deception, but in cases like this she made an exception. Sometimes the ends did justify the means.

As the conversations around them shifted to discuss the possibility of the war ceasing, the women resumed their sewing efforts.

"Em, I didn't know," Amy said over the hum of spinning wheels. "But how else can we transport these items out of here except in Mother's carriage? Our boat, while more comfortable, needs men to manage it, men the British enticed away."

"I understand, but what will I do without you here?" Emily sent her shuttle flying along the loom, quickly working in the next line of thread.

"Perhaps Captain Thomson will provide some amusement for you."

"Why would you say that? The last I saw of him, he was livid with my actions." Her inner vixen, however, delighted in the memory of his reaction. For one thing, his ire prevented him from attempting to flirt with her, enabling Emily to keep her composure.

A grin lit Amy's face. "I remember how you felt about him and, more importantly, how he felt about you before he pledged to marry your sister. Be careful, or your precious vow may be for naught."

Emily's hands trembled with suppressed emotion humming like the spinning wheels. Amy hit on the truth with precision. In order to keep to her plan, she must quell any hint of desire her heart clung to. "My vow is solid and will remain so. It is no matter if he is interested in me, as I do not return the sentiment."

"We shall see." Amy's grin contained a mix of support and teasing. "I wouldn't hold it against you should you choose to back out of the vow, not with Frank around. Shall I ask Samantha to chaperone while I am away, to be sure?"

"That is not necessary, unless she would find it amusing to spend time with me." She must master the feelings racing through her in order to maintain the calm demeanor Aunt Lucille had taught her to exhibit no matter what occurred. Her aunt had acted as her mother for all of Emily's life, and Emily would not let her down after the trouble she'd caused the woman. The fireplace popped and crackled, its warmth suddenly unwelcome in the crowded room.

Amy pivoted on her seat by a low table and caught Samantha's eye from across the room. Seeing Amy's wave,

Samantha grabbed up the pile of shirts, and, wending her way around the multitude of wheels and women, soon joined her friends.

"Samantha, would you care to visit me while Amy is away? She seems to believe a chaperone is necessary for me to keep to my vow." She did not know what Amy may have detected to make her think Emily might break her oath. But company would be pleasant, nevertheless. Emily mentally shrugged. If it made her cousin feel better, she would request Samantha's help.

Samantha dropped the shirts on the chair seat, rested her hands on the back. Her eyes sparkled with suppressed laughter as she fought a smile. "Of course. I'll bring the basil over with me for Tommy's tea to calm his tummy, as well. We'll have a nice visit."

"There, now I can leave for a few days knowing my cousin is well attended."

"I will try to stay out of trouble while you are away." Emily winked at her cousin. Catching movement at the door, she glanced in that direction and her laughter died in her throat. "Oh, fiddlesticks."

"What is it?" Amy followed Emily's glare.

The air electrified as Frank surveyed the crowd of ladies, obviously seeking her. His height enabled him to see above the heads bent over their work or chatting amicably. Raking a hand through sandy-blond hair, his gaze neared where Emily stood. She caught her breath but tamped down the surge of tension his presence created inside.

"He's here to take you home, I presume?" Samantha folded a shirt and added it to the stack on the table.

"Us, actually, I believe." Emily presented her back to her tormentor. No reason to submit to his bidding until forced to do so. Yet she could still feel the weight of his gaze when he spotted her.

"He needn't bother on my account." Samantha added to her growing pile. "I know how to handle the brutes."

"Mayhap, but we shan't ever find out as long as he is around." Emily crossed her arms. "I won't tolerate this much longer. Does he think that little of me?"

Amy chuckled. "Or that much? Ah, I fear he has seen you."

Chapter Three

$\mathcal{F}$ rank entered the large room, impressed with the many spinning wheels, looms, and women squeezed into the elegantly decorated space. The polished wood floor peeked from beneath the furniture and dresses crowded together. And the noise—he had not contemplated the volume inherent in a roomful of women and wheels. He searched for Emily's distinctive golden curls. Finally spotting the back of her head as she spoke to Amy and Samantha, Frank cleared his throat. The deep bass sound caught the attention of several women closer to him.

"Captain Frank. How lovely to see you!" Mrs. Abernathy glided to where he stood inside the open door. "To what do we owe this pleasure?"

Frank noted with satisfaction the look of resignation on Emily's face as she glanced over her shoulder at him. Her brown dress needed to be replaced with something brighter, more like her personality. Something in golden yellow with a fine white lace bonnet and matching gloves. In time he'd see to it. At least she had agreed, if reluctantly, to the captain's request for Frank to look after her safety. Their initial meeting had gone smoother than he hoped, given his new position in town. The newsman cover enabled him to both spy on the enemy and keep watch over her. She didn't know, and wouldn't, the real reason behind his role as her protector. Her father didn't want her to be forced to confess his crime, should it come down to it.

"I've come to escort Miss Emily and Miss Samantha home before the storm arrives." He noted Samantha smirking at him as thunder rumbled overhead. He bristled. Was she laughing at his concern for their safety?

He straightened the lace dropping from his cuff. When he glanced back at Emily, he saw her watching his hands. Then she met his look steadily. What was she thinking? Could she be remembering his hand holding hers, as he thought of often, God help him, even while married to Elizabeth?

"How kind and considerate of you, Frank, to see to their safety." Raising her voice, Lucille called across the room. "Girls, please, gather your things. I shall not have you soaked to the skin this time of year. Jasmine, please ask Solomon and Richard to dismantle the loom for Emily."

Samantha raised a questioning eyebrow before gathering her skirts in one hand as she crossed the room to a chair by the fireplace. What was that about? After all, he merely wanted to ensure their safety. Emily stood overseeing the preparation of her loom for the short walk home.

While the two black men broke down the heavy loom and bundled it, the three young women hugged each other in turn in farewell. Lightning flashed beyond the windows. Did they not understand the fierceness of the threatening storm? Coupled with the fact that he had postponed several important meetings so he could see them safely to their homes, he remained silent with an effort, impatient to be off.

Emily hugged her aunt fiercely before releasing her with a smile. "Farewell on your travels, Aunt Lucille."

"Be safe here." Lucille met Frank's eyes, and he nodded. "I believe Frank will see to that."

"Duty, yes, you've always done your duty." Irritation flashed across Emily's face. "That does not make it less irksome to be treated as though I do not have any sense."

"That is what you deserve for acting recklessly." Frank stepped closer to her. The sweet scent of lavender surrounded her. He inhaled deeply as he cradled her bundle of sewing. "If you had done what your father requested, you would not have ended up in such a spot last evening."

"Nothing we could not handle. A couple of belligerent British apes pretending to be tough men."

"In the middle of the street they wouldn't dare harm two ladies." Samantha turned to address the older woman. "Mrs. Abernathy, I have a few shirts finished to go with you." She handed her the small stack.

A crack of thunder shook the house as lightning again flashed outside. Frank flinched. Another southern storm to batter the town. Hopefully not another hurricane developing. Frank had slogged his way home through the remnants of the last one and did not relish the idea of repeating the experience. He'd nearly drowned in the sloppy mud and onslaught of rain. He learned later the British ships had arrived earlier than necessary to avoid that particular storm. So they were in town longer, the men more frustrated and embarrassed at failing to win the war, which led them to be belligerent. But their actions proved even worse beyond the limits of the town. Within the town's confines, the British officers could more readily hold the men accountable when they overstepped. Even so, crimes against the citizens occurred daily. All the more reason he needed to protect Emily and Tommy. He gripped Emily's arm in preparation for ushering her bodily from the room if necessary, but Lucille's voice stopped his exit.

"You sew beautifully, Samantha. The stitches so evenly spaced and firm. I'm sure the men will be proud to wear them." Lucille hugged the stack to her chest as she looked from Samantha to Emily and back to Frank. "But Frank is right to be impatient. Now off with you before the storm hits. We will send word as to when we will return."

"Farewell, Amy." Emily shook off Frank's grip and clasped her cousin's hands in her own. "I will miss you."

Samantha put an arm around Emily's shoulders. "I'll keep my word and visit you. We'll be fine."

"Is it wise for Amy to go with you, Mrs. Abernathy?" Alarm arced through him. They simply did not fathom the dangers lurking beyond the town gates, where the rule of law weakened with each mile.

The woman's mouth actually curved into a smile. "It is necessary."

"But Madam, you must protect yourselves."

"I refuse to live in fear even during a war." She laid a hand on Frank's arm. "Do not worry, young man."

Frank relented though his angst over their safety settled like cold, congealed gravy in the center of his stomach. "With the fighting so near and the British desperate for men and supplies, I beg you to not let your guard down because of talks of peace. The fighting continues despite the rumors."

He refrained from telling them of the recent ravishment of several women at the nearby town of Monck's Corner. It served no purpose to worry them. He and Captain Sullivan had witnessed the flogging of the culprits, but that did not negate the abuse the unfortunate women had suffered.

Anger curdled his stomach as he recalled Emily's bonnet in the foul British soldier's hands. The ladies did not appreciate how close they had come to experiencing the same treatment as those poor women. To take precautions seemed sensible and not an undue burden as the ladies seemed to imply.

"Now be off. Come along, Emily." Lucille took Samantha by the arm and walked her to the door.

Frank waited for Emily, but she glared at his arm as if it were a rattlesnake before slowly gathering her skirts in her left hand and wrapping her right hand at his elbow. Resisting a sarcastic retort, Frank patted her hand and smiled at her.

"That was not so bad, was it?"

She looked up at him with indignation. "Let us go."

Her animosity hung between them, palpable and intense. She used to look at him with welcoming eyes, but now those same eyes revealed distrust. He'd need to work on changing her opinion of him. For now, it mattered not. He had promised her father, and Frank's word was his bond.

Grimacing, he ushered her down the stairs to don her wrap and out the door.

He would see her safely home no matter her desires.

Emily held her head high, neck stiff, as she endured the four-block walk through the wind and darkening sky to her virtual prison. She'd left the nasty bonnet at home this morning, unable to consider wearing it before it could be thoroughly cleaned. Gusts of wind grabbed her curls, whipping them about her face. Frank's charms entertained Samantha until they reached her home on King Street, and their lighthearted debate over the best herbs for curing a stomachache allowed Emily to nurse her resentment without being called upon for her opinion. Just as well, given her mood. After saying good-bye to her friend, Frank again cajoled her into taking his rigid arm. She easily ignored the familiar heat rising through his cloak and the iron muscles beneath her hand. However, the current of awareness passing between them made it impossible for her to think straight.

Drawing on every bit of self-restraint, Emily schooled her expression and continued the normal sway to her walk, despite the unrelenting march of Frank's strides. Ahead of them, the slaves carried the loom and materials, racing the storm. She would prefer to shake off his escort and make her way home alone after the way he treated her, if doing so would not prove his point. No, better to behave as a lady rather than succumb to the delicious temptation of giving in to her wayward thoughts.

A burst of wind sent her tresses into a chaotic dance, reminiscent of Medusa's snake hair. She tugged the mass from her eyes with one hand. The long skirts of her day dress whipped about her legs, plastering across her thighs and tangling with her cloak, making it difficult to keep up with Frank's pace. A broadside blew past, and he cursed under his breath.

"Frank, wait." She slipped her hand from his arm and stopped. Richard and Solomon, striding fast ahead of them, kept moving, glancing at the dark, tumultuous clouds gathered above. Jasmine followed the men at a dogtrot to keep up, one hand holding on to her kerchief covering her dark curls. Emily longed to be with them as they disappeared down the street. She glanced up through her rioting hair at Frank and saw the storm clouds gathering in his eyes as well.

"We have no time; the storm is nearly upon us." Frank reached for her arm. "We must get ourselves safely home."

She started to follow, then blinked at him, confused, when his words seeped into her brain. "What do you mean *home?*"

"Not now, Emily. Let's go." Frank urged her to follow him, but she balked.

"Explain, or I'm not going anywhere with you." She set her jaw and braced her feet, crossing her arms over her chest. He couldn't possibly mean what he'd just said. A coldness having nothing to do with the increasing rain encased her bones. Fat drops made craters in the dirt, which soon blended together at their feet as the rain fell harder.

Frank shrugged, water dripping from the points of his tricorne hat. "Your father invited me to stay at his house until I get settled."

She caught at her rebellious locks, glaring at him as panic rose to choke her. "You can't stay with us. I won't allow it."

"Mercifully, that is not your choice. It is your father's invitation I've accepted, not yours. Can we go inside now? You're soaked to the skin."

He was right, blast the man. She could feel the tiny bumps on her skin as she started to shiver. She grew cold to her core from the deluge and the horrific truth that she must share her home with this man. How could she possibly avoid him under her very roof? At least the spacious house meant less chance of contact. And surely he'd be about town, not in the house all day. She exhaled. All would be fine.

"Finally." Frank looked pointedly at his proffered arm once again.

Emily raised a hand to shield her face from pelting rain as she regarded him. Anger coiled in her stomach and pressed for release. How dare he be so patronizing? "Honestly, Frank, anyone would think you believe me incapable of walking on my own."

A sudden blaze of lightning rent the sky nearby, immediately followed by an explosion of thunder that rattled windows in the buildings around them. Emily jumped. "Oh!"

Frank nodded grimly toward the smoke rising in the distance from behind the buildings. "Seems if the British won't bomb the patriots out, Mother Nature will have her try. We must get inside. Now!"

He tugged her along by the hand as they ran the last half block to the street door of her house. Without pause, he pushed open the door and pulled her onto the piazza. Bumping into one of the two imported rattan chairs, they hurried across the porch and through the door into the house.

"Next time, don't dally so." Frank closed the door harder than necessary.

"There won't be a next time if I can help it." She wrung the water from her waist-length hair. Shaking out her skirts, Emily focused on her sodden clothes as she started toward the parlor fire that awaited, and nearly collided with her father.

The burly man stood as though braced on board ship during a fierce storm, hands resting on his hips. Stunned by the worry in her father's expression, Emily gazed at him.

"Father?" She preferred to think her knees shook from the cold, wet clothes she wore and not as a result of his dark expression.

"Where have you been?" One of his massive hands cut a swath in the air before returning to his hip. "You should have been home before this storm hit. Have you no sense?"

Out of breath, Emily removed her wet outer garments. She took time to collect her wits before speaking. She knew better than to challenge her father when his mood matched the weather roaring about the house. She handed Jasmine the cloak. "Please dry this out for me."

"Yes, miss." Jasmine curtsied and cast a worried look at Emily's father, but stayed nearby.

Emily turned hesitantly to face his wrath. His brows pulled together in a frown as he studied her expression. She'd use verbal persuasion tactics to talk him around to her way of thinking. Though it wouldn't be easy. Emily opened her mouth to explain, when Frank cleared his throat.

"All is well, Captain." Frank took three steps forward. "I escorted Emily and Miss Samantha to their homes, safe and sound, as promised." He handed his wet cloak to Jasmine, who promptly fled the room, staggering under the weight of the wet garments. He ran a hand through his hair, drops of water falling to his shoulders. "Though a bit wet, I'm afraid."

"Yes, I can see that." Her father indicated for them to follow, then strode down the hall and into the parlor. Once inside, he closed the door and faced Emily. "Young lady, it's a good thing I asked him to keep an eye on you after you went against my express wishes, traipsing around town like that last evening. What have you to say?"

Emily cringed at the umbrage in her father's voice. The patter of the slaves filled the silence as they moved about the house doing their various chores, low voices and distant singing weaving a sense of well-being that had permeated her home all her life. Tommy's coos and giggles from the upstairs room filtered through the wood slats of the ceiling and interwove with Mary's melodious tones as the young woman cared for him. Emily plucked at her wet skirts, trying to put into words why she felt compelled to rebel against his expectations. How could she explain something she didn't understand? She looked up at him with what she hoped was a serene face.

"I'm sorry, Father, but I had to. The only other person in town who did the weaving died in that awful bombing last year. With only two of us left, the ladies need me to weave the cloth they require."

"You are not a lowly seamstress. You are my daughter, and you will do as I say. Not what the matrons of this town might ask of you."

"You would have me turn my back on those in need?" Her voice trembled, and she swallowed, refusing to allow her worry to show. He could not stop her from helping. She pictured her brothers, in tattered shirts and trousers, shivering in the crisp fall mornings. She stiffened her cold back, warmth from her growing determination thawing her bones.

Her father's hands grasped his hips as he leaned toward her for emphasis. "No, but you must be more—" He paused, his gaze flicking to the ceiling and back to her face. "More circumspect about where you go and when you leave this house. The bloody British are desperate. I'll not have you suffer at their hands."

But his clouded eyes suggested he withheld his true reasons. She searched her father's expression, his worry and concern enveloping her. She glanced at Frank, who moved to the blazing fireplace to dry his clothes. The dancing firelight accompanied by pops and hisses from the burning logs created a cheerful atmosphere in the formal parlor at odds with the tension inside her. Her cold skirts clung to her legs, chilling her entire body, and she longed for the fire's warmth. But Frank lingered by the hearth. Going to the fire with him standing there was as appealing as when she had a baby tooth yanked from her mouth. The memory of the resulting ache caused her jaw to tense.

Frank crossed from the hearth to sit on the stuffed divan in front of the shuttered window. Shivering, Emily started for the fireplace. Her father noticed her trembling.

"You're soaked through," he said gruffly. "How dare Lucille permit you to venture out into this storm? What was she thinking?"

"It was not her fault." Emily couldn't stop the glance at Frank. "The good captain was concerned about getting wet because I slowed him down. That was not my intention, of course."

"What do you mean?"

"I was surprised to learn that Frank will stay with us." Emily searched her father's expression. Only curiosity and traces of annoyance lingered in his eyes. "He said you invited him?"

"Yes, once I learned he had nowhere else to stay." He tugged on his waistcoat to smooth it in place. "He will ensure your welfare when I cannot."

"Father." Emily placed her clasped hands before her. "Please, you must allow me to do what I can for the cause. Let me contribute something meaningful to show my support."

Her father shook his head slowly. "You do not realize. With events such as they are, I cannot allow you to leave the house alone. I will not risk losing my only daughter. Your safety is my primary concern."

His scowl warned her not to argue. He tugged on the pointed edge of his vest, straining the bone buttons neatly aligned down the front. His dark blue coat with gold piping on the cuffs and lapel edges signaled his intention to leave the house. He had arranged his hair into a simple queue, so his agenda did not include town business.

Thunder rumbled in the distance, signifying that the storm now hurtled past Ft. Moultrie which was situated in the middle of the harbor, and on out to sea.

"But Father—" Emily couldn't bear it. She must make him understand. "Who will go to the market?"

"I can." Frank inclined his head as he winked at her. "I pass by the market on my way to and from the printing office."

"What about church?" Frantic, Emily glanced from her father's stony face to Frank.

"Of course you shall attend church, but I or Frank will be with you. Otherwise, you're to find something to do here until an escort is available. Enough. This conversation is over. Jasmine!" He strode to the writing desk. Removing a small bundle of papers, he studied the pages in his hand, ignoring her.

She could not let him. This was *not* over. Not yet. She hurried to him, her damp skirts still clinging to her legs. She brushed a wet clump of hair back from her face, grimacing at the sight she imagined she presented.

"Father, please. You must hear me. I feel trapped being forced to stay at home unless some man can walk with me. I've walked alone through town all my adult life. You must know I'll not live in fear."

Her father slammed his massive hand onto the richly embellished mahogany desk before him, its echo a gunshot in the room. Emily jumped and stepped backward, one hand flying to her mouth to stifle the cry threatening to escape. She was startled but not afraid. He would never harm her.

"Emily, you're trying my patience with this foolhardy notion of yours. The times have become much more dangerous for you. You must obey me." Captain Sullivan shoved the bundle into an inside pocket of his coat. His eyes flicked to the door as Jasmine appeared there. "It's about time."

Jasmine entered the room and stopped beside him, her eyes wide, and cleared her throat. "Yes, sir?"

"My cloak and hat," he barked.

Her father must be very upset to speak to any slave in such a manner. Emily gripped her hands together and waited. She sympathized with Jasmine but dared not intervene.

The slight woman bobbed once and slipped from the room. After the many years that she had worked for Emily, Jasmine knew how to handle his ire. She had served as Emily's personal attendant and housekeeper for the past ten years, ever since her father brought the twins to town to live after their aunt declared them ready to run a household.

At fifteen years, Emily and Elizabeth had assumed full responsibility for managing the small house garden, food preservation, candle making, sewing and mending, and overseeing the cleaning of the house. As time permitted, Emily also read from a Bible to Jasmine until she learned to read for herself. That was an accomplishment Emily was particularly happy about, for Jasmine's benefit and edification. If the day ever came when Jasmine won her freedom, she possessed the ability to read.

A flash of annoyance swept through Emily. It simply wasn't fair, Jasmine free to leave the house and she confined to quarters. She needed a compromise, and fast, before her father left and the matter closed without the possibility of revisiting it. She let her gaze wander the room, searching for inspiration. She turned her gaze back to Frank, his hands tucked into his jacket pockets. Tall and handsome with serious gray eyes and a cynical attitude she'd never noticed before, he was her only answer, whether she liked it or not.

"I do not fathom the reasons for the depth of your concern, Father." Emily met her father's eyes, pressing a hand on her stomach. "But if you're so worried about me, I shall renew my promise to only leave the house with a proper escort."

Her heart thudded in her ears as she waited for his response. She hoped he'd agree with her renewed vow to adhere to his demand. Once he did, then she needed to investigate the nuances of the definition of the word *proper*. Spots formed before her eyes, and she forced herself to take a breath, unaware she'd been holding it.

A light flickered in her father's eyes. She couldn't imagine what worried him so. She had never seen her father afraid of anything. Not when she was a child and slaves threatened to revolt. Not when his three sons—her equal parts loving and annoying older brothers—somberly left to fight for the fledgling country's independence. Not even when the British bombs exploded all around town, barely missing the house as they aimed for St. Michael's steeple three blocks away.

The presence of fear in her father worried her more than the threat of confinement.

"What is it?" Her voice emerged strained, and she cleared her throat before continuing. "What happened?"

"I take it you've not heard about the four women outside of town who were beaten and raped by the British soldiers?" His eyes glistened, his voice gentling, though still hot with outrage. "On their way to church, men attacked them. One poor soul even lost an eye in her fight to escape, though she did not evade

the ravishment that followed. I took pleasure in attending those bastards' whipping. Indeed I did."

Emily gasped at the thought of the poor women and of her father relishing the sight of men being horsewhipped. Or had he actually participated in laying the lashes to the British? "That's terrible. Did you—were you at the whipping?"

Her father glanced at Frank and pressed his lips together before inclining his head slowly. "Yes, that's where I met up with Frank, on his way back into town."

"Frank was there? Watching?" She dreaded hearing the rest of the story. She always pictured Frank as gentle, but first she'd seen him calmly threaten to kill a soldier, and now this. He'd grown harder than he used to be. Tougher and much more dangerous.

"He assisted with the whipping, as I did. As we have been pretending to be 'sworn' loyalists, we were afforded the opportunity to punish the brutes."

"The bastards deserved it," Frank said softly behind her.

"I never believed that you were a loyalist." Emily lowered her head, pondering the mix of relief and comfort surging through her at the revelation of this side of her father and Frank.

Men could be cruel to each other, but the idea simply did not relate to the men in her own life. However, the incident explained Frank's concern much more clearly than anything else revealed today. His participation in the punishment of villains such as those men reassured her of his position on ravishment.

Swallowing hard at the horrific images in her mind, she took her father's hands. "But surely you don't believe that would happen on the streets of Charles Town? The women here are not poor country folk without any sense, after all."

"Perhaps not. Yet I already lost my wife and one daughter, and my three sons are out there somewhere." He waved one hand in the direction of the still-shuttered windows. "I won't lose you, too."

Emily hugged him fiercely, awed at the telltale glistening of

his eyes. She rested her head against his heart, as she had all her life. The reassuring rhythm of its steady beat calmed her.

Frank coughed, and she stiffened, pulling away from her father. She looked into her father's eyes, saw his concern and love. Standing on her tiptoes, she quickly kissed his cheek. Turning to Frank, she raised her eyebrows in a silent question.

"You have no control over whether the British or loyalists harm you, my dear." Frank rose from his seat and joined them. Crossing his arms over his chest, he cocked his head as he regarded her. "They are stronger than you and grow more desperate each day."

"They've never bothered me. Not really." She forced a smile to her face, intertwining her fingers together in front of her.

Frank arched an eyebrow at her allusion to the previous evening's events but kept silent. Jasmine hurried into the room, bobbing a curtsy to Emily's father as she handed him his cloak and hat, then slipped from the room once more. Emily longed to follow Jasmine, but she must face the situation before her. She must stand on her own now and for her future.

"I would take precautions." She squared her shoulders to present a confident appearance. "I shall be fine."

"If you honor me, you shall do as I say. You must know that officers do not always behave as gentlemen. You must be circumspect with your behavior. But..." Her father hesitated, his eyes on Frank for a long moment before letting out a heavy sigh as Frank inclined his head in apparent agreement to a silent question. He held up one admonishing finger at Emily. "Very well. I prefer you stay inside, away from any chance of harm, but because I love you I shall relent this time. But do not leave the house without my knowledge and Frank as your escort, understood?"

"Yes, sir." Emily held her tongue with effort.

Worry lurked in Frank's steady appraisal of her. No, 'twas not possible. He surely didn't care about her. He only came back because of his sense of duty. She simply reminded him of his dutiful promise to Elizabeth. Emily resented the need for Frank

to escort her anywhere. Not only was he a man, but he was, well, *Frank*. And she didn't want to feel his heat and experience, yet again, their shared awareness.

"Father, I must speak with you on another matter." If peace arrived soon, she must be prepared to open the doors to her shop. She watched him with hope swelling her heart.

"I'm late as it is." He slipped his long black cloak onto his shoulders and his hat on his head. "Cannot it wait?"

Silently she nodded. The scowl on his face did not bode well for her to present her case at the moment.

"Very well, we'll talk later." Her father picked up his walking cane from its home by the desk and tapped it once on the floor. "Frank, thank you. I'll breathe easier knowing you're with her."

As though I am not standing directly in front of him. He's handing me over to Frank as though I did not think and feel for myself. A shudder moved through her as a bitter taste filled her mouth. Her father treated her like one of his nags. Handed off to someone else to care for, feed, even lead around with a bit in its mouth. If anyone else treated her thus, she wouldn't be bothered nearly as much. Well, except for Frank, mayhap.

"My honor and pleasure, sir." Frank made a small bow to her father. "I believe I shall retire to my room and dress for dinner. If you'll tell me which one is mine?"

"I've had the one next to Emily's prepared for you. Your trunk arrived earlier." Her father adjusted his hat and glanced at Emily. "With your room adjacent to hers, you can keep a close eye on her, as I asked."

"I'll do my best to keep her safe, sir." Frank winked in her direction.

Emily suppressed a cry as another shudder coursed through her. If she stayed another moment, being treated like a prized mare to be guarded, she would explode.

"If you'll excuse me, I'll go change out of these wet clothes." Without waiting for a response, Emily fled.

She raced to her room and flung herself onto her bed. The patchwork quilt absorbed the crush of her body as she lay there, tears flowing despite her resolve. She sobbed into her arm, felt the tears dampen her sleeve. Hiccupped once, twice, then realized what she was doing. The pillow beneath her crinkled as she turned over and wiped her eyes. Feeling suddenly childish, she sat up and took a deep breath. Feelings churned within her until she thought she'd go mad.

Pushing up from the down-filled mattress, she paced to her writing desk, sat on the embroidered seat of her chair, and removed the quill from the ink pot. As Thomas Payne did years previous with his pamphlet *Common Sense* that spurred men to enlist in the continental army, surely her writing could inspire other young women to stand up for their own rights. Including that of being self-reliant and independent. She anchored her turbulent thoughts on paper, settling her emotional reaction and making sense out of the jumble of ideas. Only then could she calm the inner turmoil and present a composed young lady as expected.

She scratched on the page, dipping the quill quickly as she captured her thoughts with ink and paper. Emily sat back and reviewed her words with a contented and determined sigh. She chuckled at the imagined expressions of the townspeople when they read what she had to say.

"Let's see them control this."

Chapter Four

The next morning, the pure tones of the bell hanging on the door roused Frank from his inspection of the type set for him by Sawyer, his young apprentice. With a surge of surprise, he saw Dirk Reynolds, a tall, powerful man, standing framed by the open door. Dirk scanned the bright interior of the printing office. His thick lips pressed together and his brows drew a straight line above his dark eyes. The door thudded shut behind the sour-faced man. What was amiss? Obviously irritated, he scowled like a cat that had lost its mouse. Dirk paced about the small office, straightening a stack of flyers blown askew when the door opened, allowing the briny breeze inside.

"That's fine, lad. We'll work this up after I help Mr. Reynolds." Casting a last look over the neatly aligned rows of metal letters, Frank nodded at Sawyer.

"Yes, sir, I'll get started on these." Sawyer's wide, strong hands easily grasped the heavy metal frame as he carried it to the printing press in the back room. The boy might only be seventeen, but he had the build of a smithy, with brawny arms and thick neck. Frank didn't want to face the wrong end of his fist, either.

The ever-present aromas of salt air and roasting chicken wafted along the breeze. His stomach growled. He hoped Dirk's business wouldn't take long. McCrady's chicken and dumplings would serve his hunger well. Dirk wandered to the display of public notices pinned to a board mounted on the wall.

Time to put the act to the test. Stepping up to the counter, Frank pulled out his notebook and pencil and cleared his throat. "Mr. Reynolds, what can I do for you?"

The man strode briskly to the counter. "I need to place a notice." Dirk pulled a crumpled paper from his inside coat pocket and smoothed it onto the high pine table.

Surely his hands were not trembling. Frank surveyed the ranking member of the town council, surprised at the dark circles under his eyes and the tension in his mouth.

Dirk nodded at the closely written page. "Will you carry that in your paper?"

Silently, with mounting trepidation, Frank read the notice shoved toward him. He read it again, delaying, contemplating how to handle this potential tragedy. His primary job was all about pretending to care about the everyday business of the broadside while encoding military intelligence into the printed pages. He refused to engage in actions which may injure his neighbors, unless defending those under his protection.

Slowly he raised his eyes to meet Dirk's glowering expression. "Are you certain you wish to do this?"

"I have no choice but to denounce this nonsense. I cannot be held responsible for his actions any longer."

"But he's your only son." Frank peered at him, concern a lump in his stomach.

The question remained as to the specific consequences if Dirk no longer acknowledged an heir to the impressive wealth he had built from nothing over the past ten years. Between the successful ship building business and exporting of rice from his plantation, Dirk was a prominent and influential citizen.

"No longer." Dirk pounded a hand onto the table, vibrations of anger spreading through the soft wood to tingle Frank's palm where it lay.

Frank lifted his hand to rub his chin, noting the light stubble forming there as he contemplated the man. He slid the paper back toward Dirk. "Give yourself some time to think about the ramifications."

"Don't try to dissuade me." Thick fingers drummed the pine. "You don't understand. That lazy boy wagered and lost my money, but no more."

"You're right about one thing. He is still a boy."

"When I was fourteen, I didn't have time for such foolishness." Dirk tugged on the cuffs of his coat irritably.

"Perhaps he needs a job."

Dirk looked at him with sudden interest. "Do you want Matthew to work for you?"

Frank's throat went dry. No, he couldn't support another boy and didn't need other eyes too close to the text. But who might? Surely someone in town could use the lad, keep him out of trouble and the family together.

The bell at the door rang before admitting Emily, her cranberry gown peeking from under her ebony cloak. She darted a look behind her before closing the door. Her soiled bonnet nowhere in sight, she wore a faded black one. Lavender wafted into the suddenly stuffy room, and he inhaled deeply. Her presence brightened the shop. He smiled, and she returned one, a simple enough exchange. He suddenly longed to touch her hand, her hair. Merely because she arrived in his dusty office.

But she came alone.

Frank stiffened. He and her father had made it quite clear she could not traverse the town by herself. Before he had left the house, she'd made no request to venture out. His ire grew as he gazed at her standing so calmly while his insides twisted into a knot of apprehension and, yes, blast it, anger. He suppressed the urge to berate her in front of Dirk, not wanting to embarrass her unduly, but it took all his self-control. Emily smiled benignly at him as she released the upper tie of her cloak and waited, her purse dangling from her hands.

The door chimed again as Samantha stepped inside, a gust of air frolicking in the curls gracing the ladies' napes. Frank stifled the rush of breath that escaped through his nose. She hadn't walked here alone after all. Still, Samantha did not constitute enough protection against the soldiers who roamed the streets. Damn, look at what had happened the other evening. Her father would be irate. Her father would—Inspiration struck as he watched the ladies peruse the notices on the board.

Frank turned his attention back to Dirk. "I'm sorry I don't need another apprentice, but I know someone who might be interested." He folded the paper and handed it back to Dirk. "Why don't you hold on to this for now? Let me speak to Captain Sullivan and see if he could use a strapping young lad on one of his ships."

He would likely see Captain Sullivan when he walked the ladies home. He'd protect Emily, even if that meant from her own doings. He must find a way to convince her to listen to reason and follow the simple directives he and her father had demanded for her wellbeing. If only the captain would tell her the full truth, then she would comprehend why he feared for her.

Dirk grasped Frank's hand with his own bear paw and pumped until Frank thought his arm would break. But the scowl had now transformed back into the man's normal contented demeanor. Sunshine broke through the scattered clouds outside and illuminated the small office, shining on dust motes dancing in the air. The ladies drifted to the other end of the office, looking at the set of pamphlets he'd ordered from Philadelphia and Boston.

"Thank you." Dirk finally released Frank's hand. "You've given me hope for him. I knew not what I would do with the boy."

Emily spoke quietly to Samantha, their delicate murmur adding to the sounds of Sawyer setting up the press in preparation to print the notice of the town meeting on the morrow. Frank's stomach growled, reminding him of the time. Did everyone have to invade his quiet office just when he'd planned to grab something to eat?

Frank smiled, trying to ignore the lavender teasing his nose as well as the growing hunger gnawing his belly. "Now off with you. I'll be in touch as soon as possible."

With a wave of his hand to Frank and a tip of his hat to the ladies, Dirk sauntered out of the office. The bell jangled wildly as the door thumped closed.

Frank wiped his hands on his heavy printer's apron and looked at Emily before nodding at Samantha. He worked to calm his temper before he spoke or his words would not be heard. He cleared his throat and placed his hands on the table.

"Ladies, you do comprehend it is not safe for you to be out alone?"

"Come now, Frank, do not act so aggrieved. I did not come alone. Samantha is with me as my proper escort. Her name is a *proper* noun after all." Emily chuckled at her little joke. "I needed to see you."

"It's not a laughing matter, Em. You know that's not what is meant by a proper escort." Frank shook his head at them, failing to understand their reasoning. "Why did you need to see me so desperately that you'd risk your life?"

Although formally no longer in mourning, she still wore the gold ring in remembrance of her sister. Since he could not attend, he hadn't received a similar ring when her father dispensed them prior to the funeral. A pang of regret shot through him that he'd not been able to break away to attend, yet he could not leave his comrades with one less man to fight.

Emily walked to where Frank waited, and laid her purse on the counter. "I have something, an essay, I'd like for you to publish." She withdrew a folded set of papers from the interior of the purse and clutched them tightly.

"An essay?"

Emily glanced at Samantha, who picked up one of the flyers on the counter and read it. The smooth curve of Emily's silken neck drew his attention like steel filings to a magnet. Frank swallowed hard as desire speared through him.

"It is on social deportment of young ladies in our town," Emily said. "Of how women should behave, in other words, including receiving the necessary education to enable them to run a venture."

Frank heard a note of uncertainty in her usually self-assured voice. What caused her worry?

Her eyes sparkled with a hint of challenge. Rose lips invited his kiss. The sprinkle of freckles across her otherwise pure skin tempted him to reach out and stroke her dainty nose. With a supreme effort, he restrained himself.

The pious people of St. Michael's would frown upon him making advances toward any woman so soon after he became a widower. Especially his dead wife's sister, a concept grating against their basic principles. Yet he longed to do exactly what society forbade. Not for the first time, either. One day, his desire for her would likely overcome his restraint. He hoped Emily would understand when he did make good on his plan to court her, woo her back into his life. How much longer must he deny his longing?

"Well?" Her long fingers wrinkled the pages. She gazed at him steadily, searching his face.

"I can't print your essay, Emily." As much as he'd like to help her, he couldn't.

Her smile wilted as her eyes narrowed. "Why not? You haven't even read it. Are you afraid?"

Afraid? Frank shook his head. He feared nothing and no one. Except maybe her father. And that fear was more for her benefit than his. "Your father, as well as the rest of the men in town, will not tolerate a young lady such as yourself contributing to the broadside."

"Surely everyone will understand it is only opinion, given that it is an essay." She held out the page and leaned toward him to emphasize her point.

The deep valley created by the bodice of her gown drew his eyes, and he had to work hard to swallow the lump rising in his throat. He forced his gaze back to her challenging stare.

"Well, Frank, am I right? Or is it because it's a woman's opinion and not a man's that has you shaking in your boots?"

He forced his eyes to the page shoved into his hand. Her ideas raised many points sure to provoke strong opinions.

"I cannot, my dear." He pressed his lips together to stop the wish that he could help her. "Mayhap later, after the war is over and folks settle into a more normal rhythm, but not now." He handed back the pages.

"I see." She folded the paper and slipped it back into her bag on a long sigh. She looked at Samantha, still absorbed by the pamphlet in her hands, before facing him. "Then I may as well ask my other question."

She glanced away and back at him, a touch warily. What surprise was she about to reveal now?

"I noticed the shop next door is vacant. The Widow Murray's old place. Do you know anything about it? Who owns it?"

"Em," Samantha said softly, one eyebrow raised.

"Read your treatise, Samantha." Emily stared at Frank, eyes challenging him. "This is my business."

Frank hesitated. Emily's question coupled with the warning tone in Samantha's voice alarmed his instincts. Empty shops abounded now, what with so many people having fled the area prior to the British besiegement. Add to those the people who left to escape persecution in the besieged town or who had died during the fighting. What was this about? "It's available, so I hear. Why do you ask?"

Emotions battled across her face. Her smile faded as she opened her mouth to answer. "I—"

The bell rang sharply behind them, and they turned to see Captain Sullivan striding through the door. The sounds on the docks beyond filled the small room as the wind rushed in until he closed the door with a *bang*.

"Emily?" Captain Sullivan blurted. "What is amiss? Why are you here?"

"Father, I—Nothing is wrong." She stopped and swallowed hard, glancing at Frank and Samantha. She gathered her purse before continuing. Samantha stepped closer to her side, silently supporting her friend. Emily slowly tied her bonnet strings. "Our business here is concluded. We were about to leave for home."

"I shall go with you," the captain said. "I have yet to have my dinner."

"Then we'd be pleased to have your company." Samantha inclined her head.

"Miss Samantha," the captain said, recovering. "How lovely to see you again. 'Tis a beautiful afternoon, don't you think?"

"Indeed, sir." Samantha gave him a small smile. "May my parents and I expect you and Emily for supper this evening as planned?"

"You really should go enjoy yourself, however briefly." Frank's curiosity was piqued as to what Emily almost revealed before the captain arrived. "The town feels as if it sits on pins, holding its breath. We're all waiting to find out whether all parties will sign the peace treaty."

"In the meantime, I agree that we should grasp any opportunity for a bit of merriment." Captain Sullivan bowed to Samantha. "We'd be honored, my dear. A quiet bit of fun may lighten the mood."

"Wonderful. I'll inform my parents." Samantha smiled at Frank and angled her head as she peered at him. "Will you join us for our small gathering this evening? You can complete the table for us."

Emily regarded Samantha with one brow arched, a question in her eyes.

If Emily attended, he'd happily forgo an evening of agonizing over setting broadside type for some quiet fun, as the captain so quaintly phrased it. More time spent with the fair maiden enticed him to relinquish his more pressing matters. "Thank you, Miss Samantha. I am honored by the invitation."

After everyone said their farewells, Frank closed the door and leaned his head against it in thought. Perhaps the time was right, after all, to put his plan into action.

Later that afternoon Emily rested her gloved hands on her thighs as she knelt in the dirt. The little garden appeared sad and abandoned with all the fruits and vegetables harvested and put up to eat over the winter. Several sides of venison and wild hog, mysteriously acquired by Frank, hung in the small smokehouse beyond, slowly curing over wood fires. While she appreciated his contribution to their larder, she wondered what other reasons he may have for procuring such a gift. The earthy scents filling her nose conflicted with the unease clinging to her heart.

She rose to her feet, then paced toward the kitchen. She paused halfway across the yard, inspecting the area stretching toward her from the rear of the main house, the brick cooking kitchen standing to the left, the stables to the right. The three-story brick house looked even more imposing from the back. She pulled off her gardening gloves and slipped them into her apron pocket as she surveyed the enclosed yard. An abundant herb garden wrapped around the brick kitchen and flowed into a small area behind it, the faint aromas of rosemary and mint mingling with the ever-present salt air. Solomon's bass humming accompanied a steady scrape and swish as he mucked out the stalls. A few birds twittered in the trees, hidden from view.

The scene appeared normal, yet her heart raced. As happened occasionally, she *knew* a momentous event loomed on the horizon, but what might it be?

She climbed the few steps to the kitchen door and pushed it open. The women's voices singing inside stopped as she entered.

"Miss Emily, what you doing here?" Jasmine wiped her hands on a soiled white towel before laying it on the thick wooden table in front of her. Her tan dress, sporting a small, neatly sewn patch of blue, hung to her ankles, where scarred black shoes peeked out from under her skirts. Emily sucked in a long breath. Elizabeth had discarded those earlier in the year because the soles had become too thin. Swallowing the threat of tears, Emily made a mental note to locate a better dress for her helper. Father would not want her appearing in the dining room wearing a rag. Elizabeth had taken care of the servants' clothing and welfare. Another role Emily had adopted in addition to mother to her nephew. Sadness weighed on her soul at the thought and she twisted the little gold band on her finger.

Bowls containing pecans and red apples, raw chicken cut up and ready for the stew, turnips and potatoes waiting to be prepared, covered the table in front of Jasmine.

"Somethin' the matter?"

Jasmine's sweet tenor interrupted Emily's perusal of the room.

"I'm not sure." Emily prayed for her heart to return to a normal rhythm.

She continued her quick survey of the room. Jasmine's daughter, Mary, attended the fire in the hearth where the kettle of stew simmered. A reddish-brown bean pot nestled in the ashes, steam escaping from its bumping lid. The heavenly aroma of cake baking made her mouth water. Tommy, his light tan baby dress bunched about his legs, sat in one corner inspecting a small potato, intent on exploring its dimples and curves.

Mary was comely enough to have attracted men in the past, of all races. She had transferred to town from Aunt Lucille's plantation, where the work was too difficult for her after birthing her baby, a wee child who died after being attacked by a wild dog. Her dead baby girl's light brown curls had revealed much of her previous situation. Such a tragic end to an innocent life. With so many dangers threatening young children, many women did not name their offspring until their first birthday. Elizabeth, on the other hand, named her son, Thomas Joshua Thomson, after her husband and father. Using Jedediah's middle name and her father's first name honored both men.

"How is Tommy this afternoon?" Emily picked an apple from the bowl.

"That one runs me ragged." Mary waved a wooden spoon toward the little fellow in the corner, drops of stew following its arc. "Always into something. Tommy started crawling this morning, and none too slowly neither. He'll be quite a handful once he's walkin'."

Emily replaced the apple in the wooden bowl. "That will increase your task of keeping him safe, will it not?"

"Yes, miss." Jasmine laughed. "We'll need eyes in the back of our heads to know what he's into then."

"Sure as the sun sets." Shivering suddenly, Emily looked around the room, searching for the source of her consternation.

Through the open windows the trill of a distant bird competed with the sounds of bubbling from the pots, Mary's renewed humming, and Tommy's babble. Emily's heart fluttered and raced, her breathing constricted as the feeling of impending danger built inside her.

She and Elizabeth had learned to heed their instincts. The first time this disturbing sense of danger happened, they had anticipated the horrific fire that destroyed half of the buildings in town, including the fledgling museum. Then again they knew when a hurricane would decimate the flax crop, making it impossible for them to make the material for the simplest clothing. This feeling presaged a danger. Whether large or small, something bad hovered in the air. Her hands chilled. Best to carry on with the business at hand. Try to remain calm.

"We'll be having supper with friends this evening," Emily finally said.

"Yes, miss," Jasmine said. "Your father told us earlier."

Though the floor was scarred by boot heels and scorched by hot pots and pans, the boards appeared swept clean. Likewise the table in the center of the small space glowed from scrubbing. The kitchen exhibited a remarkable state of cleanliness given the circumstances. Emily fervently wished for the day when they no longer relied upon slaves. Mayhap she'd free her personal slaves in due course. She had no power to change what her uncle and father did with the slaves, but she eased their situation in every way possible. "Jasmine, perhaps you'd like one of Elizabeth's old gowns?"

"Yes, miss." Jasmine's deep brown eyes concealed her emotions.

"And Mary seems to be fitting right in." Emily looked at the robust young woman who watched her in return. Elizabeth would have known exactly how to help the girl feel at home, relax, enjoy being part of this extended family. Why did she always feel so inadequate to the situation? "I don't know what I'd do without you to feed and care for Tommy, Mary. Thank you for that."

Mary simply nodded and smiled shyly at her.

Everyone in town knew the Sullivans took good care of their slaves. Some accused them of spoiling them, treating them too much like family to the point they didn't know their place. To her mind, this was the best way to make sure their slaves had no reason to resort to revolt and murder. She prayed someday people would be treated the same. After all, wasn't that what this blasted war was about? Independence and equality? Yet the slaves were essential to complete the never-ending work on the southern plantations and in towns. Sometimes Jasmine hired out to help elsewhere as well and earned a bit of her own spending money as a result. Normally, though, she kept busy helping Emily with the endless household chores.

The thud of Tommy's potato hitting the pine floor attracted Emily's attention. It rolled across the uneven surface, heading for the center of the room. Tommy cried out in protest of its defection, reaching out his tiny hands for it. Emily chuckled at his defiant expression as he rocked forward onto his hands and knees and wobbled after it.

"Mary's a good girl, miss." Jasmine smoothed her hands down the smeared apron protecting her dress as she glanced at the bowls on the table. "She'll do, with a bit more learning."

"I'm sure you'll teach her everything she needs to know." Emily let her gaze travel the room and back to Jasmine. "I've always trusted you to run the kitchen without much guidance."

"I try, miss." Jasmine beamed. "Mary can be a handful sometimes."

Laughing, Emily glanced at Mary. The young woman couldn't be more than fifteen years old but carried herself as though older and more experienced. "She has seen much in her short life. She could probably teach you a few things as well."

"Yes'm." Mary's teeth gleamed as she relented and allowed a smile to grace her lips.

Lord above, she was beautiful when she smiled. Her eyes lit up, and her ebony skin glowed. No wonder the men hounded her.

"Don't be thinking you can better me." Jasmine winked at her daughter. "I've years on your scrawny hide." She moved to the table and picked up the large knife to continue preparing vegetables for the stew.

"Men don't like their women plump." Mary folded a freshly laundered napkin and placed it on the stack of others on the table shoved against the far wall. "Too much of a good thing causes its own problems, you be knowing."

"You saying I'm fat, child?" Jasmine waggled her knife. "Wait 'til Miss Emily is out of here, and we'll see about that."

Mary shot a look at Emily, a hesitant grin lurking. "Miss Emily has what my man, bless his soul, used to call the perfect figure. She be honey to the flies."

"Captain Frank be one of them flies, if my eyes ain't deceiving me." Jasmine watched Emily, eyes dancing. She resumed slicing a carrot. "No problem from his side about sleeping in the next room from you, no how."

"I'll thank you to not spread unfounded rumors." Emily's face warmed. "My father invited him to stay with us."

"Mayhap he be in on it, too, then." Jasmine chuckled.

The crash of porcelain followed by Tommy's scream sent them whirling toward the fireplace. The child's mouth was wide open as he cried out.

"Tommy!" Emily started across the room, heart in her throat. How badly was he burned? She searched her memory for scraps of Samantha's conversations related to treating burns.

Jasmine reached the small boy first, his hand red from

gripping the bean pot's handle. The little potato lay amidst the broken pot and its steaming contents.

Mary grabbed the bucket of water as she raced to Jasmine, who now held Tommy in her arms. Plopping his hand in the water, Mary murmured to the boy as she wiped the tracks of tears from his pudgy cheeks. Her low voice and the soothing water calmed his frantic wails. Fortunately, he was not badly burned. He'd have a sore hand for a time, but nothing more.

Surely Emily's premonition heralded Tommy's accident and now she could relax. She let out a long breath, rolling her shoulders to ease their tension. Waited for her instincts to calm.

Unfortunately, the sense of dread remained.

Chapter Five

*L*ater that evening Emily reluctantly accepted Frank's arm on the walk to the McAlesters' for dinner. Her father had urged them to go ahead, and he would join them after he took care of a business matter. Now her only choice meant walking with the one person she did not want to be alone with.

"You look lovely, as always." Frank performed a half bow. His free hand lay briefly on top of her fingers where they curled around his elbow.

She strolled beside him, not bothering to acknowledge the compliment. Or the wayward caress of his hand. He represented everything she wanted to avoid in order to pursue her true desires. Encouraging his attentions did not factor into her plans.

What she truly wanted in life remained out of reach for her due to social propriety.

Mentally she counted her heart's desires refused her. She shouldn't open a shop. She shouldn't write for the broadside. She shouldn't be a spinster. She shouldn't dislike children. But hadn't the birthing of children been the cause of losing both her mother and sister? Although she'd tried to speak with her father, his business activities consumed his time, leaving her bereft of a moment when she could approach him with her intentions. Her thoughts swirled like cream whirlpools in her morning coffee while Frank chatted on, filling the silence.

Minutes later she roused from her musings as they mounted the steps to the McAlesters' brick home. She loved the adorable quaint cottage nestled among its array of plants and trees Mrs. McAlester chose for their medicinal uses. However, Samantha's reputation far surpassed her mother's as a healer. Indeed, she knew more about delivering babies and healing illness or bandaging wounds than either of the two Dr. Cunninghams, young or old. Emily tried to smile when Samantha opened the door, but apparently failed.

"Are you alright? I'm so glad you made it safely, what with Frank's requisite escort." Samantha ushered them briskly inside and collected their cloaks. "Mother and Father are in the sitting room."

"Have they been away?" Emily followed Samantha down the hall. "I've not seen them around town."

"Mother and I have spent some time over the last few days tending folks in the Neck." Samantha paused in the door. "The slaves out that way had a time lately with the change of the seasons and the cold snap gave them the grip something bad."

"Samantha, darling, surely this is not appropriate before-dinner conversation." Cynthia McAlester regarded them from her place beside the fire. "Come in, all of you. Would you like some sherry? Aaron, darling, pour our guests a drink, will you?"

Aaron, dressed like the distinguished gentleman he was, tilted his head in acknowledgment of the request. He crossed from where he sipped his brandy by the mantel to the decanters arrayed on a sideboard.

"Emily, dear," Cynthia continued, "where is your father?"

Accepting the crystal glass of amber wine from Aaron, Emily sat down in the chair across from Samantha's mother. "He had business that could not wait until morning. He will be along shortly."

"Such a serious businessman." Cynthia shook her head on a sigh. "It's a shame he pays more attention to business than family."

"He's a loving father." The woman's tone raised her hackles.

Good manners prevented her from saying more.

Frank stood beside Emily's chair, swirling his brandy gently in the glass he held in long fingers. His presence so close to her, his sleeve brushing hers with each movement of the glass, increased the tension within. Her nerves hummed with awareness. She searched for an excuse to put distance between them without making the movement obvious.

"His poor wife thought so, may she rest in peace. Or she wouldn't have given him six children, now would she?"

"Six?" Emily shifted away from the masculine heat invading her senses to clear her head. "You must be mistaken."

"Four boys and twin girls makes six," Cynthia replied. "Oh, that's right, my dear. You wouldn't remember the fourth boy. The poor thing died as an infant."

"I didn't know." She had another brother? Frank's fingers lightly gripped her elbow, silently offering her support, even as his touch combined with the revelation spun her senses.

"Many children die as infants." Frank lightly shrugged. "It happens, and life goes on."

"I suppose." Emily stood to shake the feeling of unreality surrounding her. So cavalierly stated, the loss of a life. "It is difficult to prevent illness and accidents."

Cynthia tossed her head and examined Emily. The mantel clock ticked four times before she spoke. "One would think his death would dissuade her from having more children."

"What do you mean?" Emily gripped her glass, finally relaxing her fingers so it wouldn't shatter.

"My dear, she hazarded having you and Elizabeth within a year of the little infant's burial."

Emily glanced at Frank, and he frowned at something he saw in her face. Taking several swift strides, he stood in front of her, searching her eyes. "I believe we should change the topic before my lady faints."

"I'll not faint." Emily cleared her throat and struggled to clear her head from the cotton that seemed to be filling it. "This is all so surprising, 'tis all. I'm fine. Honest."

"Are you sure you'll not collapse on me?" Frank took hold of one arm.

He'd like that, to rescue her, but she did not need his support. "Yes, so please release me." She indicated his hand cupping her elbow.

His grip sent currents of desire through her, igniting her senses and making her heart thump harder. Reminding her of the heat of his lips upon her hand for one chaste yet sensuous kiss years before. Some secret, hidden part of her longed to experience the seductive heat again, but she squashed the desire.

Samantha chuckled, drawing her attention. "Speaking of dangers, I see you've managed to defend your right to escape the house."

Did her friend have to raise that issue? She wondered how her father felt about failing to safeguard her lost brother. Is that another reason why he stayed adamant about her behavior? She pursed her lips briefly before forcing them into a smile. "He can be a tad overly protective, but I suppose he feels 'tis within his rights as my father to protect me, though I do wish he'd not be so demanding."

"Yes, he must see to your well-being, darling." Frank shifted his weight, closing the gap between them. "Unless I'm about, that is."

"I heard you're staying with the Sullivans." Aaron's silver hair, pulled into a queue with a black bow at the end, framed his narrow face. His sharp green-gray eyes seemed to absorb everything. "Something about your brother's house confiscated by the British?"

"They've seized it as an office and quarters for Major Bradley and his aide." Frank's mouth tightened into a flat line as he spoke.

"More's the pity." Aaron shook his head in sympathy. "You'll likely never get it back from what I've seen and heard. In fact, I hear General Leslie wishes to strip Charles Town of as much of its wealth as possible before the British troops and loyalists embark the waiting ships."

Frank's heat increased beside her, though his mouth relaxed into a pleasant expression. She shook herself, forcing her eyes to look somewhere other than his lips. The air hummed with tension.

His eyes glittered as he nodded once. "Surely Leslie's intention will not be realized. I will recover my family's property. One way or the other."

"The soldiers tend to be ruthless about any patriot's property, and your parents were devoted to our country's cause." Aaron dragged one hand down the length of his gray beard. "The British invade patriot homes whenever they like, whether civilians live in the house or not. Barge in and take whatever they want and destroy what's left."

A loud *bang* sounded from the front of the house, halting the conversation.

Emily darted a look at Frank and gasped. His hand already held a pistol aimed at the door. Samantha straightened to her full height and waited with hands resting at her side, eyes serious. The entire group assumed the still positions of a tableau, silent and watchful. Footfalls sounded in the hallway. Aaron started for the door while Cynthia held her hands clasped tightly in her lap.

Aaron's words echoed in Emily's mind. Her pulse throbbed in her ears. Soldiers? She pictured the threatening hulk of the soldiers in the street and tensed even more as the sound of footsteps drew nearer.

"Hello! Where is everyone?" A deep voice rumbled in the hall.

Emily relaxed, recognizing the voice. "Father has arrived, I believe."

Moments later her father breezed into the room. Dressed in his finest attire adorned with gold buttons, he cut a striking figure.

"Captain, glad you could make it." Aaron met him at the parlor door, shaking her father's hand. "Business finished for the day? May I pour you a brandy?"

Her father glanced at Aaron before bobbing his head once. "A whisky, if you please."

Frank relaxed at her side as he slid the weapon back into the secret pocket from whence it had appeared. The speed of his reflexes both surprised and impressed her as much as the extent of the changes he'd undergone while away. Who was he now?

"Here, Captain, there's room here on the sofa." A brilliant smile lit Cynthia's eyes.

Surprised, Emily looked to her friend.

Samantha gazed at her mother, blinking several times. So she had also noted the distinct change in the woman's voice. What did it signify?

"Interesting, don't you think?" Samantha whispered, leaning closer to Emily.

"She is very happy to see him, isn't she?" Emily sneaked a look at her father, startled to see him sitting on the chair she had vacated earlier. Curious that Cynthia wanted him to sit so close beside her. "I did not realize our parents had become such good friends."

Samantha eyed Emily. "Me, either."

"Shipping is doing a booming business now the British run scared, eh, Captain?" Aaron handed him a drink.

"It's easier with so many ships in the harbor." Her father sipped as he watched the other man and then swallowed, his face friendly but guarded.

"Good news for your imports then. You've built up a surprisingly successful enterprise despite the embargoes and sanctions."

"I do my part for the benefit of South Carolina."

Emily listened to the men's conversation with confusion. What were they talking about? The last time she checked the books at the shop, they suggested a comfortable living but nothing extraordinary. Indeed, fewer shipments had arrived in the past year, leaving them to rely more on the meager resources available in Charles Town. She must have made a sound of disbelief, for her father suddenly shifted his gaze to her.

"Is there a problem, my dear?" His smile didn't reach his eyes. "Is my nose grown too long, perchance?"

"If it had, I would not tell you." If Emily could joke her way out of this uncomfortable conversation, it would be the best solution. "Given how utterly mean you've been to me lately."

The big man laughed out loud. "I'd do anything in the world for my daughter."

"I'm sure, sir, but I believe dinner is served." Aaron rose and offered his hand to his wife. "Dearest?"

Rising easily, Cynthia swished her way out of the room on his arm. Emily watched the obviously loving couple leave, followed by Samantha and her father chatting amiably. That left Frank, standing too near her, waiting.

She looked up into his smiling eyes, and his charms pulled her in despite her resolve. Stiffening, she stepped away from him, intent not on fleeing so much as not staying.

"Em, you've forgotten something." Frank's voice made her pause.

Her cheeks warmed at his arrogance. She had not given permission for him to speak to her thus. "Do not refer to me so familiarly. Now, what is it you think I've forgotten?"

"Me." He gazed at her, his fingers closing around her elbow in an electrifying embrace.

"I think not." She eased away from him. Aware of Frank showing interest in her. An interest she must deny for both of their sakes. "But we should join the others."

He crooked his arm, a gentle smile on his lips. "Yes, we should."

He stood there, all brawny and confident. Her body's reflexive reaction to him dismayed her. She could not allow her physical response dictate her life, her future. Fiddlesticks, he meant nothing to her. She drew in a breath as the truth hit home. Liar.

She sighed and laid her hand on his arm, allowing him to escort her in to supper. Reminding herself that he was just a man. A handsome, witty, intelligent, and, yes, a very dangerous man.

"The McAlesters prepared a lovely repast, didn't they, Miss Emily? Perhaps next time you'll permit me to escort you home as well." Frank tugged on his sleeves, mechanically straightening the froth of lace draping from each cuff, his eyes fixed upon her. "Such a lovely evening begs for sharing with one's special someone."

Despite the tiny pang of guilt that shot through her heart at his pained expression, his flirtations met their match in her determined resolve. "I'm sure you understand my desire to spend time with my father." Emily gripped her hands together.

She would not succumb to Frank's advances. Her emotions did not matter. She could tame them, given enough time. Men tried to understand, perhaps, but they did not risk death each time they wanted to have children. No, they planted their seed and waited for the results. Her father's attitude proved a case in point. Would the woman, and the child, live or die? They may as well roll the dice to determine the outcome.

She sniffed. She could never share her thoughts with her father, who glanced at her questioningly. She shook her head at his silent inquiry and returned her gaze to Frank, who stood on the steps. Behind him the full moon floated amidst the stars of a clear late autumn sky. A whip-poor-will sang from some hidden place in the trees surrounding the cozy home.

"I must apologize, but I am not feeling well." In truth, Emily never felt quite herself when she stood next to Frank, always on edge, heart aflutter, heat suffusing her entire being. "Father is anxious to see me home. If you'll excuse us?"

Her father's perusal warmed her face into a blush. She blatantly bent the truth to the point of breaking, but he said nothing.

"Come see me when you return," her father said to Frank. "I know you're anxious to check in at the printing office before retiring this evening."

Frank bent in a half bow. "Yes, sir, I must ensure Sawyer

accurately prepared the broadside for the press in the morning. I shall seek you out in about an hour at home."

Emily's stomach tightened at the reminder of where he intended to sleep that night. In the room next to hers. Her cheeks warmed, thinking of him lying in bed next door. Hearing any sound she made as she moved about. Her own feelings aside, he remained the one fully responsible for little Tommy. "Be careful, Frank. As you both insist on reminding me, the streets won't be safe until the British leave."

"I will seek the safe haven of your home posthaste." Frank's teeth flashed against the evening darkness. "At your sweet request."

Emily bristled at the innuendo echoing in his words as he strode briskly toward his office. She stared after him, steeling herself for the night ahead.

"Are you sure you're feeling ill?" Her father gazed at her. "Is something amiss?"

Clasping one hand around his arm, she smiled at him though her thoughts stayed on Frank. Her heart calmed without Frank's heat and energy surrounding her, and she shivered with the loss of warmth. "May we go home, please? I am tired."

"Of course, my dear. You said you wished to speak with me on a pressing matter?"

The moment had finally arrived to reveal her wishes to him. "Yes, sir, I need your assistance to effect a plan for my future."

"Plan? What sort of plan?" He glanced at her, then surveyed the way before them.

"I wish to open a shop but I need your blessing to do so." The words hung in the air, tantalizing and awful.

Her father barked out a laugh. "My dear, I thought you had some terrible news to tell me, not this joke. Come, let's get you home."

"I'm not joking, Father." She let him propel her toward their house, feeling as though he'd slapped her. She had anticipated it being difficult to convince him, but she hoped he would at least take her seriously. Not refer to her plans as a joke. "The

Widow Murray's old shop has perfect dimensions and lighting to suit my needs."

"My dear daughter, please desist with this ribbing you're giving me. No daughter of mine will lower herself to the status of shopkeeper as long as I live. Your future is to be a good wife and mother of many children. You needn't worry your pretty head with the dirty business of making money."

Emily started to reply, to counter his argument, but suddenly she heard men talking behind them. She looked over her shoulder and a frisson of fear swept down her back at the sight of the loyalist major and a couple of other soldiers following them. Her father stiffened and stopped his banter, maintaining an even pace beside her. He seemed focused on where the men ranged behind them in the street. She assumed that, due to his military experience, he anticipated their actions—and more importantly their motives—more than she comprehended.

Unease washed over her. Loud voices were interspersed with boisterous laughter behind them. She kept pace with her father, wishing the enemy threat would disappear from their lives so she could move on with her plans.

She really wanted to write her thoughts out to share with others. Not just lighter fare like the satire Frank refused to publish. She proposed that women should be considered equal to men throughout this fledgling country. The fight for independence involved more than merely white men having their freedom. Rather, everyone stood to benefit from the resolution of this conflict. All citizens. White men. Black men. Red and purple and green men. Likewise, all women. Indeed, all people, free or slaves. Surely the city leaders could understand that, if nothing else.

She had read an essay written by Judith Sargent, an insightful woman in Massachusetts who argued against the men of the colonies who believed girls, or women, did not possess the mental capacity to learn complex topics. The stupidity of the idea that women would become ill if educated equally to men angered her. That notion coupled with her father's belief, that the British soldiers and officers considered colonial women nothing more than spoils of war, increased her alarm for all women.

Although she would continue to put forth a brave facade, she remained afraid. It meant more to her to be the woman her mother and her beloved sister would expect rather than the querulous soul threatening to emerge from within her. How did one endure a war with one's emotions, sensibilities, and sense of peace intact?

God help me. She longed for quiet and the assurance of a peaceful life. That the British would be chased out of the colonies and the new country would take root. She believed it soon would happen. But the delay tried her soul.

But what if the British didn't sign the peace treaty? What retaliation would King George inflict on the people who dared defy him? Her pulse pounded in her ears. Her bosom rose and fell as she attempted to quell her rising panic. *Oh my Lord, please protect us.* They would be ostracized, like the loyalists before the bloody British occupation. Her father and brothers who fought so valiantly would be punished for believing folks should control their own destiny. Perhaps experiencing the love of a good man, such as Frank, even if it resulted in death in childbirth, may prove better than succumbing to such a dire future. Death loomed before her, no matter the path she took. Her choice merely determined the means and timing. *I don't want to die! I have too much I want to do and experience.* She swallowed around the fear lodged in her throat, and clenched her father's arm.

"What, child?" he asked, looking sharply at her. "Are you all right?"

"What happens if the British win this war? I mean, what happens to us?" The last words came out on a quaver and a hitch.

"Do not fret." He patted her arm. He inhaled and exhaled slowly before continuing, as though hesitant to voice his opinions. "The British would not dare to blame you for any of the war. The men will bear the burden. You need not worry on that point."

"But that's not right, is it? I have an opinion as well as you do." Emily paused midstride to attract his undivided attention. "Why is my opinion not considered?"

Her father chuckled. "Daughter, you jest. Women have no rational understanding of politics, and therefore men could not chastise them for their failings." He patted her arm yet again. "You'll not be blamed for my actions. Now stop with the jokes this evening."

Bile bubbled to the back of her throat, burning so it brought tears to her eyes, making them sting and smart. Surely she'd choke on the disappointment consuming her.

How dare he, of all the men in her life, belittle her knowledge, her learning, her opinions? He and her brothers had taught her, for mercy's sake. However, he revealed a startlingly low opinion of her intelligence.

Damnation.

Bloody hell.

She closed her eyes, relying on her father to guide her as she attempted to cool her anger. She chewed her lower lip, forcing herself to remain calm so she did not trigger his temper. She did not believe he'd harm her, but with the British soldiers so close behind, the results may be disastrous.

"You there!" a deep voice called from behind them, tugging on her memory again. "Captain Sullivan?"

She pivoted to see who spoke to them, feeling as though she recognized the timbre of the voice. The bloody loyalist officer who had encouraged his men to accost Samantha and herself trailed after her and her father. He seemed familiar, and yet she couldn't place him. He appeared dashing and handsome, no doubt. But he wore the blue coat of a loyalist. His pretentious wig, that only those loyal to the king dared to wear, needed curling and freshening. His green eyes reflected no depth, no insight into his soul or what he valued. Yet he reminded her of someone she once knew. She searched his face, looking for recognizable features, but the echo of her father's words distracted her.

"To whom do we have the pleasure?" Her father stopped and pulled her closer as he addressed the major.

"My apologies, sir. I hoped you'd remember me. Major John Bradley of the light horse regiment." He tipped his hat to Emily's father.

Emily's muscles tightened like a wet leather strap drying in the sun. Of course. John. She gazed in shock at her former admirer.

"My apologies for not recognizing you in that uniform. How fares your father?"

"I know not." John cleared his throat as he returned her father's steady appraisal. "I have not spoken to him in some years now. Not since he lost his senses and became a patriot." He sneered as he spat out the last word.

Emily stared at the man she once knew. John had certainly changed during the intervening years, transforming from a kind, happy lad to a hardened, suspicious man. His loyalist views conflicted with everything Emily believed.

Growing up on neighboring plantations, she had fantasized he embodied her ideal man, coming to rescue her and spending the rest of their lives together like in the stories. His strong features and lighthearted attitude had mirrored her outlook on life. He had kissed her—the first boy to do so—when she turned fourteen. Heat rose in her cheeks as the chance encounter that led to the clandestine intimacy played in her memory.

She had been exploring the expanse of fields at her uncle's plantation, checking on the apple and plum trees and the pasture fences for her uncle while riding her favorite mare. She paused at a stream to let her sweaty horse drink. John rode up on his way home, crossing the path winding between the two properties. He dismounted, and they had talked and laughed while their horses rested. The hesitant kiss he gave her, not more than a light placing of lips together, had tantalized her senses. Although many years ago, the memory of that day shone like a polished silver cup.

Emily shivered, ice creeping into her soul as she looked on

the man John had become. Although attractive, his eyes glittered with hate. His expression fixed on her father with malice in the tight lips and drawn brows. His once-silky black hair poked out unattractively from under his disheveled wig. She shivered again. A whirl of sadness and disgust spun through her. No girlhood crush should make her sad for him. By becoming a loyalist, he became her worst enemy, worse even than the British. He became a turncoat.

"What can I do for you, Major?" Emily's father waited patiently, his voice guarded. His arm tensed beneath Emily's clammy palm. Her fingers trembled, and he laid a massive hand on top of her slender fingers. His small act afforded her a welcome sense of protection.

"I've heard of your efforts to support the townspeople," John said. "You're a valuable mentor to many in town; thus I seek your advice."

A veiled threat lurked behind his words, encased in his hard tone. Emily waited for what followed. Her father did not know of the several clandestine rendezvous she and John had shared while growing up. The lazy summer afternoons when her aunt chased her outside to find shade and rest from the perpetual household chores, times when they spent talking and laughing—and kissing—beneath a spreading live oak tree, Spanish moss draping to the grass. Revealing that past would only open new hurts. She relaxed her grip before she left fingernail marks in her father's cloak.

"Your words are too kind," her father replied easily. "May I be of some assistance?"

"Actually, you can. I have heard of some illicit activity occurring under the veil of darkness." John stepped closer to her father, piercing him with his cold gaze. "I am hoping you know who is involved in this cowardly privateering. I mean to determine who defies the king's laws. The traitors, when I catch up with them, will find themselves hanged for their acts."

How absurd. The king's influence in America waned with each passing day. But John's attitude and claims suggested the enemy had not relinquished the hope of being victorious. Perhaps the concern for her safety held more credibility than she cared to admit. The muscular arm beneath her fingers flexed and tensed, but her father's voice remained even when he replied to the barely concealed threat.

"I cannot help you, I fear."

"Perhaps you have cause to fear me," John countered. "I wouldn't want to deprive your lovely daughter of yet another family member, and so soon."

Emily gasped, recalling that he had called her by name, obviously recognizing her when the soldiers accosted her and Samantha in the street, and still he had done little to stop them. He'd not only become suspicious but abusive.

John raised a forefinger in front of her father's face, though her father did not back away. "Tread carefully, Captain."

"Surely you have the wrong idea." She would not allow him to abuse her father's reputation. "My father is an honest merchant."

John studied her as if she stood on the newly arrived slave auction block. He surveyed her, first up, then down, his gaze lighting briefly on hips and breasts before fixing to her face. A flare of recognition lit in his eyes as he repeated his deliberate appraisal of her body. Forcing herself to maintain her poise, she endured his roving eyes as they returned to her chest, then down her waist to her hips, returning once more to her eyes. The heat in her face intensified as his lips curved.

"That remains to be seen." His smooth tones belied the sudden spark of lust in his eyes.

Stiffening, Emily swallowed. "That is a fact." She moistened dry lips. "My father's reputation is well-known throughout the state. He's fair, honest and hardworking. That is how he made his fortune here." She stepped closer to emphasize her point. "He need not be a pirate or smuggler to accomplish that, unlike some other desperate souls."

"Emily, that's enough. Major Bradley, rest assured you will find nothing to suggest I am involved in anything so—what did you call it?—oh yes, *cowardly* as you propose." He tipped his hat to the younger man. "I must see my daughter home, out of this chilly air. It is not good for her health, and she has a child waiting for her return."

"A child?" John asked, obviously startled. "You have a child?"

Tommy. Although Mary saw to his day-to-day comforts, his needs presented the perfect excuse to end this uncomfortable conversation. Her head filled with ideas she wished to capture on paper as well. Emily grabbed at the excuse of a child to tend with both hands. Curiosity lit John's eyes and she wondered at the reason. "My nephew, Tommy. Father, we should go."

"Yes. If you'll excuse us, we'll be on our way." Her father angled his head in invitation to continue their walk home.

Returning home became more urgent with each step and the more she thought of what needed conveying in her next essay. Yes, she had much work to do.

Chapter Six

*D*arkness still blanketed the sky as the little boy's crying awoke Emily from a fitful sleep. Hadn't she just placed her head on her pillow moments before? She snuggled her face against the cool linen, reluctant to leave the warmth of her bed. Once she and her father arrived home the night before, she'd spent several hours committing her thoughts to paper. Then, at the risk of infuriating both her father and Frank, she slipped out of the house. Her late-night trip to the printing office to drop off her controversial essay, written using the fictional name Penny Marsh, left her with few hours of sleep. Fiddlesticks. Fortunately Mary would rise and tend the boy. She relaxed, prepared to drift back to sleep.

Tommy cried louder.

Forcing open her encrusted eyes, she moaned. Darkness surrounded her. The rest of the house slept undisturbed. Samantha's visit later today could not come soon enough. She needed those basil leaves. The previous day's many adventures made the day a long one, caused first by the anxiety of merely asking Frank to publish her work. She'd spent several previous nights scratching through inept, convoluted phrases she dare not show to anyone, let alone publish. Atop that they'd enjoyed dining at the McAlester's, the revelation of her secret brother, coupled with the strain of Frank's attentions and then her encounter with John. She meant to ask her father about her fourth brother, but John's accusations and threats had pushed the thought from her mind. Now Tommy chose *this* night to have colic.

The one night, she recalled with dismay, she'd given Mary a reprieve from caring for him.

Fiddlesticks.

"I'm coming, Tommy." Slowly she eased from her comfy bed and lit the lantern on her bedside table. She paused to stretch the stiffness from her back. Tommy wailed louder. "Coming."

She hurried into the nursery across the hall. Moving to the cradle, she anxiously tried to hush him before he woke the entire household. Lifting him from the cradle momentarily silenced his distress, only to resume offending her ears once he squirmed at her shoulder. Her annoyance rose, even as the expected twinge of guilt at her own frustration pricked her conscience. What bothered him that he wailed all night? Emily checked his diaper and found it wet. Again.

This should not be her problem. This should be her sister's problem. Though the thought was unkind, she couldn't deny its underlying truth. Tears threatened, but she swallowed them, patting the little boy on the back. He cried louder. Huffing out her exasperation, she crossed to the pile of clean diapers and stared at the stack, counting slowly to ten. Jasmine had showed her several times how to do this seemingly simple task, yet it remained a magician's trick. At her age she should know how to change diapers, but she did not have the experience of younger siblings to tend. Thus she started as a novice at caring for children. Muttering to herself and the child, she snatched a clean cloth and clumsily changed the wet one for a dry one. All the while, Tommy cried until he was hiccupping, tiny gasps of air between tonsil-revealing wails of discomfort.

He couldn't be hungry, as Mary had fed him prior to retiring to her room out back next to the stable. Perhaps it was the colic, then. Samantha planned to visit late morning and bring the promised basil. Feeling decidedly inept, she paced the room, crooning to Tommy as she contemplated possible ways to quiet her nephew.

She needed help, and she knew where to find it.

Joggling him against her shoulder, she hurried down the stairs to Jasmine's room. A light shone from beneath the door. Probably couldn't sleep for the crying babe. As Emily approached, the door swung open. A sleepy-eyed Jasmine stared owlishly. She wore the new shift and robe Emily had found for her, its belt loosely tied as though accomplished in a hurry. Jasmine eyed the infant warily before blinking at Emily. "I heerd you coming."

Emily grunted. "He's colicky. What can we do? Something must quiet him." Frustration surged through her, but she held her tongue and her temper.

"Don't know that it's colic at his age," Jasmine said. "But I've been told if you jump over someone's grave while holding him, it will cure it. Sure 'nough."

Emily chuckled. "Not in the middle of the night, if ever. Perhaps some warm milk?"

"I'll fetch some right away." Relief flickered through Jasmine's eyes as she bobbed a curtsy. Then she slipped past Emily and scurried down the hall and out the back door.

"Tommy, please." Emily paced the hallway while she waited for Jasmine to return. He burped and cried louder. "What is wrong, little one?"

Children should be born with the ability to talk. God had it wrong if he thought this wailing was communication. Frustrating, yes. Worrisome, absolutely right. But wailing only told someone that one was unhappy. *Bah.* Anger and vexation warred inside her until tears at her ineptitude threatened. There must be a better way to raise children. One that did not require a person to walk the hallways carrying a heavy bundle of boy all night.

She paced into the library and paused at the front windows. Interrupting the continual patting on Tommy's back, she pushed open the heavy shutters. At this hour, few if any people would walk by. Her hand automatically returned to patting the child's back in a vain effort to comfort him.

The sun edged into view on the horizon, sending flaming fingers shimmering across the water. The sky softened from its star-studded blackness to deep gray and red tinges. Tommy's crying obscured the normal sounds of morning. The beating of the waves. The call of the sea birds welcoming the new day. She gazed on the heads of the dayflowers outside reaching for the dawn's early light to coax them to face the morning.

Her mind wandered as she waited for Jasmine's return. She imagined the day she opened her shop, hanging her signs in the windows, mannequins dressed in shawls, hats, gloves, and other garments she'd made and decorated with embroidered designs. Her days filled with customers and collecting monies to pay her own way in life. Tommy squirmed on her shoulder, nearly falling over her arm, and she caught him and sighed. One day she would have her shop and not have to worry about either birthing or caring for any babies. At the moment one seemed as bad as the other.

"Miss Emily!"

Emily jumped at Jasmine's voice in her ear. She turned from the window to see her maid holding a bowl half-full of milk and a small spoon.

She eyed the spoon warily. Shifting Tommy into a cradled position in her arms, she pondered her next move. The spoon hadn't worked very well before. Glancing around the room with its many imported furnishings and antiques, she shook her head. "We should go to the dining room."

As they hurried down the hallway, Tommy buried his head into Emily's breast, pausing his crying briefly before turning away from her and wailing once more. Mary, as the wet nurse, allowed him to suckle her, but Emily had no capacity for *that* form of feeding. She hated to wake the woman on her one night off as well. Despite her servant status, it seemed only fair to give her a break now and again. But if the child needed to suckle to eat, the spoon would never work no matter how much they tried.

Inspiration struck as they passed into the dining room. She settled onto a straight-backed wooden chair positioned between the table and the banked fire.

"Fetch my sewing box and gloves. Hurry!"

"What you need with sewing things?" Jasmine hesitated in the act of leaving.

"We'll put the milk in a glove and he can suckle from that." She hoped.

Understanding optimism lit Jasmine's eyes, and she hurried from the room without another word.

It took both of them to pour the milk into the tightly woven glove. Once Tommy felt the warm milk in the glove's finger, he latched on to it with his toothless gums and suckled hard. The culprit seemed to be hunger, after all. Blessed silence descended over the house for the first time in an hour.

Emily cradled the boy in one arm, the other hand holding the leaky glove while Jasmine stoked embers in the hearth into a morning fire. Emily needed a clean shift, but at last peace surrounded her. Sunlight eased through the windows, reaching for her, casting shadows across the floor. Tommy's eyes closed, his cheeks flushed from crying. Content like this, she easily tolerated him. Even stirrings of affection flickered in her heart. His little mouth pulled on the glove finger, nearly as much milk going into his mouth as dripped onto her night shift.

Finally the boy's movements slowed. Drowsy tugs replaced the frantic sucking. Then his mouth relaxed and dropped open as he succumbed to exhaustion.

She carried the sleeping boy up the stairs to his cradle. Back in her room at last, she slipped off the milk-soaked garment, cleaned herself, and donned a dry gown. With a heartfelt sigh, she eased back onto her mattress and longed to sleep the rest of the day.

The warble of a songbird outside the window lulled her back to sleep. As her eyes began to drift shut, Frank's voice murmuring in his sleep in the room next door made her heavy eyelids fly open. *Fiddlesticks.*

Later that morning, Emily worked on mending her favorite dress. Again. A noise at the door made her look up.

Samantha stepped into the parlor carrying a basket covered with a green-and-white striped cloth.

"What do you have there?"

"Fresh basil as promised." Samantha peeled the cloth off the basket, revealing a neatly tied bunch of green leaves. The sweet aroma filled the sunlit room.

"I'll have some tea from that myself. It smells wonderful." Emily cleared her throat, trying to erase the exhaustion-induced rougher tenor of her voice.

"It will help the little boy's stomach when it bothers him again. You sound tired, my friend. Did Tommy have an upset overnight?"

"A touch. Mary is bathing and dressing him now that he's finished his breakfast. I thought of a new way to feed him when Mary is not available." She shared her new method discovered in the wee hours of the morning.

Samantha chuckled. "Good thinking. Perhaps we can improve on your idea so that it doesn't require fresh clothing each meal."

"That would be appreciated by all, I believe. I have few enough gowns now without having to clean them every day."

"Perhaps we should sew some new gowns for ourselves." Samantha fingered the fabric of her skirt. "Mine are sorely needing replacing."

"As soon as this war ends and our men come home, and not before. In the meanspace, it wouldn't feel right."

"The fighting will end ere long." Samantha pulled a bound book from the basket, laying it beside the herbs before settling next to Emily on the sofa. "The British are confined here, same as the rest of us. They have nowhere to run but back to England."

"And good riddance, when they go." Emily eyed the book. "What do you have?"

"My commonplace book." Samantha pressed her lips together for a moment. "I decided to make some notes, with your assistance."

"About what?" From the concern in Samantha's eyes, Emily hoped she erred in guessing the topic. Elizabeth. The idea of reliving her sister's death made her chest tighten against the painful images brought to mind.

"I wish to learn more about making childbirth safer for the mother through documenting what goes right and wrong during the birthing process. After all, animals manage to have babies without fear of dying. Perhaps my efforts will help women safely have children."

Emily sank back in her chair. The memory of Elizabeth straining to deliver Tommy replaced her view of the elaborately decorated room. She pictured Elizabeth fondly holding him, gazing with love on her child, a love shining like moonlight on the ocean on a clear night. Followed by her distress a few days later, her pallor and sweating before her expression stilled and she no longer saw anyone. Emily twisted the little ring, recalling the feel of her sister's limp hand in her own. She tasted salt and slowly pulled a handkerchief from her sleeve to dry her cheeks.

"I am sorry." Samantha laid a hand on Emily's arm. "I know you miss her, as you should. But she will always be part of you. You have her child to remind you of her every day, so you will never forget your sister. That should be some comfort as well."

"It should." Emily dabbed her eyes. She tucked the damp cloth back inside her sleeve and stared at the fire burning in the fireplace. Something about the dance of the flames fascinated her. She could stare at it for hours, thinking, wondering, planning. Ignoring the pain in her heart.

"What do you mean, it should?"

"Tommy is not my child, and yet he's my responsibility. I want my sister back, not her child. I want more from my life than to be tied to the house." She shrugged and frowned at her friend. "I want to learn new things, go to new and distant places, meet new people. I want more than this."

"You can still have those things. He won't be a baby forever. He'll grow up and become his own person, with your help along the way."

"I don't want to raise a child, don't you understand?" She rose and paced the room, twisting the gold ring so hard it almost flew from her finger. How could she explain? She took a deep breath and gazed at her friend and confidante. "I… I sometimes think I hate the boy."

Samantha stood and glided to where Emily paused at the chests nestled between the front windows. "You don't mean that, surely."

She nodded slowly. "Sometimes, I do, yes. When this war ends, I shall start my apparel shop and be my own person, and Tommy will be Frank's responsibility alone."

Samantha regarded her for a long moment. "I know you're struggling. Give it time, and you'll see you do not have to resort to extreme measures."

"I won't risk my life. Not like Mother did." Recalling the conversation the previous evening before dinner, she gazed at her friend. "Did you know I had a fourth brother?"

"No, I didn't." Samantha shrugged. "It's not uncommon, though, for women to not speak of their little ones who die."

"It's tragic that no one but your mother remembers him." She brushed at her gown, smoothing the worn fabric. "I meant to ask Father about it last night, but other events intervened."

Samantha studied her, pursing her lips in thought before relaxing her mouth into a slight smile. "I'm sure your father recalls the boy. For now, let's start with your mother. Maybe the events surrounding that long-ago day will be less painful to contemplate."

Emily clasped her hands in a silent prayer for strength. All she knew about her mother stemmed from what others shared with her. The secondhand recollections resided in her head like songs heard at the tavern, echoes of someone else's experience and imagination.

Samantha returned to the little table and picked up the book, opening it to a page half filled with her neat script. "What do you know about how she died?"

"Not much." Emily moved to stand by the fireplace. Snippets of stories floated through her mind like dust motes in the morning sunlight. Jasmine sang a haunting gospel tune in the kitchen out back, the scent of freshly baked bread drifting into the room. In the distance, a mockingbird shared its medley of songs.

"Anything you recall may help." Samantha strode to the bookcase and lowered the writing desk door to create a flat surface. Within the compartment resided the tools needed to make notes from the plethora of books surrounding the desk. She laid the book alongside the quill pen resting next to its stoneware ink pot, and then retrieved a side chair.

"She didn't have any problems delivering either of us. Not that anyone noticed. She sang to us when we were both in her arms, did you know that?"

Emily sat down on the couch, watching Samantha with wet eyes. She swallowed the tears with difficulty, refusing them release. Wanting to help her friend, she drew a deep breath and let it out as she counted to five.

"What a lovely welcome into our world she gave you. That's a precious gift."

Emily wrinkled her nose. "She apparently loved every one of her children with all her heart. Though she only lived a little while after we were born. Something to do with the afterbirth not being shed completely, I think, led to the infection that stole her from us. She cried out in pain, my father told me, grabbing her stomach. He held her hand, never leaving her side. He watched her gasp and close her eyes, never to open them again."

"Did a midwife attend her? Was there no one there to assist her?"

"Yes. I don't know who, a newcomer to town, I believe. Perhaps a childhood friend of Father's, as I recall. But what could she do?" Emily shook her head. "From what Father said, it all happened too quickly."

"Did anyone send for a doctor?"

Emily laid her head on the tall back of the couch and studied her friend. "Doctors in this area weren't of much use back then. They hadn't the same training."

Samantha pressed her lips together as she dipped the quill and scratched in the journal. She apparently struggled to remain silent, to not say whatever bothered her. Ever since returning from caring for her ailing grandmother, her reticence to share her thoughts had become more and more apparent.

"Let's talk about Elizabeth if you're ready." Samantha looked at her, unsmiling. Her quill pen hovered above the page, ready to capture Emily's next words. "It seems your sister had a similar experience, didn't she?"

"Yes, she lived two days after Tommy's birth before succumbing to infection."

Emily wrapped her arms around her waist, holding her pain inside. Two days filled with Elizabeth's laughter and singing, her beatific expression every time she gazed on her newborn son. A maternal connection to the boy Emily would never have, even if she wanted to. A tiny voice chided that she did like the boy and one day she might even grow to love him, but she silenced it. Her dreams of husband and family had transformed into her nightmare.

"When did you notice the signs of illness?" Samantha held her quill poised.

"The evening of the first day, Elizabeth seemed restless, and when I asked if she was all right, she said her stomach ached, likely from the contractions. She looked so happy I didn't press the issue. But I should have. Tarnation! I did mention it to your mother at the time, but she agreed it probably meant nothing."

"My mother?" Surprise registered on Samantha's face. "Mother attended Elizabeth as the midwife?"

"I assumed you knew." Emily was taken aback. "My apologies, I forgot you were in Savannah when Father asked her to tend Elizabeth, when she first discovered she was with child."

"And when she passed, I had gone to the Neck to tend to

several slave families who needed aid." She sighed, a long-drawn-out exhalation. "I'm sorry I failed to help."

"You had other obligations. Amy stayed here, along with my father and your mother. We did all we could."

The front door banged shut, and the sound of heavy boots on the wood floors echoed into the room. "Emily! Where are you?"

"In the parlor."

She considered following up on her earlier conversation with her father, but with Samantha present, it simply wasn't appropriate to have such a delicate intercourse. Hopefully after Samantha left, her father would listen to her plans. If he was in a good mood, of course. Emily's father hurried into the parlor, charging the atmosphere with his presence as he had done all her life.

"Yes, sir?" Emily detected the fresh tang of sea air carried on her father's long cloak.

"Miss Samantha." He nodded at her before turning to Emily, his bushy brows arched. "What have you been doing today, my dear?"

"Samantha and I have spent the morning talking about how Mother and Elizabeth died." Emily's voice wavered on the last word. She swallowed to clear her thoughts and voice.

"Such a sad conversation for a beautiful fall day." The hefty man folded his arms and shook his head. "Why are you dwelling on such a subject?"

Samantha waggled the feather of her pen. "I thought I'd make notes on the circumstances surrounding healthy childbirths and compare those to stillborn births and infant mortality." Replacing the quill, she gazed at him. "Can you recall which midwife assisted your wife?"

"Naturally. Your mother."

Samantha blanched. Emily feared her friend would faint from the sudden loss of blood to her head.

"My mother?" Samantha blinked in puzzlement. "I had no idea she lived in Charles Town so long ago."

"She's an old family friend," Emily's father said. "I became acquainted with her shortly before she moved into town. So when she did, and my wife announced she expected another child, I naturally requested that she tend her. Unfortunately the little boy did not live. But she also helped in delivering Emily and Elizabeth, and look how well they turned out."

Emily sensed he withheld more to the story, given the guarded expression he wore. "So you asked her to attend Elizabeth."

"Naturally. Cynthia has been a good friend for many years. I trust her to do her best." Emily's father put his hands on his hips. "However, I sought you out because I've been requested to go on a short sea voyage."

"For whom?" Emily folded her hands and laid them in her lap. "Isn't that risky with so many enemy ships at anchor?"

He shrugged at the question. "I received the request at the town meeting this afternoon. The British have stepped up measures to locate those in town who have aided the patriotic cause in a last-ditch effort to punish this town. Frank will return to the house soon, of course, to look after your safety. Prudence requires caution."

Ignoring the burst of annoyance coursing through her, setting her teeth on edge, Emily approached him. "Yes, Father. But a voyage? For how long?"

"A few days, perhaps a week. I don't want to miss telling my famous ghost stories, after all."

"Or infamous." Emily tried to recover her good humor with an effort of will. "Where are you going?"

"I can't say but I'll be fine. Don't worry."

Samantha shook off the concern in her eyes. "Perhaps we should ask Amy to dream up some new stories in case you're detained."

He feigned horror at her suggestion, then laughed. "Only if they prove spookier than mine. I'll not have any happy ghosts in my house."

Chapter Seven

*G*lad to finally reach the outer bounds of Charles Town, Frank sighed. Returning home to Emily and Tommy made his trip away tolerable. He'd slipped out of town with the excuse of researching the validity of a news item, but in truth to rendezvous with an aide-de-camp of General Greene. Hidden upon his person, he carried letters of instruction to be given to key men working behind enemy lines. If caught with them, he'd be hanged.

He reined in his horse as he approached the sentry, watching the young British lieutenant in the pendulum-like plodding that served as guard duty. After exchanging the requisite formal credentials, Frank paused at a sound behind him. A dusty pair of grays with black manes and tails pulled a light carriage bearing two women up to the guard and halted. He recognized the carriage as well as its occupants.

"Why, Mrs. Abernathy and Miss Amy, you've returned at last." Frank urged his horse over so he could greet them properly.

Amy scrutinized his face but only smiled. Odd, she usually returned a greeting more rapidly. What had they been up to on their little excursion to the Abernathy plantation? His suspicion hummed at the intriguing question.

The lieutenant sauntered over to Amy's side of the carriage

and grinned up at her, tipping his hat in greeting. "Ladies. Your papers?"

Mrs. Abernathy handed over the scrunched document with a rueful pout. "We arrive tardy for when we expected our homecoming."

"Late?" The young man looked at her with raised brows, then peered at the pass.

"We should have returned yesterday, but it couldn't be helped." She shrugged, a slight lift of shoulders.

"I'm not authorized to permit anyone with an expired pass." The sentry's shoulders drew back as he straightened his spine and fingered the paper in his hand.

Frank smothered a sigh. The officious lieutenant obviously planned to adhere to the regulations today. Why the heightened awareness of procedure? Mayhap something had changed for the British and not for the better. Amy didn't seem to notice, or hid it well.

The lady in question grimaced. "It's hard to imagine that so many ill-timed events could happen in such a short span." She let her breath out in a rush, her eyes searching the soldier's face.

Frank gentled his high-spirited mount and hid a smile. Amy could spin fascinating stories, as their circle of friends well knew. Discerning fact from fiction provided much entertainment for her avid audiences at parties.

"Indeed?" The soldier didn't look as though he believed her, but still listened.

Another dramatic sigh and then she continued. "My poor granny felt better after a dose or two of our good doctor's medicine. Too good, perhaps, because she decided she wanted to sit on the front porch and breathe some crisp fall air."

"Amy, please." Lucille frowned. "The lieutenant has no care for our misfortunes."

Despite the frown, Emily's aunt seemed to suppress a grin. Frank stifled his own reaction. This should be interesting. Frank's horse shifted beneath him, the leather tack creaking with the movement.

"She had just sat down in her favorite rocking chair when a hornet—you know, one of those that sound like a whole swarm of bees chases you? Well, it buzzed past her, startling her so she rocked backward violently. The chair overturned, throwing her to the floor. Unfortunately, in all the fluster and tumble, she sprained her ankle and broke her wrist." Amy twisted in her seat and leaned closer to the young soldier, inviting his attention to where a lace kerchief nestled in the plunging neckline of her golden gown, tantalizingly hinting at creamy mounds beneath the fabric. Her eyes crinkled as she followed his gaze. Fanning herself with one hand, she succeeded in redirecting his attention back to her face. "We sent for the small town doctor because he lived closer, and he patched her up as soon as he could, but not soon enough that we could return yesterday as scheduled."

"How horrible for her." The lieutenant's gaze drooped again to where the pulsing slip of lace obscured the valley between Amy's breasts.

Amy bobbed her head in agreement, her mouth twisting into a wry grin. "We thought so too at first. Then the doctor turned out to be a school chum she hadn't seen in ages." Amy shrugged. "Who knew they'd end up rekindling an old crush from way back then."

"That's one way to renew a friendship." Frank chuckled. "Will you be seeing Emily upon your return?"

"That depends on this young gentleman giving us entrance." Amy adjusted her skirts and fluffed the lace at her bodice. She peered into the young man's eyes, batted her lashes once, twice.

The lieutenant followed her movements with a slight frown. When he licked his lips, Frank cleared his throat, startling the infatuated soldier.

"Well, sir, will you grant them leave?" Frank's horse dipped his head to scratch his nose on one leg, nearly unseating Frank with his sudden downward movement. Gathering the reins more firmly, he pulled the stallion's head up.

"I don't suppose fine ladies such as you could be any

trouble." The lieutenant handed back the pass. Tipping his hat once more, he waved them through. "Travel safe."

With a slap of the reins, Mrs. Abernathy set the carriage rattling into motion. Nobody spoke until out of earshot of the smitten lieutenant.

"Now that's to bed, what has you out of town, Frank?" Amy asked.

"News printing business." The less they knew about his clandestine activities, the better for everyone. However, he wanted to confirm his thoughts about their activities. "I do hope your grandmother is feeling much better."

"Grandmother?" Amy blinked twice slowly and grinned. "Why, whatever do you mean?"

"As I thought." Frank laughed with the ladies as they rode back into town.

Frank braced his tired hands on the heavy leather apron hugging his hips and stretched his screaming back muscles. He had spent hours hunched over the metal trays of letters, ones reset three times already and still not aligned properly. Having to place the letters in backward so they printed right side up and reading left to right when his mind kept drifting to Emily's face, her scent, her laugh, frustrated him on many levels. He slammed a hand onto the thick wood table.

A folded paper glared accusingly at him from one corner of another table set at right angles to the first. He had found the pages when he unlocked the door. The pages were signed by Penny Marsh. He did not recognize the name, which was downright mysterious. British guards ensured the town remained closed to comings and goings at night. So who might it be? Someone wanted him to be at odds with the entire community, not just part of it. He slammed his hand down again to hear the satisfying *thump* followed by the high, tinny sound of the metal tiles wavering in their slots. Suggesting men sold women via marriage into bondage as often as they sold slaves would see him shot. Or worse, hanged. Marriage did not equal slavery. His parents had demonstrated that to him through their love and caring for each other.

He considered his marriage to Elizabeth, forced on him by his own sense of honor. He had not wanted to marry anyone at that juncture in his life, with the war all around, but could not abandon his brother's child or the woman having it. His brother had died for the very cause he now worked to support. He would thus honor his brother's sacrifice. His conscience had balked at walking away from his responsibility. Nor could he let an innocent child endure the shame of being labeled a bastard. The war may take the boy's father away, but his uncle would see to it he grew up proper and with pride.

He scrutinized the small square metal tile with a raised E on it before shoving it into its space on the iron composing stick. He allowed that what the essayist claimed held a measure of truth. A woman enjoyed the protection of her father until she married, then trusted her husband to protect and provide. She relinquished her claim to any property in the agreement, exchanging any former sense of freedom. But marriage still did not equate to being bought and sold like slaves. Not at all.

Dare he print this inflammatory essay? He wiped a rag across his beaded forehead before the sweat dripped onto the waiting galleys of set type. The wooden trays marched up the table, the painstakingly set tiles secured in place. He selected an A and placed it next to the E, cursing when the edges refused to meet squarely. Yanking it out, he threw down the stick.

Damnation, this business served only to tie him down in one place. Yet his duty to the general to masquerade as a loyalist meant he needed an occupation acceptable to the British. The broadside enabled him to communicate with his patriot counterparts easily, though the job felt like his own version of slavery. He took a deep breath and frowned at the rows of compartments before him, each holding a different style and shape of letter.

In truth, he wished he could board the next ship for anywhere across the ocean. The thought forced his gaze to the double windows at the front of the little shop. Outside, the bay shimmered in soft moonlight. The moon hung low in the sky, a luminous disc suspended above the sleeping town. He'd sent Sawyer home hours before, knowing it might take all night for him to finish his clandestine task. The one he dreaded each week.

Setting the letters in line after each line of text remained the least appealing aspect of the printing business. Sawyer then ran the press the following morning, while Frank inspected and prepared the papers for distribution. Another day chained to the shop. If he were forced to remain a printer after the war, he'd hire more lads to assist. For now he meant to keep to a minimum the number of people aware of his activities.

Sighing wearily, he retrieved the composing stick from the table. Best to continue or he'd not sleep tonight. Too many nights awake, thinking about Emily, turned him into a grizzly bear by day. For once, he'd make himself sleep after he finished this blessed chore. He bent his weary back to the task.

Not more than a quarter hour later, the sound of footsteps on the street made him raise his head. The person walked purposefully toward the shop's door. Mayhap word of some emergency had roused some other unlucky soul from a good night's sleep. He stretched his back and headed for the door, feeling satisfying pops as his spine released the tension that built within while hunched over his work. Few people ventured about town after dark, the fear of drunken British soldiers enough to keep them locked inside their homes. The light footsteps neared, a shadow passing the window before the person paused. He stared at the knob as he crossed the room, waiting for it to rattle and wondering who hazarded to be about town at this time.

The shape of the woman's silhouette passing the window finally registered in his mind, and he knew.

Could it really be her?

A paper slipped under the wooden door, the gleaming surface blocking his ability to identify the late-night visitor. The mysterious Penny, surely. He must know for certain.

Dropping the stick, he took three long strides to reach the door, twisting the key in the lock as he yanked it open.

Damnation. Alarm raced through him. "Emily?"

Emily stood ready to flee, one hand at her throat as she stared at him. Dressed in a flowing black cloak and matching bonnet, her pale face glowed in the moonlight. She looked fragile as she lowered her hand to clutch the dark fabric closed tight against her chest.

Rage and fear blended into a feeling so intense his heart nearly escaped the confines of his chest. All the perils she recklessly courted raced through his mind. He grabbed her hand and hauled her inside the store, slamming the door behind him. "Are you daft? Do you not understand the danger?"

She continued to stare, her mouth opening and closing like a catfish in the Cooper. He noticed her trembling and felt the anger build when he needed it to dissolve.

"I am fine."

"No, you most certainly are not. Look at how you tremble in your shoes." He scowled at her, shaking his head. "Your father should tan your hide for defying his express orders."

She raised her chin and glared at him. "He should not treat me like his slaves. Nay, his slaves are allowed to come and go freely from the house. He has imprisoned me in my own home."

Her words echoed those in the mysterious essay, confirming his suspicions. "Do not—" Frank held a hand up before her, noticing with growing dismay glistening tears in the corners of her eyes slowly slip free and course down her porcelain skin. One tear tantalizingly paused at the edge of her ripe mouth before she swiped it away with her palm.

She sniffed, retrieving a kerchief from her purse to dab her eyes. Eyes that brimmed with anger. He blinked. What right did she have to be angry with him? His hands clenched into fists at his side. She, who flaunted her father's wishes, parading about town as if enjoying a church picnic.

"My apologies." She glared at him, no hint of remorse in her posture or her voice. All trace of tears vanished like so much spilled water on a hot summer's day. "I know how you despise any sign of emotion. Do not take that attitude with me, though. I shall not stand for it."

She did not need to be rude. Of course he did not mind *emotion*. People *emoted* all the time around him, and he did not care. He—no, more to the point, he and her father were only looking out for her. Frank straightened. See now, even he was *emoting*.

"Do not attempt to avoid the bald fact that, number one, you have absolutely no business being out of the house at this time of night." Frank held up one hand and pointed at a finger as he counted off his very valid reasons. "Number two, you're alone, for goodness sake! Have you absolutely no regard for your father's feelings? How would *he* feel if something disastrous befell you?"

He held a finger to her lips when she dared to open her mouth to speak, ignoring with difficulty the sudden intense desire shooting through him. Grimly holding on to his anger to distract himself from the unwanted reaction, he detected an echoing shimmer of awareness reflected in her wide eyes. This flagrant disregard for her well-being could not continue. "I'm not through."

She closed her mouth, pressing her pink lips together into a mutinous pout, and he nodded. The desire to kiss her speared through him, but he grimly continued his harangue.

"Finally, it was *you* writing those missives of dissent you call essays?" That new comprehension set his heartbeat pounding in his ears. "What will your father say when he learns of this betrayal?"

"Betrayal?" Emily frowned at him, her lovely eyes clouding. "I have not betrayed anyone. You dare to betray me with your lack of insight and understanding. 'Missives of dissent' indeed!"

Emily actually came near to shouting in her intensity. The trembling he'd noted earlier transformed into quivering resentment, pulsing toward him as she glared at him through narrowed eyes.

She'd gone too far now by traipsing about town after all he and her father had said to impress on her the risk to her person. He needed a fitting punishment to force her to comply.

"Emily, please, hear me." He stalled for time as he racked his brain for an appropriate response. Despite her current agitation, she possessed a captivating golden beauty, with dark blonde locks, eyes that drew him in, and rosy lips begging for his kiss. No wonder the damn soldiers paid so much attention to her.

"Does this mean you will not print this one either?" Emily waved at the paper on the floor neither bothered to retrieve. "Is this the end or the beginning of my writing?"

She wanted the farce to continue? Her father's reputation hung in the balance of Frank's words as surely as hers. Yet the controversy could serve to bolster the circulation of the paper, which meant it would be easier to continue his secret communications. Something to consider.

"If it's going to raise as much of an uproar as I suspect…" Frank hesitated as an idea dawned. Yes, that would work. "I will on one condition."

Wary hope replaced the anger in Emily's gaze. She clutched her purse, her chest quickly rising and falling as she waited.

"Condition?" she whispered, then swallowed.

Frank nodded at her awareness of the import of his next words. "I wish to court you, Emily."

"Court me?"

The glimmering hope in her eyes changed to worry. She glanced away from him, her gaze flitting from one object to another around the room like a bird suddenly caged.

"Yes, I do wish to court you properly. And you must agree to wait for me to escort you, no excuses. This is for not only your safety but for my peace of mind." Frank closed the distance between them. He laid her purse on the counter behind her and gently enfolded both her quivering hands in his. "You can't deny you're attracted to me as much as I am to you."

Emily tugged on her hands, and he let them slide out of his.

The departure of their warmth left his empty and cold.

"If I say no?" She raised her chin, her hands grasping her upper arms in a defensive gesture, barring him access to her. "What then?"

"Simple, my dear. I tell your father what you have been doing."

She gasped. As he knew she would. Surprise, worry, and finally resignation worked across her features.

"You leave me little choice," she said evenly. "You must know this is blackmail. And more importantly, I shall make no commitment to do more than wait for your escort. Though it goes against my desires."

He tapped an ink-stained finger to his stubbly jaw as he contemplated the light blush rising up her neck to color her cheeks. Desires indeed. She did care for him, her expression said as much.

"Actually, I want to say one more little thing regarding that." Feeling like a cat about to pounce upon a bird, Frank stepped forward. He wouldn't bite, but the game did entertain. "You must at least pretend to enjoy my company, which I believe will be easy for you to do."

"Why would you presume so?"

"I know you, my dear."

Her bow-shaped mouth pursed as she watched him, one foot tapping the wooden floor. "I have a condition as well." When Frank raised a brow in silent question, she continued. "You must agree you will not censure the content of my essays. I shall have free rein to write on whatever subjects I choose."

"Within reason, yes, of course."

"Whatever I deem reasonable." She folded her arms more snugly across her well-endowed bosom. A challenge glittered from under her furrowed brows.

When she wet her lips with a dart of her pink tongue, she won. Marrying anyone other than her had torn his heart, nearly killed him inside, but he had upheld the obligation to the child. He'd do it again if necessary. Though, thank goodness, now she was agreeing even if reluctantly so he could pursue the quarry he desired. His feelings for Emily had continued despite her apparent reservations. He needed only to convince her of his sincerity. Perhaps allowing her to write what she pleased took a big step toward his goal.

"Very well. I grant you free rein with your topics and in exchange you shall permit me to court you."

"Agreed." She reached for her purse, then let her hands fall to her sides as she regarded him.

He took her hand in his and kissed the back lightly, then caught her gaze. "We shall have a magical time together."

She huffed but said nothing. Good. His hastily constructed plan worked. He would win her over to him. It might take patience, but patience he had.

Emily sighed. "I do not wish ill of you, Frank. In fact, it is not you in particular, but men in general I wish to avoid." She turned from him, preparing to leave. She bowed her head and stood still, her breathing ragged, as though fighting her own emotions.

He could not let her go in such a state, nor alone. Grasping her arm, he pulled her around to face him. Fortunately, her eyes held no pending waterworks. She searched his face but persisted in her stoic demeanor.

"What did you mean, men in general?" Frank lightly touched her chin to force her to continue to look at him. And *only* him, if he had anything to say about it. So beautiful, yet with such pain in her expression. He wanted to remove that look from her face once and for all.

"It is of no matter."

Her usually lilting voice flowed soft and serious. Obviously her new predicament, his creative form of "punishment," suppressed her reactions. She would not regret spending time with him. She would enjoy their courtship. He'd make sure of it. "Trust me, Em. You won't regret agreeing."

Emily examined his expression, looking for laugh lines crinkling in the corners of his eyes. Or the dimples deepening beside his mouth as he smiled with mirth. Nothing. Frank wanted to court her. Why? Not because of the essays, surely. Or perhaps little Tommy's care hovered uppermost in his mind. Her mind whirled with possible motives for this absurd yet inexplicably tempting idea.

Court her? He must be teasing. Firm lips compressed with no hint of a smile or frown. Waiting for her response.

"Do you approve?" Frank winked at her, breaking the silence.

"Of course not. I know you jest." She waved a hand in the air as if to shoo away a pesky fly. "I will care for little Tommy without this pretense."

"More is needed from your promise than Tommy's care. Your agreement to my courtship also comes with your promise to await my presence before emerging from home." He shook his head as he gazed at her. "I will not print your missives without that vow."

"Are you serious?" The intensity of his perusal ignited a hot flush in her neck, rising to warm her cheeks. A smile curved his mouth, revealing white teeth, dimples deepening. His fingers caressed her heated face, eyes fastening on her mouth before sliding to meet her gaze.

"Indeed, I am. You fascinate me. I cannot stop watching you."

Quivering with the conflicting emotions battling inside, she held her ground. "I am not some caged creature for you to stare at, sir."

Emily's physical reaction to his touch was as out of control as her emotional dismissal of his unwanted affections. The whirlwind consuming her composure left her longing for support, but she dare not show him any weakness. She must master the unnerving reaction. She clasped her hands together to still them.

A waft of night air filtered in through the gaps around the

door, refreshing the stale air inside. The salty tang mixed with the scent of ink lingering in the shop. The night watchman strolled past the office, calling out, "Ten o'clock and all is well."

When Frank stroked her cheek with the backs of his fingers, she raised her chin and pulled away. He should not be so bold. Her conscience chided her for being too loose and fast. She shouldn't permit this audacious behavior. She closed her mouth, agitated it had fallen open without her permission. His eyes darkened as they fixed on her lips.

Her inner quiver matured into visible trembling under his scrutiny. His kiss seemed inevitable unless she prevented it. "You cannot force me to court you, Frank. I'm a grown woman."

"Yes, you are." He stepped toward her, invading the buffer of air she imagined protected her.

"It's late." She refused to step back and give him the pleasure of her retreat. Besides, the edge of the table rested at her back. She had nowhere to go but toward Frank, which she would not do. The air fled the printing office, suddenly suffocating her. Sweat snaked down the valley between her breasts at the realization she must extricate herself and quickly. What if Mary and Tommy needed her and she was not there to assist? The entire household, especially her father, would learn of her clandestine undertakings. That simply would not do. "I must go home."

Frank's dimples carved tiny crevasses in his cheeks, and radiating lines framed his twinkling eyes, reminding her of rays of sunlight shining through a cloud. Why did he grin so?

"I suppose, if you really will not allow me to be with you then I must reveal your late-night activities to your father." His knowing smile confirmed his sincerity.

"You wouldn't." Keeping her arms locked around her helped her pretend some sense of control. She envisioned her father confining her to the house under armed guard, never to venture forth until the war ended. Whenever that might be. Worse, he would take away her writing materials if he knew about her essays. Searching Frank's face, her fear of her father's wrath stayed uppermost in her mind. She had no choice.

Her shoulders sagged. Her father must not discover who authored the inflammatory opinion pieces she hoped would spark the entire town into debating their merits, if they found any. At least the conversation would start. Not only would Father be angry and embarrassed, but he may even consider her actions a disloyalty to his authority and his trust. Worse, he would be right.

"I will, but only because you leave me no option, my dear. But do not despair." Frank traced a finger lightly along her cheekbone, skirting her lip and down her chin. "I will be an eager and attentive suitor."

Her body leaned toward him despite her resolve, tingled over every inch where his finger trailed. But how could she agree and still maintain her reputation, let alone her vow?

The memory of kissing John under the live oak tree years before flashed through her mind. She courted then without marrying, though he had intrigued her for a time. She certainly could experiment in such a way again. Without any commitments, of course.

Examining the man before her, she acknowledged her attraction to him on a purely superficial level, though she resisted any emotional interest. Frank's dark blond hair put emphasis on a sculpted jaw and intelligent eyes. Broad shoulders stretched the fabric of his coat, suggesting the strength of the muscular arms beneath. His breeches fit snugly, hinting at powerful thighs and hips, as well as revealing strong calves.

Courting did not mean a death sentence. Nor a marriage contract. Courting merely meant a temporary situation she could end anytime she chose. She could survive this.

As if sensing her change of heart, Frank moved closer until only an inch of charged air separated their heated bodies. Emily dragged in a breath and let it out on a ragged sigh.

"We should determine the ground rules." Emily searched his eyes for his agreement.

"Such as?" Frank paused, his gaze roaming her face.

"Such as how long we'll pretend to be courting."

"Hm. I'd think at least three weeks. That should be enough time."

"For what?" Holding her breath, Emily waited.

"To know each other well enough to determine whether we should marry."

Emily opened her mouth but no sound emerged.

Frank stood so close his breath stirred the curls tickling the sides of her face. He smelled of peppermint, wool, and the tangy aroma of ink from the press. His eyes became deep pools she wanted to lose herself in as he studied her.

"I should give you fair warning, my love." Frank trailed a finger over her parted lips. "I plan to kiss you."

His deep voice flowed over her, through her, fueling the sensations smoldering in her nether regions.

Her pulse quickened, as did her breathing. When he clasped her upper arms to pull her to him, lightning shot through her veins. Who knew a man's mouth could be so utterly fascinating? The way his lips moved as he drew closer to her, parting slowly in anticipation of meeting hers.

Fortunately, he kept a firm grip on her or she would have collapsed to the floor. She started to refuse him, to remind him how inappropriate a kiss would be between them, alone without a chaperone, but no sound emerged. Closing her mouth, she stared, tempted by what seemed inevitable.

His head dipped lower.

Sensation competed with emotion as his lips sought hers. His kiss, warm and firm, radiated through her until even her toes tingled. On a low moan, he pulled her closer. She pressed against him, craving him. His embrace tightened as his tongue plundered her mouth, one hand cradling her head. He tasted delicious, of peppermint and rum.

After awhile, Frank gently eased his mouth from hers. She clung to his shoulders, needing his strength and stability after being rocked to her core. She should be angry about his audacity and presumption. *Should.* Instead, she longed for a repeat performance. Sensations swirled through her, conflicting desires and expectations filling her mind.

"Thank you, my love." Frank relaxed his grip, enabling her to push away and stand on her own, though he kept one arm loosely around her. "I needed that."

She smiled, tentatively touching a finger to her sensitive lips. "I enjoyed the act as well."

"You sound surprised." He squeezed her to him, then released her. "You hurt me with your surprise."

"You really shouldn't have presumed to kiss me. Enjoyable or not."

"Perhaps. But you wanted to establish the bounds of our courtship."

"With an illicit kiss?" She shouldn't deceive him or herself. Another act to conceal from her father. Even so, she'd do it again.

Frank reached for her hand, caressing her thumb. "Yes, so you'll know touching and kissing constitute essential ingredients of our private times together."

"You think highly of yourself, don't you?" Emily withdrew her hand on principle, though she had to force herself to refrain from leaning into him, once more engaging their lips. He drew her like a magnet. She must maintain her distance from him or she'd either burst into flames only he could quench, or break into pieces, never to be put back together.

"I'm confident. There's a difference." He wrapped his arms around her in a long hug, folding her inside his protective circle. "Now, my dear, it is past time I walk you home."

Frank excused himself to retrieve the lantern from its hook by the back door. Emily picked up her purse from the table and waited silently for him, her body singing even as her mind whirled in confusion over this surprising turn of events. Slipping on his cloak, he locked up the shop and they walked the few blocks home in silence, Emily pondering the predicament she now found herself in.

Once inside, he paused by her bedroom. His lips touched hers in a long, gentle kiss before he slowly released her. He reached around to open the door. Emily moved toward the opening, her escape from the tangle of emotions swirling within her. Soon she would be alone to sort through her thoughts and feelings.

Frank stopped her before she stepped over the doorsill. "I'll inform your father of my intentions tomorrow morning. Good night, my love."

Her heart fluttered at the endearment, but she stiffened her resolve to remain aloof. "My name is Emily." If he didn't use endearments, perchance she might keep him at arm's length until the three weeks elapsed. It was a hope, even if only a glimmering one.

He smiled at her attempt at resistance. "See you on the morrow, Em."

He made a half bow as she dashed into her room, heart racing at the sound of her name on his lips.

Chapter Eight

The next morning, Frank rose before the sun and dressed with particular care. An important day lay ahead, one that could easily change his future as well as that of the love of his life.

He entered the dining room and went to the sideboard to peruse the breakfast offerings. Filling a plate with fruit and hard cooked eggs, he took a seat and began to eat. Jasmine brought piping hot coffee to wash down his meal. Ere long the captain strode into the room and quickly loaded a plate with eggs, link sausage, and buttered toast.

Settling onto the chair at the head of the table reserved for the master of the house, Joshua peered at Frank. "I trust you had a good night."

"I did, thank you. In fact, I have news to convey." Frank laid down his fork to give the captain his full attention.

"Business or pleasure?" Joshua bit into his toast and chewed.

"Pleasure. Actually, personal." Frank squared his shoulders and steeled his spine. This conversation was harder than he'd thought it might be. "Emily has agreed to allow me to wait on her, sir. If that meets with your approval."

"She's willing for you to court her?" He took another bite as his eyes gleamed with delight. "Very good. You have my blessing."

"Thank you, sir. I would like to begin this very day."

Emily strolled into the room as Frank lifted his cup. She paused just inside the doorway to study him before she went to the sideboard to fix her plate. Had she heard their conversation? He gulped the hot coffee and then lowered the cup to the waiting saucer, keeping his eyes on her graceful movements. She soon joined the men at the table with her breakfast, sitting across from him. Jasmine returned with the coffee pot and filled cups as she eased around the table.

"Emily, Frank tells me you have agreed to his courtship. I heartily approve."

She swallowed a bite of sausage. "Thank you, Father."

"I'd like to take you for a long stroll and then have our dinner at that new eating establishment uptown. Would you enjoy such an outing?" Frank acted nonchalant, cutting a bite of egg with fork and knife, but his gut swirled with an unfamiliar insecurity.

She nodded as she sipped her coffee, her gaze open and inviting. "I've heard good things about the menu at the Gray Pelican, so yes. I look forward to it."

"Very well. I'll return from the shop around two." He smiled at her, relieved and anxious to show her a nice afternoon in his company. He dug into his breakfast.

Later that afternoon, they sauntered along East Bay toward the small battery located at the point, her hand wrapped around his arm. Seagulls soared above, swooping down to land on the wharfs. A string of brown pelicans cruised just off shore, flying north. Sunshine warmed his shoulders almost as much as having Emily on his arm warmed his heart. He greeted several townspeople with a nod and smile but otherwise kept his attention on his woman.

My, how he liked the sound of that. She was his and no one else's. If he had his way, she would always belong to him alone.

As they passed the Exchange, he pulled her to a halt. "I pity the people held prisoner in the Provost dungeon. It's not a fitting place for anyone."

"It's a beautiful building turned to awful purposes." Emily's hand tensed on his arm.

The Exchange stood as one of the grandest public buildings in the states. Three stories tall and made of red brick, it housed a basement at ground level, an exchange and customs house on the first floor, and a Great Hall on the top floor for meetings and important gatherings. The Hall doubled as a ballroom for the socialites. It was the site where delegates were elected to the Continental Congress and where the town's citizens first heard the reading of the Declaration of Independence. Now it was a prison for patriots.

He kissed her lightly on the lips. "Let's not dwell on the matter on such a lovely afternoon. Come, let's move on."

She shivered as they continued down the street. They passed the group of buildings known as Rainbow Row, each painted a different pastel color. Past the small tavern that had existed in town for decades and was a favorite haunt of the sailors. The wharves bustled with activity, the harbor beyond filled with more than one hundred ships at anchor. He longed for the ones flying the British flag to be gone.

"Have you seen Ft. Wilkins?" Frank glanced down at her upturned smiling face.

"No, what is that?" She aimed her lovely eyes at him, soft as moonlight.

"It's a small battery used for defense. It's near the oyster mound."

"With my father's concerns, I've not been able to see much. While I'm not enamored with looking at military apparatus, I am intrigued by the oysters. Did you know that nobody knows the purpose of the mound?"

"It's a matter for debate." He pulled her closer as another couple approached, wrapping his arm around her waist until they'd passed. "I believe it's where the natives, you know the Indians, discarded the oyster shells before white men arrived."

"It's very big and interesting." She straightened her bonnet after a gust a breeze tugged it askew.

"So do you want to walk down to see it?" Her answer would tell him more about her interests.

"Yes, that would be nice."

"Then let's keep going." He smiled at her, pleased with her choice.

They walked several blocks with only a few words exchanged. He appreciated the easy conversation as much as her companionship. Relief at not being pressured into small talk swept through him. Their exchanges may be intermittent but were meaningful. When they reached the huge mound, she stopped at his side.

"That's astonishingly huge." Her delighted and surprised expression made him grin in response. "It always impresses."

"Yes, it does."

She smiled up at him, glancing back to the amazing sight repeatedly. "Thank you so much for bringing me back here. I like contemplating the past and how people have changed over time. But after all this walking, I'm parched and hungry."

"Then let us head for the Gray Pelican and solve both problems." He ushered her back up the street and turned onto Tradd, heading west a few blocks to the site of the new tavern.

The widow who ran the cheerful establishment insisted on decorum and provided both fine meals and entertainment. As a result, Frank had no qualms taking his lady inside for their afternoon dinner. The only down side was that the widow was a loyalist, so she welcomed him without reservation. If she knew the truth, he'd be turned in and trouble would follow.

He stopped outside the door and pinned Emily with a serious look. "Remember, I'm a loyalist soldier. Don't say otherwise inside these walls, understood?"

Surprise widened her eyes as she nodded. "Understood."

He pulled the heavy door open and led her inside the brightly lit room. A bearded man played the piano in the far corner accompanied by a fiddler, his bow flashing across the strings.

Frank led her to an empty table near a front window and

pulled a chair out for her to sit upon. Then sat in the opposite chair, glancing out the window to watch people hurrying about their errands.

She sat upright in her chair, gazing about the busy tavern with interest sparkling in her eyes. "This is a lovely place. Do you come here often?"

"No, I just heard of it the other day and came to see what sort of place it might be. Once I did, I thought you might like it. I'm glad you do."

A buxom young woman with a white mop cap on her brown curls approached the table. She told them the menu and took their order and then sashayed away to retrieve their meals and drinks. While they waited, Frank drummed his fingers on the white linen tablecloth.

"Anxious?" She smirked at him, laughter in her eyes. "Or hungry?"

He chuckled and stilled his hand. "Hungry mainly. Chicken and dumplings will hit the spot this afternoon."

Her good humor flooded his chest with pleasure. Sitting across from her and sharing in her day made everything right in his world. Well, mostly. If he didn't have to deceive he'd be set to rights. Soon that would end. As soon as the Britons left Charles Town.

The girl brought out two tankards of cider and deposited them in front of each of them. She gave Frank a long look, leaning forward to give him a glimpse at her ample cleavage. He merely thanked her and kept his attention on the woman he cared about.

Emily lifted one brow with a knowing smile on her lips but made no comment on the brazen girl's attempt to flirt with him. "I haven't had any dumplings in a long time. I'll have to ask Jasmine and Mary to make some soon. Father would enjoy them as well."

"If he's in town, I'm sure he would."

Joshua came and went on business, making frequent short voyages. Privateers seized merchandise intended for the British but which the Americans desperately needed. Depriving the British of their necessities and luxuries was worth the risk to the ship's crew. The sooner their supplies were depleted, the sooner they'd be forced to abandon the city. Joshua Sullivan acted heroically even if most citizens remained unaware of his bravery.

"I'll have to arrange for them when I know he'll be home." She clasped her fingers together and laid them in her lap. "That's not much of a challenge."

"I'm aware of how efficiently you run the household, Em. It's obvious."

"Thank you for the kind words. I do my best."

He leaned back as the girl sashayed back and placed steaming plates in front of them. This time he didn't bother looking her in the face, but inhaled appreciatively. "Smells delectable."

Emily stabbed a bite of dumpling and ceremoniously put it in her mouth and chewed slowly. She nodded and speared a bite of chicken. "It's very tasty."

He sampled the chicken dish and glanced outside as he chewed. The shadows lengthened down the street suggesting the late hour. He needed to return his love to the safety of her home before darkness settled on the town. "Let's eat and then I'll walk you home."

She met his serious gaze with a pout. "Must you ruin the moment with reality?"

If only he could profess his true feelings for her, but she wasn't ready to hear that reality. He grinned at her and took another bite of the savory food. "I'm here to help. Now eat and enjoy."

Emily paced the bare boards of the hallway, little Tommy snuggled against her shoulder. Only a couple of days had elapsed since she enjoyed the late-night excitement with Frank at his printing office, yet it seemed weeks. Had it only been days since Frank squashed the offensive assault by the British brutes? So much had happened it seemed much longer.

The early afternoon sunlight drew attention to dust motes dancing in midair and sparkled the silken threads of her pale green skirt. Grinning with happiness, she pivoted on one foot and sauntered toward the rear of the house. Through the window of the back door she noticed the little garden struggling to retain its colorful flowers despite the arrival of fall.

Tommy snored softly in her ear. The boy grew heavy to carry. She had abandoned the idea of sitting with him. As long as she kept moving, he seemed content, though her thin slippers faced certain ruin as a result. She shifted his weight, holding him securely with her left arm, and stroked his back with her free hand. He rooted against her dress, finally turning his head so she could see his closed eyes and open mouth. The scent of lavender wrapped around her nose as she gazed on the sleeping boy.

The back door jerked open, and Emily ambled toward it, inhaling air ripe with smoke from the cooking fires along with the pungent maritime scent. Jasmine halted when she spotted Emily approaching.

"Tommy's asleep." Although stating the obvious, Emily didn't want Jasmine to make any unnecessary noise.

"Yes, miss." Jasmine shifted the scarred wooden bowl brimming with apples from one hip to the other and eased the door closed. She turned questioning eyes to Emily. "You're doing fine, miss."

Emily reached the woman and paused. "What do you mean?"

"I've been seeing how you handle him, and you's learned quickly. You're a natural mother."

Emily began shaking her head before her maid finished speaking. "No, I'm not. I need advice, but am not sure who to ask." Questions plagued her mind, not only about caring for an infant as it grows, but also about her future, her writing, and most important, how to manage this courtship problem.

Jasmine peered at her for a long moment, waiting to be allowed to prepare the afternoon meal. At Emily's nod, Jasmine slipped into the dining room, out of sight.

Alone and feeling lost—a ship without a sextant to navigate her path—Emily walked up and down in the quiet house. Having no real mother nor being one herself, her motherly instincts never developed. She didn't feel comfortable sharing any of this with her aunt, for fear of the disappointment she suspected would haunt that fine lady's eyes. Had she learned nothing from her teachings over the years? Apparently not.

Emily paced the hallway, contemplating her dilemma.

What did the future hold for her?

A tiny boy needed her to be a mother when she didn't know how to be one. The thought made her tighten her spine. Guilt slid through her before she relaxed. Elizabeth had wanted her to step in and be the mother she had planned to be for her child. Emily's stomach clenched, her breakfast rebelling at the turmoil in her heart. Elizabeth naturally loved and cared for others. Her sister's smile and good nature had won over many slaves and the old women at church alike. Emily wished she possessed the patience of her twin.

Tommy stretched in her arms and yawned, his hands fisted as tightly as his eyes. She watched, fascinated, when he opened them and the emerging color hinted at the brilliant blue of his father, Jedediah.

Frank's slate-colored eyes, on the other hand, evoked a sense of strength overlaid with the energy of a stormy sea. When he looked at her, she struggled to recall her vow and the reasons she'd resorted to it. Indeed her armful of baby right now provided a reminder of what she wished to avoid. So why did she think of Frank? She shook her head at the mystery of how thoughts connected in her brain. She needed a distraction.

"Let's venture outside, shall we?" Emily tucked the end of the blanket around him. At the sound of her voice, Tommy blinked at her. "It's hard to wake up sometimes, isn't it? Some fresh air will do us both good."

The sun warmed her face even as the light breeze pulled a stray lock of hair into her eyes. Wrapping it behind her ear, she shifted Tommy into a more secure hold and babbled to the child, grateful for the sun warming her skin.

Fortunately, he seemed to enjoy the outdoors. How much could he see? How well did his eyes work? Could he smell the dying flowers all around him? When would he start walking? Running? What would she do when he became a little boy playing in the street with the other children?

Preoccupied by her thoughts, she wandered through the garden, making a mental note to remove the suckers from the artichokes, trim and dress the asparagus beds, and sow the radish and lettuce. She chatted with the boy about the flowers preparing for a long winter's nap and the birds darting among the leaves and branches, searching for fallen seeds and scurrying bugs.

"They don't want to be caught out in the cold, and the danger of frost harming them. Every creature and plant has to protect itself."

A blue jay swooped in front of her and landed beside a nearby rosebush, where the white petals clung to the green stems in a vain hope of surviving the coming winter. An errant gust caught the petals and freed them from their grip, the delicate blossoms tumbling to the ground.

Tommy squirmed in her arms, and his eyes scrunched up, ready to start wailing. "Tommy, baby, please." Fussing over the child, Emily started walking toward the house.

"I'm glad you found time for a walk outside."

Emily raised her eyes at the familiar voice. "You're back!"

In short order, a smiling Amy embraced Emily and then confiscated Tommy. The flash of light glinting from her gold chain necklace caught the boy's attention.

Emily propped her fists on her hips in frustration as Tommy stopped screwing up his face to cry and became entranced with the small gold balls spaced on a fine chain around Amy's neck. "How do you do that?"

Amy chuckled and tossed her curls. "It's natural for women to know how to care for children."

"Not for me." Emily swallowed the frustrated panic filling her throat as she paced beside her cousin. Despite Jasmine's assurances, she did not feel as though she would ever be comfortable as Tommy's mother. Mayhap she'd learn from Amy's example if she paid closer attention. They went back inside the house, entering into the dimness from the bright sunlight. "It's time for his afternoon tea, so to speak. Let's change his diaper and then take him to Mary."

"I'll carry him." Amy joggled Tommy in her arms, his eyes widening in surprise. Her laugh floated down the stairwell as they climbed the last few steps. She paused at the top and peered at Emily. "Perhaps he senses you don't want him around."

"Not wanting him has nothing to do with it." Emily crossed her arms and returned Amy's gaze.

"Then why do you keep foisting him on others to care for him?" Amy pried Tommy's fingers from her necklace and waited for Emily to respond.

"I don't." Emily grimaced, remembering her conversation with Samantha earlier. "Perhaps I have, but he's not my son. I try to ignore the resentment that my sister didn't live to rear her own child. She wanted that more than anything else in this world."

"Granted, but plans change. My arms shake from holding Tommy. He's an armful of a little boy, isn't he?"

"Definitely." Emily took Tommy into her arms and she led the way into the nursery where she expertly swapped the soiled diaper for a pristine one.

"Amazing how you've perfected the task in such a short period of time." Amy chuckled and clapped her hands twice. "Well done."

"Fumbling and practice, and lots of both, too." Emily patted the final fold in place and picked up Tommy, who cooed and burbled in response. "Come along, little one, time for supper." Pleased by Amy's compliment, she grinned, happiness diffusing through her. "If you're hungry, we can grab a snack as well."

Amy bobbed her head in eager agreement. They deposited the boy with Mary and soon sat together at the dining table. Autumn sun filtered through the lace curtains, dappling the worn floor boards.

The chores associated with caring for an infant were never ending. Emily thanked the good Lord for her slaves' assistance. This experience made her even more aware of how the forced limitations on a girl's education prevented her from learning necessary skills, such as how to treat wounds as well as learning about the government, history, and nature.

Emily felt unprepared for either aspect of her life.

Hmm, that thought could be spun into an essay. She'd need to ponder the subject more when she had time to think on it, while puttering in the garden or dipping candles.

"I met General Greene while I was away." Amy spread apple butter on her corn muffin.

"What was he like?" Emily bit into a slice of apple, juice dribbling down her chin. She dabbed her face with a linen napkin to remove the sticky rivulet.

"He personally thanked us for the cloth and boots."

"Is he as kind as they say?"

"Yes, quite the gentleman. His gratitude made me feel like we really helped. And…" Amy paused for effect, eyes gleaming.

"Must I beg?" Emily leaned forward.

Shaking her head, Amy grinned. "And he said they will retake the town whether or not the peace treaty is signed. Either peaceably when the British evacuate, or by force if necessary."

"How much more of this waiting must we endure?" Reclining against the hard-back chair, Emily sighed. "It's interminable. I cannot even recall life prior to the start of this war."

"Seems like it's been all my life instead of a third of it."

"How long will you stay in town this time?"

"Not long, I'm afraid. Mother asked me to help her again. Alone this time."

Emily stared in horror at her cousin. "Must you? What if you're caught?"

"I won't be." Amy prepared another corn muffin and took a delicate bite. "I'll wear my widest skirts so they won't see anything I tuck underneath. I've already sewed a few things into the waist. I'll be fine."

"What will you take?" The sentries searched the wagons and carriages with swords, spearing into piles of clothing, looking for people trying to escape the confines of the town without proper passes. More than one smuggler had suffered death on the spot.

"General Greene said they need whatever lead we have to make ammunition." Amy lowered her voice, casting around to ensure no one overheard. "But keep that to yourself."

"Oh, Amy. Please be careful."

Amy patted Emily's hand in reassurance. "I've watched how Mother does this. I'm sure I'll have no problems at all."

Emily's instincts quivered despite her cousin's calm assurance. "I hope so."

Chapter Nine

*E*qual education indeed. Why does a young girl need formal education?"

The question, more of a declaration actually, made Emily look up from her weaving. The ladies gathered in the upstairs parlor of Aunt Lucille's house turned out to be fewer than usual, a direct response to the stepped up surveillance by British soldiers. The enemy searched for spies and patriots even as they prepared to evacuate the city. As a result, the group of women indulged in more gossip than sewing. She'd been silently composing her next essay, one forming around the radical idea of how women should be able to represent their own interests and even sign contracts, when the woman's voice broke through her thoughts. Frank had grumbled about the essay in question but held to their deal. She listened to the ensuing conversation with interest.

Darlene Walters stumped her way across the parlor, her long skirts rustling with each step. Whatever she said guided the other townswomen. Change in such an atmosphere became hopeless, because the others acted like sheep instead of individuals. The situation rankled Emily's nerves. How could they fall into step so easily with one person's point of view? Surely their brains functioned independently.

"Wh-y, Dar-lene, just like that lil ol' paper said, so's they can teach their younguns how to be proper citizens." Fanny Norris, a petite woman sitting to Emily's right, set her chair rocking, her painted fan waving before her face. A newcomer to the town after her husband's death at the battle at Cowpens early last year, she spent all her effort supporting the aims of the patriots and spoiling those of the British. Across her lap lay an unfinished shirt, its left sleeve dangling. Her southern drawl infused the atmosphere, painting smiles on the other ladies' faces.

"It's such a grand idea for our new country," another woman added. "Don't you agree?"

Emily paid close attention to the discussion, though she made a show of passing the flying shuttle back and forth, and tapping the weft thread snuggly into place after each pass. The rhythmic motion of weaving provided a steady beat as a counterpoint to the ladies' conversation.

"The men sure do not like the concept of girls knowing as much as boys, I can tell you." Aunt Lucille continued spinning as she spoke, barely glancing up to gauge reaction.

"It's about time somebody had the gumption to state things as they are." Samantha pulled a needle through the finely woven linen shirt in her lap, her stitches evenly spaced, before looking up at the other women. "Girls have been denied a proper education for far too long."

"What's she afraid of, then, that she doesn't put a real name on the article?" Darlene gripped the arms of her chair and leaned toward Samantha. "Nobody's ever heard of Penny Marsh."

A nervous chill crawled up Emily's arms as she listened to them discuss her essay, hearing their views of the thoughts she had committed to paper. They even debated the points in her essay. A glow spread through her, chasing away the chill. Glancing around the circle of five women, Emily tried to determine if anyone suspected her as the mysterious writer.

"We-ell, I think the lass is smarter than you's give her credit for," Mrs. Norris said. "She knows to keep her true self hidden so she's not persecuted by this town."

Emily needed to join in the debate in case they suspected she did indeed hide something. "Who is to say it's not a man using a woman's name?"

Laughter met her suggestion. Emily's neck and cheeks warmed, but she kept her hands busy with the shuttle and her feet moving on the treadles. Still, she must leave it an open question.

"A man?" Darlene harrumphed and shook her dark curls. "Why would a man pretend to be a woman? Who ever heard of such a thing?"

"If the author wanted to remain a secret, what better way than to pretend to be of the opposite sex? No one would suspect him, if so." Samantha knotted the thread and bit off the end, her gaze taking in the ladies watching her.

Darlene sat back in her chair and looked at Samantha. "I still say *whoever* it is has no business stirring up trouble when we have hope this war is finally drawing to an end. Must we now battle between the men and women of our town?"

"'Tis an old battle, Mrs. Walters, although not a visible one," Samantha said.

Emily nodded, pleased Samantha defended her opinion. She dared not share with any of these ladies the true identity of Penny Marsh, for fear she'd be ostracized from the group and by extension the town. For a lady of her status, propriety forbade her to sink to the level of printing her thoughts in a common broadside. These women had provided her support and comfort during the trials of the war, the loneliness of her brothers being away, the fears for their safety. Even during Elizabeth's pregnancy and subsequent illness, they had stayed stalwart in attention and caring. Emily wanted to change the town's opinion regarding the proper roles for women, even if it meant facing the possibility of being shunned for her views. First, she needed to have her say, then she'd step from the shadows into the sunlight.

"I've not had any issues with the men in my family," Darlene snapped.

"That's because they's afraid of you." Fanny's subsequent chuckle elicited laughter from the entire group. Except for Darlene, who glared at the slender woman.

"Now, ladies, resume your tasks," Aunt Lucille said. "We must finish this today so we can deliver our items tomorrow."

Samantha folded the shirt in her lap and laid it on the pile beside her. Emily marveled at the speed and precision of Samantha's needle. That woman could sure whip out shirts. Emily preferred the artistry of embroidery, what she considered painting with floss. Over the years, she'd created pictures of flowers to hang on the parlor wall as well as pillows to place on the couch. Adorning her gowns with seed pearls and sequins had given way during the war to making pants and shirts for the militia. Soon she'd be able to start replacing her gowns, once the merchant ships were allowed to freely pursue their trading.

"You are leaving today, Mrs. Abernathy?" Samantha asked.

"Tomorrow at first light," Aunt Lucille replied.

"Pray be careful, as I heard through a member of my father's church that the British suspect some ladies of smuggling supplies into and out of town. They may be more diligent in their inspection of your carriage."

Amy frowned, concern in her eyes. "Surely propriety will stay their hands from searching our persons, though."

"I wouldn't count on that." Samantha lifted a shirt by the shoulders and shook it out. "Remember that soldiers do not behave the same as gentlemen."

"I'll keep it in mind." Amy smoothed her skirts with both hands, then folded her hands at her waist. "But we have to try."

Emily caught her breath, sudden unease gripping her. "Please be careful. I fear you'll be caught and…and punished." What an understatement. Smugglers risked imprisonment or being shot on the spot. Amy's friendship meant the world to Emily. Contemplating life without her in it so soon after the loss of Elizabeth caused Emily's throat to constrict.

Lucille nodded once, her eyes distant. "Anything else?"

Samantha hesitated, making eye contact with Emily. Her

friend's steady gaze made concern swell in Emily's chest. Why did she look at her with such worry?

"My father told me the British know privateers operate from this town. Some prominent ships' captains may even be involved." Samantha's emerald eyes held Emily's for two ticks of the long case clock standing against one wall before sliding on to other surprised faces.

Emily stiffened as she stared at her friend. Her tone suggested Emily's father fit the description. A privateer? Never. His moral fortitude precluded such deceptive behavior. Yes, he continued to export items but he did so openly to survive. Aunt Lucille had reared her to never deceive, as her father wished. Of course, a few times she couldn't prevent a slight deception, but always for a good reason. And never in order to circumvent the law. Still, Samantha's look suggested she knew more than she said.

Lucille caught Emily's eye, offering a slight nod and smile of encouragement. "Perhaps Emily could check with Frank, to see what he's heard." At Emily's start, she added, "Given that he's a relative and all."

The weight of eyes drew her attention. The circle of women waited for her response. "I don't know if Frank would be very helpful."

While she knew Frank's true leanings, she could not reveal the truth to these ladies for fear of undermining his efforts. Should word reach Leslie, Frank's very life hung in the balance.

Lucille nodded. "I understand your reluctance, dear, but if you could ask him, discreetly of course, I'd appreciate any information you glean."

Fiddlesticks. Even when not in the room, everything centered on that man. Perhaps Amy had been right to worry about him.

The expectant eyes of the women rested on her.

Emily sighed. "I'll see what I can discover."

The fog enveloped the harbor and clung to Frank's black boots as he strode toward the docks. His forest-green cape danced about his legs with each stride. If only he had received word sooner, this crisis could have been averted. Despite the late-morning hour, the fog refused to relinquish its elusive grasp on the town, clinging like a fretful child.

He tugged his tricorne lower. He should have dragged himself from his warm bed earlier this morning, of all mornings, but he had stayed out later than intended. Emily's kiss haunted his memory. Distracted by the image, Frank started when a young boy dodged into the street in front of him, nearly tripping him as he darted between the wagons and people going about their business.

"Bloody hell!" Delays today spelled disaster. "Watch where you're going, boy!"

Resuming his former pace, Frank hastened toward the cutter tying off at the end of the wharf. His boots resounded on the planks, scattering the handful of seagulls searching the sandy banks around the pier. The white-and-gray birds disappeared amidst a flapping of wings into the cottony air.

"Captain Davis!" Frank hailed the grizzled hulk of a man descending to the dock. The British standard hung limply from the ship's mast. Manheim Davis's dark clothing provided a striking contrast to the swirling white mist as he approached. The muffled shouts of sailors sounded through the clinging dampness.

"Cap'n Thomson, how fine to see you. None too soon, neither." Davis's lips parted around the stem of his clay pipe. Fragrant cherry smoke mingled with the scent of rain.

"You're early." Frank fell into step beside him, their boots thudding on the planks as they paced back toward the busy street. "We did not expect you for another week."

The pale disc of sun hovered behind the flowing mist. The cry of gulls circling the two men seemed distant compared to the hearty voices of the crew on the *Gallant Enterprise*.

"Had a favorable wind." Davis tapped the pipe bowl against

the heel of his hand, knocking the glowing embers onto the damp ground, landing with a faint hiss. "Helped that the British don't care about jars of pickled snakes and painted masks."

Relief loosened the knot in Frank's stomach. "Excellent."

Though the Charles Town Museum, one of the first natural museums in the colonies, had officially closed its doors during the war, Frank secretly helped Captain Sullivan and several prominent members of town continue gathering specimens from around the world. Importing these wonders helped assuage his wanderlust. One day, though, he would board that boat with Davis to explore the world and identify and obtain incredible wonders and historic finds to display at the museum. The pieces of history and culture hid in an isolated warehouse for safekeeping from potential pillagers and the British until they could reopen the museum. They planned to open as quickly as possible by continuing to build the collections until the fighting ended.

Captain Sullivan had ensured the safe arrival of this particular shipment, adding thirteen crates to the cargo hold. His connections spanned the world, and through them he identified and acquired, in one way or another, the items most important to the museum. Davis excelled at circumventing the watch of the British inspectors and managing to deliver the requested goods.

A resounding thud on the ship's deck drew the men's attention to the *Gallant Enterprise*. A large crate was surrounded by four brawny sailors. A gust of wind lifted and tossed the fog. Colorful markings announcing a number of ports became discernible, dotting the crate's surface. The men hoisted the heavy crate and began moving it toward the dock to where a nondescript wagon waited. Within the box were the articles desired to replace the ones destroyed in the horrific fire that had raced through the museum four years earlier. And one special item only a few select men knew about.

"Do ya have me money?" Cautious jade eyes studied Frank from a face resembling dried tobacco leaves.

Frank looked around, ensuring no one observed them. *Blasted fog.* He couldn't see much of anything for it. But then, the fog aided their clandestine exchange as well. He pulled a folded envelope from his cloak pocket. "When do you leave?"

Davis slid the envelope out of sight. "In a month. Can't come and go too often or they'll grow suspicious. More than they already are, that is."

"What happened?" Frank peered at the serious expression on the captain's face, dreading his next words.

"Aye, they boarded her as we entered the harbor." The grin that erupted onto his face sported two matching gaps on either side of his upper jaw. "They did not know what treasures they beheld when they looked upon me cargo, so they let us in."

The tense coil of fear released inside Frank's chest. "Thank God."

Davis shook his head. "Next time we probably won't be so lucky. They'll ask questions in the meanspace, be on the lookout for why I'd be hauling such junk in from foreign ports."

"In the event, that is a risk we'll have to take, I'm afraid." Frank rubbed a hand over his jaw as he thought. "Waiting a few weeks may reduce their curiosity."

"Or give them more time to tighten the noose." Davis shrugged. "Either way, I have to make the runs. Who'd take care of me Jenny otherwise? But I won't hang for it, neither."

Jenny was frail and needed special help from the ladies in the rural town where the Davises inhabited an imposing house along the river. Davis risked much but refrained from risking capture so he could tend his wife.

"The wagon driver has directions for where to take the cargo." Captain Sullivan's boxes came with specific separate instructions, provided in a wax-sealed letter only for the driver's eyes. Frank looked back to where the men struggled to lift the heavy containers onto the wagon bed. The team of horses tossed their manes and stamped their hooves impatiently.

"Did you tell him to drive carefully? Those glass jars have water in them, you know."

"The alcohol in those jars preserves the organisms. The driver knows what to do. Thanks again for your skillful and experienced endeavors on the museum's behalf." Frank clasped the other man's powerful grip.

"Now who is that, pray tell?" Davis indicated with his head someone approaching from behind Frank.

"Captain Davis, just the man I'm looking for."

Dread swept through Frank as he turned to face the man with the razor-sharp voice. John Bradley.

"Major." Frank's face remained neutral while he assessed the officer before him.

"Captain Thomson, how fortunate you're here as well. We have unfinished business, you and I." Bradley glared at Frank, then dragged his gaze back to Davis. "I understand you brought an interesting assortment into port."

"If you be into dead reptiles." A puff of smoke rose from the pipe bowl, masking Davis's wary eyes.

"Nothing contraband." Frank puzzled over what possible business existed between them. His plans for the ultimate return of his brother's house stayed unknown to the man, so that couldn't be the matter at hand. Why did the bastard care about the shipment anyway? Bradley did not perform inspections. "I requested those preserved animals for my personal study."

Bradley's stony eyes narrowed. Sniffing, he smirked at Frank. "Indeed. I had no idea you, a mere newsman, entertained ambitions of a scholar."

Coiled tension gripped Frank's innards, but he gazed steadily at Bradley, pretending to wait patiently for him to continue. Inside, he seethed at the slight. *How dare he?* This damned turncoat did not deserve to live. Frank forced himself to not react to the man's attitude. He could not reveal his true feelings or face imprisonment. Masquerading as a loyalist enabled him to protect his family and their property from the vengeful hands of the enemy, as well as provide the inside information needed to win this war. But it didn't mean he liked the sham.

Davis coughed, breaking the taut silence between the two men.

As if coming out of a trance, the turncoat shrugged lightly. "I'm sure you gentlemen are busy, so I won't detain you longer than necessary. Captain Davis, if you'd be so good as to produce your ship's manifest for my inspection." He held out a hand, open palm ready to accept the requested papers. When Davis did not move, he snapped his fingers twice and again held his hand out.

Frank balled his hands at his sides, twitching with eagerness to find purchase on Bradley's face.

Davis pulled his pipe from his mouth, a frown replacing the indifferent expression he'd worn. "Me manifest has already been inspected and stamped, as you well know, sir."

Why did Bradley need to see the manifest? Although apparently aware of ships coming and going, the major's rank held him above the task of import ships' inventories or challenging the captains regarding their cargo. What did Bradley want and why? His stomach tightened at the thought of Bradley discovering the special item, the smallest box in the entire shipment, yet the most valuable. Much rested on Frank along with his friend and fellow patriot spy, Benjamin Hanson, delivering one small silver box into the right hands.

"Come now, Captain, that is not possible." The grimace transformed into gloating. "Surely, you do not think I was aware even of your arrival until now?"

Davis scowled at the major, the ship captain's shoulders hunched against the mist settling onto his hair and beard. "You ordered the men to board me ship at the mouth of the harbor. The poor crew nearly drowned at the mixing point of the Cooper and Ashley with the open sea and trying to navigate them waters."

Bradley barked a mirthless laugh. "Nonsense. Now, produce the papers or face the consequences."

Knowing those consequences meant Davis would go to jail, and likely hang if the blasted turncoat inspected the cargo too closely, Frank squared his shoulders, preparing to settle the dispute.

If it came to blows, so be it.

He could use a little fun.

"Major Bradley, if I may. You have my word as an officer. I have seen the approved manifest and, at any rate, the goods are now well on their way."

"On their way where?" Bradley gripped both of his hips.

With an effort, Frank maintained a relaxed position, flexing his fingers slowly. He shrugged. "Into storage, if you must know. I'll not display them until this dispute ends."

"Yes, once the British quell this uprising."

Frank shook his head before he could stop himself. Bradley apparently operated under the false impression that the British had any hope of winning the war. After Yorktown saw the British surrender a year ago, everyone knew it was over. Despite having lost many battles, the Americans held all but two cities now. In a matter of months America would secure its independence once and for all. In the meanspace, he must maintain the farce he played or risk revealing his mission. He assumed a bored expression. "I simply do not want to chance damaging the items."

Droplets of condensed fog clung to Frank's hair and beaded on his wool cloak as he waited for the major to speak.

"Your newfound allegiance will only protect you so far," Bradley said.

"Far enough to ensure the safety of my personal property." Frank's hand curled into a fist, though obscured by the drape of his cloak.

"Perhaps, but it does not allow you to interfere in the king's business."

Frank dipped his head once, hiding the anger building inside him as he schooled his expression. "Granted. You're acting on his behalf?"

Hard green eyes drilled into Frank's steely gaze. "If you talk with Miss Emily's father, tell him I'm watching him. You may be off the hook, because you signed that oath of allegiance and fealty to the king, and I don't possess evidence to the contrary. *Yet.* But if Captain Sullivan makes one false move, I will arrest him for treason."

This discussion headed into treacherous waters Frank preferred to avoid. Suspicion of his or Joshua Sullivan's actions by this bastard could only lead to more trouble. The air sizzled with tension. Bradley glared at him, and Davis shifted beside him. The major really thought he could be a true adversary. Bradley was simply a bully. Frank forced his fist open.

"May we go?" Frank would rather walk away than risk charges of attacking this peon. Yet the prospect of landing a fist on his face continued to tempt.

"Be careful what company you keep, Captain Thomson, because I'll be watching." With that, Bradley swung around, his cape billowing, and stalked away.

"Pleasant fellow," Davis said sarcastically around his pipe stem. He remained silent until Bradley could no longer be seen through the fog. "What now?"

"Now we tend our business." Frank shook his hand. "And Captain?"

"Aye?"

"You heard the man. Watch your back."

The grizzled man winked at him before striding off into the dissipating wisps of fog.

Frank watched Manheim disappear into the mist before shrugging off the encounter with Bradley. Benjamin should be back in town ere long to take over control of the special shipment. And none too soon for Frank's peace of mind. The mysterious little box had already brought unwanted trouble into his life.

Chapter Ten

"I can't believe the old women think Frank will have inside information about privateers, or who the British suspect to be one." Emily grumbled to Samantha as they walked home from the sewing circle behind the two black men, sworn to ensure they arrived unharmed, later that afternoon. Frank had urgent business to attend to and could not accommodate her request to go to the sewing circle. Richard and Solomon strode easily in front of them, despite trundling a wheelbarrow filled with the pieces of the loom back toward Emily's home. The sun dipped behind the houses, and Emily quickened her steps. If she hurried, she'd be home early enough to snatch some writing time before dinner.

"Watch what you say." Samantha chuckled, easily matching her pace. "Whether true or not, one of them may hear you."

"I don't care." She did, actually, but at the moment, with no one around, Emily felt safe to say what she thought. On that topic at least.

"You will if it comes to pass. How would your opinions reflect on your father's upbringing of you?"

"Hurry and we won't have to worry about being overheard."

"We're practically running down the street now." Samantha lengthened her stride to match Emily's quick march. "We don't want to overtake the blacks after all. What's the rush?"

"I have tasks to take care of before dinner."

They strode past several two-story houses with shuttered windows. Thoughts whirled through Emily's head. She let her gaze skate over the familiar and comforting architecture. Homes in Charles Town boasted a variety of wide front steps or side entrances through a porch, with a hitching rail or post at the street's edge to hold visitors' horses. Most homes included a garden beside or behind the house, used for growing vegetables and fruits as well as flowers.

How could she discreetly ask Frank what he knew so he did not suspect the motives behind her interrogation? She wondered how much to reveal about Aunt Lucille's and Amy's smuggling efforts. Did he know they were smuggling? If not, she didn't want to be the one to tell him. He printed the broadside, so maybe he did know something useful. But drawing secrets out of him had been a challenge as long as she'd known him.

They had first met while in their late teen years, after she and Elizabeth moved into town to run their father's household. Their father had introduced them to Jedediah and Frank at church one stormy summer morning. Emily's eyes had met Frank's, and she couldn't refrain from seeking out those steely depths, again and again. His infectious smile had summoned a response from deep inside her. Even though he seemed to share his deepest thoughts as his eyes connected with hers, his feelings hid safely from scrutiny.

Perhaps he made such a trustworthy spy and officer because of the many layers of his personality. Now, it confounded her how to prompt him to reveal details about possible crimes by her father without telling him why she needed to know.

Climbing the few steps to the piazza, she heard Tommy crying. They had resolved his stomach ailments, thanks to the basil tea. What now? Pushing open the door, she stepped inside, Samantha close behind.

"Thank goodness you're here!" Jasmine rushed down the short hallway. Tommy squalled in her arms, his mouth open, tears streaming down his face. "He's been snake bit!"

"What?" A charge swept through Emily hearing Tommy's pain-soaked wails. It tore at her heart as his eyes met hers and he cried harder.

"A snake in his cradle." Jasmine paused for breath, tears trailing down her cheeks, too, as she handed over the red-faced child into Emily's waiting arms.

"His cradle? How?" Fear replaced the pain. She frantically searched the boy for signs of the telltale puncture.

"I dunno!" Jasmine cried. "He started wailing and when I went to check on him, the snake slithered under the drapes in his room. I shouldn't have left him."

"It's not your fault." Emily glanced at Samantha. What do we do for him?"

The child continued to bawl but interspersed his vocal hurt with hiccups of tortured breaths. Memory of the ten-year-old daughter of a neighbor last year who died from the bite of a snake flashed through her mind. The girl perished in her despairing mother's arms within hours. Emily tightened her grip on the boy. She wouldn't let that happen.

"I'll make a fleabane salve." Samantha pulled her red leather pouch of dried herbs around in front of her and rummaged within its depths, trotting down the hall toward the kitchen.

Emily barely noticed her departure as she tried to calm the baby, all the while searching frantically for the puncture wound. "Where is the bite?"

Jasmine yanked up the sleeve of the gown and showed where the fangs had left two round punctures. A red knot surrounded the bite. Emily placed a hand lightly on the wound area, and it warmed her palm. Poor baby.

"Get me a rag and some water. Hurry!"

Jasmine raced away, her tiny shoes pounding on the floor boards. Emily cuddled the baby as she trailed the girl down the hall. She headed for the dining room, where a fire always burned with a chair placed nearby. Her legs felt like water. "You'll be fine, Tommy. I promise."

Where had that vermin come from? Snakes didn't normally

frequent the garden or venture into the house. She rocked Tommy in her arms, crooning softly to him, reassuring him. And herself. He would be all right. He had to be.

Jasmine hurried into the room with a cloth and a basin. Emily took the cloth, soaked it, squeezed it out, then laid it on the wound, trying to ease the pain until Samantha returned.

"I hope this helps. I'm not sure it will."

"Miss Samantha will come back soon, miss." Jasmine took the cloth and soaked it again, wringing it out before handing it back.

The back door banged open. Samantha strode into view, a small bowl in one hand, her mother following her.

"It is good for him to cry so," Cynthia said.

"Mrs. McAlester, what a surprise to see you!" Emily forced a polite smile, wondering how she heard of Tommy's troubles so quickly. "What brings you here?"

"I was walking to the printing office to place an ad for my services, when I saw Samantha out back in your herb garden and stopped to see if she'd care to join me." The woman peered at Tommy, leaning in close to inspect the wound. Her head blocked Samantha's view of the child until Emily waved for Samantha to move closer. She frowned and pulled back, glaring at her daughter. "She told me what happened. I thought I might be able to help."

"He's alive, that's what is important." Emily exposed the arm to show Samantha the puncture. "I'm glad you're here. You always know what to do."

"Not always." She slid a look at her daughter. "She's not using the proper herbal combination for this, but I can't convince her of that."

"Mother, you're mistaken." Samantha held Emily's gaze for a long moment. "Trust me, friend, this will work to counter the poison in his system."

Confused by the bickering between mother and daughter, Emily relied on her instincts and her friend. "I do trust you. Please, go ahead."

"Obstinate, that's what you are." Cynthia shook her head. "I wouldn't have used fleabane in that mix, that's for certain. Snakeroot. That's what you need. Don't say I didn't tell you, though."

Emily caught the hesitation in her friend and smiled at her.

Samantha tipped her head and silently smeared the paste onto the boy's arm. "That should help."

With a weary sigh, the older healer shook her gray head again. "I can see I'm not wanted here, so I'll be on my way." She glared at her daughter, gathering her purse in her hands. "I'll see you at home."

"Farewell, Mrs. McAlester." Emily tried to smooth over the tension in the room but failed. "Thank you for your concern."

"Let me know if you need my help," she replied tersely. "I've served this family for many years without complaint."

"I understand, ma'am. Thank you. It's meant the world to my father."

Cynthia stared at her. "I've done my best for him all these years, despite the troubles we've had. Such tragedies to endure." She sighed and pulled her shawl around her shoulders. "Is the Allhallows dinner still on for next week?"

"Yes, we'll have it despite all that happened this year." Emily glanced at the gold band on her finger. Her sister had loved the celebration her entire life, and Emily refused to end the tradition now. "Elizabeth would have wanted us to enjoy the food and friends, I'm sure."

Cynthia nodded as she glanced at Samantha. "We'll be there, as usual then."

After she left, Emily turned to Samantha. "What's the matter? You frowned at her the entire time."

"I'd rather not say until I know more."

"About?" Emily's curiosity piqued when her friend became so mysterious.

Samantha shook her head, her lips tight. "Please don't press. Tell me how Tommy fares."

Since Samantha refused to talk about the exchange between

mother and daughter, Emily followed her lead. "He's settling. Looks like your choice works despite your mother's doubts."

"She has her ways, and I have mine. They don't always agree."

"It's wonderful we have so many who care to tend to this little boy."

He had the entire family and their friends looking out for him. Knowing others could step in and help eased some of the burden.

"Always a pleasure to be with this little guy." Samantha brushed a finger across the downy cheek. "He's like my own brother."

"I know you love him, maybe more than I do." Tommy squirmed in her arms, his cries weakening. She kept a firm hold of him, watching him settle even more as the initial shock faded. "How do you know so much about plants and medicines? Did your mother teach you about them?"

Seeing Samantha's nod toward Jasmine, Emily looked at the young black woman. "Is the snake gone?"

"Yes, miss. Solomon took care of it, though he didn't much like it." She shook her head, a mischievous grin forming on her face. "No, miss, he said 'twas like handling the devil himself."

"I want to keep a close eye on Tommy. Jasmine, please move Tommy's cradle into my room, near my bed, and make sure it is cleaned and prepared for him. I'm sure he'll need it before long."

"Yes, miss." She bobbed a curtsy and withdrew.

Emily waited until the door closed. "You were saying, Samantha?"

"I learned much of what I know from my mother. But I also spent time with a Cherokee medicine man while I…visited my grandmother earlier this year."

Emily noticed the slight hesitation in her friend's explanation. "You talked with the Indians? Why would you do such a dangerous thing?"

Samantha set the bowl on the table and sank onto a side

chair. "Curiosity, mainly. And it wasn't any more dangerous than visiting a doctor."

"So you went to see an Indian doctor?" The Indians on the frontier were known to side with the British during the war and therefore not to be trusted. "You risked your life and your reputation. Why?"

Looking at the fire shadows dancing on the wall, Samantha let out a long, slow breath. "Because I had hurt my leg and needed help, but didn't trust the town doctor. I did not have what I needed to heal it." She rubbed her right thigh as she spoke, finally turning to face Emily again.

"How did you hurt it?" Emily studied Tommy's face, leaving Samantha to answer when ready. Her question had hovered in her mind ever since her friend returned to town limping. She waited, hoping the silence between them presaged the revelation of her friend's mysterious injury.

Tommy stopped crying, his eyes drifting closed though he didn't feel relaxed enough to actually sleep. The long silence from her friend drew her attention. She peered at Samantha, noticing the way she examined the room, her gaze lighting briefly on the ivory carvings on the mantel, then to the sketch of the town square hanging on one wall, and back to the child. "Well?"

"A bad cut…from an accident."

"My goodness! If it's still bothering you, it must have been very bad. Mayhap you should see the doctor about it."

"I'll be fine." She tapped her leg to prove its strength. "There's no need to impose on a doctor."

The tension in Samantha's posture indicated she felt defensive, on edge. Emily regarded her for a long moment. She couldn't let it go so easily. "But it's been months. It should have healed by now."

"It only aches sometimes." Samantha shrugged lightly. "That's when I rub it."

"I see." Healing skills apparently involved more art than science. Emily gazed at the boy. His little body felt warm in her arms, his breathing fast and shallow. "Will this little one survive? I mean, will the fleabane really protect him from the venom?"

"It should. I don't know if I used enough or too much, but the fever will continue only until the medicine has a chance to work. Babies have different reactions to the herbs than adults do. We'll know more by this evening."

"That seems such a long time considering how many children have died from these invaders." Emily swayed with Tommy cuddled in her embrace. "Need I worry?"

"Nay, he will be fine. I treated him within a short period." Samantha peered at her. "You do believe me, don't you?"

Emily smiled in response. "I need to send for Frank. He'll want to be informed." The little body seared her inner arms. "He's burning up. Do you think mayhap we should call for the doctor?"

Samantha's brow furrowed as she stared at Emily. "We don't need old Dr. Cunningham yet. If he gets worse, we can send for him. His body must fight the venom, so there is internal heat."

Samantha finally showed her defensiveness. Emily held her tongue, deciding to trust her friend's judgment. Samantha resented being questioned about her role as healer in the town. Doctors employed somewhat suspicious treatments that did not always work. Samantha's reasons seemed based upon her experience and knowledge, so Emily slowly nodded in agreement.

Samantha touched the boy's forehead. "He will sleep now. If you'd like, I'll sit with him and keep an eye on him."

"Thank you. I would feel better if you stayed, given your training. Unless you have other obligations?"

Samantha shook her head. "Come, let's lay him down."

"I wish I knew more about healing." Emily stood with Tommy snuggled close. "I feel so helpless."

"It's not too late to learn, my friend." Samantha brushed gossamer strands of hair from the boy's forehead. "Even as you teach him what he needs to know, you can learn right along with him."

"But I should already know things." Frustration raced through Emily. Why had they kept her from learning so many things? Only recently had she realized the limited extent of her education. The more she learned, the more questions popped into her head.

"You possess more knowledge than you realize." Samantha opened the door to the bedchamber, and Emily gently laid the baby in his nest of blankets. "Nobody can learn everything, especially not in fewer than three decades."

"All the more reason to have started sooner." Emily pulled a chair closer to the cradle, recalling to mind the stack of crates in the corner of the nursery across the hall. The shipment of baby furniture and clothing her father obtained from India had been a godsend, or so she thought at the time. "I wonder how many more vermin are in those crates delivered recently."

"We should have them removed, to be certain." Samantha sat in the rocking chair. "When you go down, perhaps you can send someone up to haul them out of here."

"I will. And thank you again for being such a good friend. I'm fortunate to have met you at the market last year. Your friendship has been a blessing."

Samantha smiled at her, a touch of sadness lingering in the corners of her mouth. "We'll see if you still feel the same way after I investigate why your mother and sister actually died."

Emily stared at her friend, conflicting emotions warring within. "Indeed."

The street in front of the Exchange swarmed with a mix of townspeople and soldiers. Frank took up a position on the fringe of the crowd near a small tree and waited, trying to gauge what urgent news needed to be relayed to the entire assembly.

An armed guard stood at the street-side steps leading down to the dungeon's door. Hopefully the British wouldn't find the thousands of pounds of gunpowder hidden within the depths of the basement.

The arrival of another contingent of loyalist soldiers caused a stir in the crowd and drew Frank's attention. He stiffened away from the tree. *Damnation.* John Bradley led the group.

No point in focusing on Bradley when he represented one small fish in this ocean of deception. But damn it, he wanted his house back, the one he and Jedediah had built. In good shape. He may eventually be able to reclaim it, but in what condition? From what he'd heard, little hope remained of securing possession of the place intact. For many patriots, loyalists confiscated their homes and the British destroyed them before they departed.

But Frank had a plan, one certain to yield the desired results. He merely needed to bide his time and plant the right seeds of doubt into the appropriate ears of the loyalist forces. He knew how to handle that. If only they'd remove themselves from the besieged and beleaguered town, he wouldn't need to force the issue. He'd simply reclaim the house.

He returned Dirk's salute as the councilman crossed the open area in front of the Exchange, heading to intercept Captain Sullivan, no doubt. Although Frank had suggested to the captain that Dirk's son would be a good lad to sign on as an apprentice, the captain had not committed to hiring him. Being responsible for the education and ultimate livelihood of a lad took some adjustment. A heavy weight rested on Frank's shoulders, resulting from the knowledge that Sawyer depended on him, unaware of how little Frank actually understood of what being a newsman entailed. He could masquerade like the best of them, though, and ensure no one ever suspected the deception.

He'd come to terms with the necessity but longed for the day the farce ended. Still, an honest living suited his plans better than spying and undercover operations during this bloody, devastating war. The fighting had nearly ceased throughout the states, except for around the last British occupied cities: Charles Town and New York. Once the peace treaty displayed the appropriate signatures, even that skirmishing would end. The

British would go home to their own shores and leave Charles Town in peace.

A dark head with darker beard appeared on the edge of the crowd of men and women gathering for the town meeting. Sergeant Graham served as a trusted aide to General Greene for two years now, and had come to Frank's rescue on more than one occasion. Simply put, Frank owed Graham his life. Acknowledging the silent request to join him, Frank wended his way through the growing mass of people.

The notice issued last evening called for an assembly of the townspeople for a special announcement. No word as to what the announcement might be, though. Curious about what the occupation forces wanted to say to the city's residents, Frank guaranteed he attended. If nothing else, he'd have news for the paper.

Dirk had indeed caught up with the captain. A quick handshake between the two men suggested they'd reached an agreement. It looked like young Reynolds had secured a new apprenticeship after all.

"Captain Thomson," Graham said when Frank reached him, "good seeing you."

"You have word?" Frank continued to let his gaze roam the crowd, appearing to have a casual chat with an acquaintance and hoping no one grasped the true importance of the conversation. Despite the cooler fall air, sweat gathered at the small of his back.

"Aye, we have what we need. You're to stay in place and continue as planned."

"Understood." Frank smiled as Mrs. Manning strolled past on her husband's arm, looking as fresh as a newly opened pansy. After all the horrors the town had witnessed, the Mannings reflected the resilience of the people. If they also reflected the future of Charles Town, the sweet promise of independence yielded hope.

A contingent of British officers arrived, including the commanding officer, General Leslie. The tall man climbed the steps leading to the airy level of the Old Exchange two at a time. Once in position to look down on the gathered people, the general raised a hand for silence. A hush spread through the crowd packing the street.

"It's been brought to my attention that some of you feel it is acceptable to support the patriotic cause within this town." He paused and looked out on the crowd, a smile tugging at the corners of his mouth. "I assure you, that until an official peace has been settled, to do so continues to amount to treason."

Frank grimaced at the gasp followed by smattered clapping the man's declaration elicited.

Apparently pleased with the reaction, the general continued. "I've ordered an increased diligence from my officers to ensure our enemies are not to be found within the town limits as long as British troops occupy it. The security of this town is my highest priority. That is all." The general descended the steps, surrounded by several of his officers.

Realizing he'd have to step up his efforts to reclaim his property, Frank peered at Graham.

"Can you do something for me?"

A hard glint shone in the man's eyes as he looked at Frank. "Anything you need, sir, I'm your man."

Frank stepped closer. "Here's what I want you to do."

Hours later Graham met him at McCrady's as he'd asked, sidling between the groups of men talking and drinking. A low cloud of pipe smoke swirled lazily in the air. His uniform showed signs of a tussle. Grimly, Frank ordered him an ale.

"Did you have a problem?" He gestured to Graham's askew hunting shirt.

"Nothing I couldn't handle." He gulped his ale and set the bottle on the table. "You were right."

"You managed entry?" Frank held his breath, anxious for news as to the status of his former home.

"Aye, and so far it looks in fair shape." The man hesitated, then resumed. "Mostly, that is."

Coldness settled on Frank's shoulders as he sipped his drink. "Tell me."

A quick nod and a gulp preceded the man's tale. "The main floor parlor is their headquarters, you know. They've made some…changes to it."

Frank gripped the blue bottle. Jedediah had invested a great deal of time and money into perfecting the cedar inlaid floor and massive stone fireplace. If they destroyed his brother's work, he'd seek his own kind of revenge. "Go on."

"The floor's been stripped out and replaced with pine. I think I seen the red wood used for the major's travel chest. Least, the chest were made from thin strips of wood, like the flooring."

"The bastard… What else?"

"Sorry for it, sir, but he's taken down the drapes and gotten rid of them. I couldn't discover where they went. My gut says they're aboard one of them ships at anchor." He took a long draught of his ale.

An outburst drew their attention toward the back of the room. Two sailors proceeded to settle their disagreement with fists. Grunts and thuds filled the crowded room, competing with the laughter and cheers urging them on. Shaking his head, Frank turned back to Graham.

"They'll pay for that in the morning, I dare say. But, what of the furnishings? The table I built?"

"Nowhere I saw. Probably used for firewood, knowing the man."

Frank slammed the bottle onto the bar, breaking it into five large pieces, ale spilling across the scarred surface. "Bloody hell!"

The barkeeper appeared suddenly and discarded the pieces, mopping up the mess with a towel. "Get ya another?"

Frank shook his head, then focused on Graham as the barkeeper stumped away. "I imagine he's stripped anything of value from the place as well?"

"At least it is still standing. The house can be repaired after they evacuate."

Frank hunched his shoulders as he shook his head. "It's not over yet, friend. The Britons are capable of anything. They're desperate enough to wreak havoc on everything left behind. We've seen that before."

"Aye, but it will be over soon if the treaty is signed as expected."

"Keep your eyes open, and don't let your guard down." Frank tossed coins on the bar. "Tomorrow I'll put the wheels in motion to get my house back before the major destroys it."

Chapter Eleven

The sun had finally burned away the fog when Frank managed to tear himself from the printing press later in the afternoon. Solomon had arrived earlier to request him to call on Miss Emily as soon as possible, but he needed to complete his work before he could answer her summons. Perhaps he should have left sooner, but he trusted Emily to handle matters until he finished his urgent task. His back ached from leaning over the channels to align the type precisely.

Tomorrow the paper must be printed, including the secret message intended for General Greene. He had spent hours laying out the new edition, ensuring the coded message appeared in the upper right corner of the specific page as required. To a casual reader, the advertisement for doeskin ladies gloves was innocuous. Only if one knew the decryption method could one read the information about the enemy troop activities.

As the day marched toward evening, he longed to see Emily. To hear her voice and breathe her scent. Cleaning his ink-stained hands on a rag, Frank sent Sawyer home. As he left, he paused and scanned the area, Sawyer's tan-clad bulk with dapper tricorne retreating down the busy street. Puffy clouds drifted across the pale blue sky, a light wind cooling Frank's cheeks. The afternoon lingered in its infancy, and for many folks closing shop this early would be considered scandalous. Men labored along the wharfs, the strike of hammers pounding wooden lathes into barrels echoing against the buildings facing the harbor. Free from the confines of the shop, he inhaled the bracing sea air. He'd kept Emily waiting too long already. He strode down the dirty avenue, his steps decisive.

Memories of his time at Oxford floated in his head, sparking the longing stoked by the war. Sketches and engravings of the Coliseum in Italy and of the Great Wall of China teased his imagination. He wanted to see those vistas in person. He craved the feeling of the majesty of the Himalayas or the beauty of the Orkney Islands. His thirst for adventures yielded insight and understanding about other cultures, other ways of life, yet remained unquenched. One day he would be free to travel to places denied him because of the war. For now, another mission lay before him. See Emily.

Before entering Emily's home, he studied the street, searching for anything unexpected. A couple of boys ran by, calling to a mate down the road. A watchful pair of older brothers herded a group of young girls down the street. Late afternoon sun lengthened the shadows of the now five-year-old trees, planted as a sign of the hopeful future of the town, lining the road. Several sparrows hopped and fluttered along the side of the road, searching for their afternoon repast.

The door creaked behind him, and he turned to find Jasmine grinning at him. "Captain Thomson, what you doing standing out here? Come in. You don't need to knock."

"Is Miss Emily home?"

"Yes, sir. I expect you'll want to see Tommy, after all he's been through this afternoon. Poor boy." Jasmine shook her head slowly and opened the door wider to allow him to enter.

"What happened?" Apprehension and guilt shot through Frank at her words. His boots echoed on the planked floor as he surged into the house, barely refraining from running down the hall. The scent of wood smoke from the fireplaces greeted him. He should have come home right away.

"All is fine now. Miss Emily will tell you about it, I'm sure. She's upstairs with the little one and Miss Samantha."

The rustle of skirts whispering in the hallway alerted him to Emily's approach.

She paused in the door, and he had to look twice to ensure the vision before him lived and breathed. Would he ever become accustomed to her beauty? Her splendor swept his breath from his body. Her alabaster skin emphasized her pink lips and bright blue eyes. He only half saw the light brown gown, noticing only how it emphasized her hips. A white collar embroidered with tiny flowers peeked from the neckline, tantalizingly obscuring her cleavage.

"Frank, I thought you'd surely arrive sooner. My apologies for interrupting your work, but I knew you'd be concerned about Tommy."

She must think him daft, standing there gaping like a fool. Frank hurried to her with hand outstretched. "I want to hear all about whatever happened. But first, my dear Em, I must tell you how lovely you are this afternoon."

She watched him approach, unsmiling, head tilted to one side. Whatever was wrong had obviously been taken care of and the details would wait another moment while he drank in her loveliness.

Frank lifted her hand and pressed a kiss on its back, assessing her expression as he did so. The delicate scent of lavender surrounding her satisfied his craving. To be near her equaled heaven on Earth. The concern in her eyes finally registered. "Now tell me, what happened."

She quickly related the incident to him. "Samantha treated him with a salve she made."

"You didn't summon Dr. Cunningham?" Using folk medicine when a perfectly trained doctor lived blocks away? Science and medicine had advanced greatly over the past decades, and still people continued to surprise him by sticking with old wives' tales.

"Doctors don't always have a high success record, compared

to the experienced healers we enjoy in town. Besides, I trust my friend to do what's best."

"And I trust the good doctor will have more education and training behind his methods." Frank stared at her for a long moment, not fathoming how she could defend the old ways. "You should have sent for the doctor immediately."

Emily stiffened, eyes narrowing. "Samantha is trained in healing and assured me he will recover. You've left him in my care while you're off doing whatever it is you do all day. Trust me."

"I do." How could she not be concerned about the boy's welfare? He took a deep breath to calm his agitation. "I wish to see him."

"He naps, so I'd prefer you wait."

"His breathing? It's even?"

"Yes. Samantha assures me his fever will break while he sleeps. She's staying with him to ensure all goes well." Emily laid a hand on his and gazed steadily into his eyes. "He'll recover. We have matters well in hand. Give it time."

A snake in the house was a serious matter, but his long delay left handling it to others. Obviously he could do nothing for Tommy now. He took another deep breath. Perhaps the Fates gave him this chance to take the next step in his plan. His shoulders relaxed, the tension easing. "If you're sure we're not needed here, would you care to walk with me? We won't be away long, and I have something I'd like to show you."

She raised her eyebrows as she smiled at him. "Now that the commotion has settled, I'd love to. Where shall we go?"

"To show you the secret collection." Frank tried but failed to resist the temptation of kissing her hand again. He wanted to share his pride and joy with her, to gauge her reaction to their wonders. The additional crates should be safely stowed inside. It wouldn't hurt to make sure the bloody turncoat hadn't stumbled upon that particular treasure trove, either.

"A collection?" She cocked her head curiously. "What kind?"

Her expression stopped him. It seemed her beauty increased each time he saw her. Her golden hair fell lightly on her shoulders, pulled back on the sides and held in place by ivory combs carved into elephants linked trunk to tail. The silver flecks in her eyes twinkled with curiosity. Lips parted to hint at pearly teeth. Lips begging him to taste them.

"Are you all right? You seem distracted."

He could stand all day and marvel at her loveliness. Instead, he shook off the longing for her kiss and winked. "It's a surprise. Get your things and I'll show you."

When they arrived at the warehouse, nestled between two much larger buildings on a side alley, he pulled a key from his inside pocket and soon swung the massive wooden door open. He hoped she'd be impressed with the assortment of specimens hidden inside the apparently decrepit building. The air of decay helped mask the treasures within, and the high, darkened windows kept the prying British eyes from peering too closely. Once the war concluded, he'd move all these fascinating objects to a beautiful venue so everyone could enjoy the benefits of his and many other men's labors.

Pulling a lantern from the hook inside the door, he lit it before leading Emily into the dim interior. Flickering lamplight created dancing shadows on the walls and ceiling. A slight breeze accompanied them, stirring the layer of dust coating the mounds of boxes and crates.

The scrabble of unseen claws echoed in the quiet. Emily inhaled sharply beside him. When she didn't squeal in fear like other women of his acquaintance, he felt stupidly proud of her. Barrels and crates surrounded them, some with their lids pried open and left askew. Others huddled against the wall, splattered with markings from ports Frank longed to visit. One day he would, too, if he had his way. The vast quantity of crates reflected the extent of the growing collection. As long as the collection remained safe, the natural museum had a chance of reopening and continuing to inspire the townspeople.

"Where did all this come from?" She surveyed the vast warehouse.

"All over the world." Her delight brought a smile to his lips.

"How did it get here?" She glanced at him then let her gaze slide away to peruse the room.

Of course she would ask that question, one he wouldn't answer for her own good. And her peace of mind since it involved her father's clandestine affairs as well. "Does it matter? Come." He took her elbow and propelled her through the winding aisles of the storage area. "I want you to see these. Are you cold?"

She trembled beside him, but she shook her head. "Did Father arrange for any of these things? He's been so cagey about his clients."

"I really wouldn't know about his business." Did she suspect the truth of her father's secretive endeavors? "Why do you ask?"

She gnawed her lower lip for a moment. "There's a rumor that the Britons know of the privateering, even a hint of several captains involved."

He scrunched his brow as he looked at her. "Your father is one of them?"

"I hope not." She glanced away and then met his carefully blank gaze. "What do you know about it?"

He shrugged, keeping his expression clear of the shock careening through his chest. "Nothing."

"Like I thought." She sighed and donned a grin. "What else did you want to show me?"

Relief at her easy acceptance swept his shoulders. "It's not much farther. Over here."

She followed him without a word. Satisfaction flowed through him when she did not hesitate to accept his proffered arm, draping a hand on the dark fabric.

Several shelves spanned the back of the building and boasted a group of straw-stuffed birds and liquid-filled glass jars in an assortment of sizes displaying a montage of specimens. If it were not for Benjamin's efforts and subtlety, the collection would not be safely ensconced in this discreet location.

Without thinking, Frank gravitated toward the largest of the containers. The two-foot-tall jar, showcasing a black python in a contorted position, intrigued him. Beside the python rested another smaller vessel with brown speckled quail eggs bobbing in the cloudy fluid, and in yet another the heart of an antelope. He looked away from the crimson, chambered organ, the illusion of it slowly beating within its glass prison too much for his imaginings.

"What's in those crates?" Emily motioned to the piles and stacks filling the center of the immense warehouse. The lantern in his hand fought the darkness of the room. In this light, tarpaulin-covered windows hid beyond the illuminated pile. With Emily at his side, the dim space changed into a romantic haven. The lamplight danced across pearly skin, her lips in sharp contrast. He wanted to taste them but hesitated, knowing she only reluctantly entered their courtship.

"Mostly preserved animals." Taking her hand in his, he led her between the stacks, pointing out various features. "Somewhere out there is a hyena from Africa, a bristly hedgehog from England, and an orangutan from Sumatra, too."

"What is an orangutan?" Emily turned lovely eyes to him, and they tugged on his heart, drawing him closer to her.

"An orangutan is a type of primate, with long orange hair all over its body. Its name means 'man of the forest.'" He enjoyed sharing his knowledge with her. Would she want to journey with him if he could amply pique her curiosity? "They were once mistaken for people hiding in the jungles."

"How peculiar, to refer to a monkey as a person." She moistened her lips, and he forced himself to look away from the quicksilver tongue before taking a steadying breath.

"It's one of the great apes, not a monkey." Frank patiently explained the difference even as his gaze drifted around the room, lighting briefly on each shadowy object.

The far-ranging collection filled him with pride. He envisioned a time when people brought their families to explore the wonders of the Earth in this little harbor town. He imagined the sandy streets paved with cobblestones. The young trees planted several years ago growing tall and strong, shading the sidewalks for the pedestrians' comfort. More houses would line the streets with more families to live in them and what would become lush courtyard gardens.

He imagined the beginnings of a peaceful town full of happy and contented citizens, unlike the current fear permeating everyone. After the war ended, all the town's plans and dreams could be made to come true. Would he live to see those changes? He looked at Emily and smiled. They would see them together.

"Do you wish to travel to the places where these things originated?" Emily swept her gaze around the large building. "I imagine they must live very differently there from what we're accustomed."

"I yearn to go to faraway places and experience how others live." Frank looked at her with renewed respect. "I did not know you wanted to travel as well."

She nodded furiously. "I want to know so much, to understand more than I do. I feel like I've only had a taste of life's treasures."

"This America we're creating will enable us to live as we choose. I plan to travel more than ever and bring back items from far away to share with others here. To broaden not only my education but those of the people, and of the children, like Tommy, in particular."

"Girls, too?"

"Of course. All children. Like you so eloquently said in your essay, we must educate our children in order for them to be fit to continue our new country."

"Thank you." Emily graced him with a radiant smile.

He squeezed her elbow, tugging her toward him. Her mouth pursed as she looked at his eyes, his lips, and back again. His world reduced to her lips, his flaming need to touch them, taste her essence. He turned her to face him, his hands skimming up her arms to her shoulders, inviting her into his embrace. Relief and desire blended within him as she stepped closer, her face tilted up, eyes on his mouth.

The contact of their lips ignited a series of tiny shocks, combining and building, finally bursting into a wildfire of desire. Deepening the kiss, he plunged his tongue into the sweet inner region of her mouth. Instead of satiating his desire, her sweet elixir intoxicated him, fueled his need. He never wanted to stop, to break this intimate connection with her. Wrapping his arms around her, pulling her breasts tight against his chest, reveling in the firm softness of the twin globes he dreamed of catching with his hands. Not yet. But soon.

The sound of the massive door swinging open tugged at his consciousness. He ignored it. When the whisper of a breeze brushed his cheek, though, he knew they had company. He reluctantly parted his lips from hers. Emily's eyes stayed closed until a sudden shaft of light illuminated her face. Her lips, plumped from his kiss, tempted him again. Perhaps one more…

"Frank, I didn't expect to find you here."

At the interruption, Emily blinked and stepped away from Frank, leaving him bereft, to face the visitor.

Even though Frank hadn't heard that deep voice in two years, it could only be Benjamin. His stalwart friend with extremely poor—or mayhap perfect—timing. Emily inhaled sharply and smoothed her hair, staring over his shoulder. He reluctantly dropped his hands from Emily's arms and turned to greet the new arrival.

"Finally decided to make an appearance?" Frank clasped Benjamin's strong hand and accepted the brief half hug they'd adopted during years of sporadic militia training as an acceptable brotherly greeting. His friend looked much the same as the last time he'd seen him. Maybe a bit more muscular, as expected given the nature of his assignments. Weak spies would be useless, after all, ferreting information from the British across the southern colonies. From the adventures Benjamin had shared with him in the past, he needed to be burly enough to extricate himself from dangerous situations.

"I came to check on our investment, after hearing of the troop ships in the harbor." Benjamin gave a final pat to Frank's back before stepping away. His eyes landed on Emily, and she moved closer to Frank. "Miss Sullivan? You're looking lovely, as always."

"Thank you, Major Hanson. It has been too long since we've enjoyed the pleasure of your company at dinner." Emily smiled at him, her happiness at his presence apparent in the glow of her eyes.

A worm of jealousy wiggled through Frank at the joy she expressed in the simple smile directed at Benjamin.

"Perhaps we can rectify that while I'm in town." Benjamin performed a half bow.

"I'm sure we'd like that." Her expression hopeful, she sought Frank's agreement. "Wouldn't we, Frank?"

"Of course. I believe Miss Abernathy will also enjoy seeing you again."

"Amy? My apologies, I mean Miss Abernathy?" Benjamin grinned. "She's in town?"

Emily nodded once. "I know she'll be glad to see you again, Major. We're having our Allhallows Eve celebration next week. Perhaps you'd care to join us?"

Benjamin took her hand and squeezed it. Frank tried hard not to glare at his friend. He couldn't possibly know what had transpired between Frank and Emily in his absence. Indeed, Frank couldn't say what it might lead to at this point. After all, Emily, though being courted, was still a single, available, and enticing woman.

"I'd like to very much." Benjamin touched his lips to the back of her hand before releasing it. "Perhaps even sooner, if the situation allows."

"Situation?" Frank moved closer to Emily's side. When she smiled up at him, laying her hand on his arm, he relaxed. A little.

"I received your message." Benjamin's brows lowered as he regarded Frank. "We need a plan in place to avert further interest in certain, shall we say, imports."

"What kind of imports? My father has many imports in the house and his shop from around the world. They fascinate me as much as seeing all these curious and strange items this afternoon. You've got my curiosity piqued, sir."

Above Emily's eye level, Frank shook his head at Benjamin, alarm in his heart. He tried to telegraph caution in one simple movement. *No, don't let her know about her father's business. She need not know a word about it. No good could come of her awareness.*

"We'll talk later." Benjamin silently acquiesced to the subtle warning. "I'm sure Miss Sullivan is not interested in discussing a subject as boring to women as politics."

Emily stiffened beside Frank. She wouldn't take the slight easily, given her penchant for knowing and understanding the ins and outs of current events. Frank placed his hand on top of hers, and she glanced at him before turning her gaze back to Benjamin.

"Pray tell, Major, why I should not know what occurs in my town?"

Emily spoke evenly, perhaps too evenly for Benjamin's own good. Frank could have told him that her measured tone indicated annoyance strapped down under strict control. At least temporarily.

Benjamin chuckled. "Women have no need to worry about anything outside of the domestic domain they rule over with such aplomb. It's the men's job to be watchful and protect our women and children from danger and unnecessary worry."

"Unnecessary?" Emily's tone contained a razor's edge.

Her hand trembled beneath his, but Frank did not let go.

"Miss Sullivan, I believe, does not agree with your opinion." Frank tried to diffuse the tension radiating from Emily's quivering body. He felt her anger coursing through her. Felt the heat of her racing pulse against his fingers. "She has always been well versed in the politics of town."

Benjamin shrugged then winked. "A fact that most likely caused her brothers no little discomfiture, truth be told."

Frank winced when Emily gripped his arm tighter.

"Excuse me?" Emily blinked owlishly. "My brothers taught me about politics and strategy and other supposedly men-only topics. Topics not so complicated as you seem to think. Perhaps women have the greater intellect after all."

Squaring his shoulders, Benjamin straightened to his full height and grinned at Emily. "Then pray explain why girls grow up so ignorant of the world."

"That's simple." Emily sniffed with disdain though kept a pleasant expression as she lightly shrugged. "Because men are ultimately cowards."

"Cowards?" Benjamin's eyes widened and sparkled with mirth. "Why would you say such a thing?"

"Cowards, because they fear if women discover man's fallacy that women cannot learn, they will be overruled and women will run the town councils. We'd be better off, that's for certain."

"That's blasphemy!" Benjamin chortled at her statement.

"Why, because women do not go to war over trifles, and therefore we'd have peace more often than not?" Emily glared at Benjamin, her hands on her hips.

Frank stood speechless. Not from her opinions. No surprises there. No, Emily herself radiated with ardor. She exuded beauty and femininity even while livid with affront. Her skin glowed with the intensity of her passion. Blonde curls bounced when she finished nodding to emphasize her point. Stunned, Frank could only watch the vibrant woman pin Benjamin with her stare.

"Despite your protestations, my girl," Benjamin said somewhat stiffly, "I'd rather leave the discussion for later."

"Over a pint at McCrady's, no doubt." Emily dropped her hands to her sides, though they clenched and unclenched repeatedly. "I may join you just to prove my point."

"You would not dare be so brazen. Captain Sullivan would never allow such behavior from his precious daughter. But if you want to take on your father's ire, feel free to join us."

"Do not put it past her." Little did Benjamin realize how often Emily disobeyed her father's wishes in order to fulfill her duty as she saw fit. Unsure as to why Emily pushed Benjamin thus, Frank still felt the conversation quickly spinning out of control. His job was to protect Emily, not allow her to fall into more trouble. "Miss Sullivan has other obligations this afternoon, so she really cannot and *must not* accept such an invitation."

He prayed she'd agree with his intervention so she did not yet again earn her father's disapproval. A mutinous frown emerged on her face, darkening her lovely eyes, but lasted only a moment before clearing away. Relief settled over Frank as her expression cleared.

"As much as I would dearly love to take you up on your challenge, Major, we'll have to do so another time as I'm afraid Captain Thomson is correct." She squeezed Frank's arm. "In fact, I'm sure we must be going. Frank?"

"I had not realized the time. Excuse us, Benjamin. I'll send word when we can pursue this discussion further. Lock up on your way out, will you?"

He quickly ushered Emily away from Benjamin, steering her around the boxes and crates as they made their way to the door.

"I look forward to dinner, Miss Emily." Benjamin's laugh echoed in the cavernous building. "And becoming reacquainted with Miss Amy."

Emily woke to snuffling and whimpering. Moon glow illuminated the cradle by her bed and its tiny occupant, arms flailing and head thrashing. "Tommy!"

She pushed back the quilt and rushed to his side. Her fingertips encountered searing heat when she touched his forehead. Lifting the baby, she hugged him close and hurried down the hall to her father's room. Bursting inside, relief washed over her when she saw him waking before she said a word.

"Father, Tommy still has a fever." Panting from her run, she paused to catch her breath. "Please. We need the doctor."

"Now, my dear, calm down and let me see what we have here before we wake the poor man from his rest." He slipped on his dressing robe over his night shirt, tying the belt in one fluid motion. He looked at the boy, felt his head, a frown lodging between his eyes. "Should have done this earlier, but you convinced me not to worry. The old ways are never as good as a trained doctor, I always say."

Going out to the hall, he hollered for Solomon and sent him to fetch the doctor. He turned back to confront his daughter. "Now we wait."

Wait? She shook her head. "We need to cool this fever or he'll die. A wet cloth may help." Emily hurried with Tommy out of the room and downstairs to the dining room and its ready pitcher of water.

"Likely not." Her father trailed after her.

"I have to do something in the meanspace." She sponged cool water onto the child quietly fretting in her lap. "I hope Solomon hurries."

"He's fast and trustworthy. He won't come back without the doctor."

Twenty anxious minutes later Emily heard the front door open and voices in the hall.

"Where's the child?" Doctor Cunningham strode into the room, a black leather bag in hand, a young man silently following him. A frown marred Dr. Cunningham's usually pleasant features. He caught Emily's eye and held it. "Well? I haven't all night."

She stared at the men, uncertainty sweeping through her. Upcountry Cunninghams were notoriously loyalist, especially the family led by William "Bloody Bill" Cunningham, who attacked a group of patriots at Clouds Creek November past. She didn't know if the men before her sided with the loyalists as well. If they could help Tommy, what difference did it make? Her grip on the baby tightened as she met his gaze. "I'm sorry for disturbing your rest, but thank you for coming so quickly, Doctor."

"What have we here? A snake bit him, I'm told." He took the silent baby from Emily's arms and turned to the fair-haired man standing behind him. "This is my son, Dr. Trenton Cunningham. He has more experience with venomous injuries than I do, so I asked him to accompany me."

"Thanks again for coming." Emily appraised the younger man. His broad forehead and generous mouth showed his displeasure in tense lines while the skin around his startlingly blue eyes displayed small lines radiating from the outside corners. "I understand it's inconvenient."

"Call me Dr. Trent. You should have sent for us as soon as this happened." Trent's eyes were dark and concerned. "The delay may cost this child his life."

He turned his attention immediately to the boy, listless, lying in the older doctor's arms. The elder's deference to the younger man showed his pride and trust in his son's abilities. The lack of motion and sound from her nephew propelled a wave of fear and regret crashing through her. She couldn't determine whether he even breathed. Trent's frown deepened, but he ignored her. What had she done?

As much as she resented Tommy living when her sister had died, she could not bear to lose him now. His smile and babbling worked into her heart until life without him seemed unimaginable. As Samantha had said, he embodied the only living piece of Elizabeth left.

Frank. He should be summoned. She caught Jasmine's eye where she stood at the door, and then walked to her.

"Jasmine, go wake Frank. He'll want to be here, I'm sure." She'd make sure to keep him informed whether he responded or not. She wouldn't give him any reason to mistrust her again.

"Yes, miss." Jasmine scooted out the door, and her slippered feet pounded up the steps.

Emily watched the young doctor inspect the wound and then raise his worried gaze to her.

"I need a tub of cold water." Trent pinned her with accusing blue eyes, and she swallowed the protest forming in her throat.

Hurrying past the speechless Mary, she rushed upstairs and retrieved the small tub from the nursery, lugging it back into the dining room. She poured cool water from the urn into the tub, and Trent placed the baby in it, reaching automatically for a cloth to sponge him.

"He'll warm this up in no time as hot as he is."

"I'll fetch more." She hurried to the door where Mary lingered uncertainly. "We'll need towels to wrap him in."

She grasped the back of a chair to support her shaking legs. She must stay strong for Tommy. The wisp of a girl nodded once before running from the room soundlessly. With a sigh, Emily followed her trail toward the open door.

Footsteps thudded on the floor boards, and Frank suddenly filled the door, two vertical frown lines between his eyes. His presence calmed her ragged emotions, her overwhelming fears for her nephew. Her eyes smarted, but she forced the tears back as she crossed the short distance to take Frank's hand in hers.

When he didn't look at her, she feared he'd lost faith in her. "I'm sorry."

He continued to stare over her head at the scene unfolding behind her for a moment, then she felt the weight of his look. "What have you to be sorry for?"

"I should have sent for the doctor earlier after all. I didn't think—"

"We all trusted Samantha." Frank's deep voice pulsed with anger as he interrupted her. His scowl deepened, and he raked a hand through his hair, a sure indicator of his distress. "My brother's son may die because of a miscalculation."

"But Samantha assured me he'd be fine." Her voice failed her.

Had her trust in Samantha's abilities killed Tommy? She glanced at the small body in the tub. Trent gently bathed him in the tepid water, his face serious. She looked back at Frank. He had every right to never forgive her for endangering his nephew, his charge. How had they gotten to this place of enmity and mistrust? Insistent tears finally won the battle and coursed down her cheeks unheeded.

"At least a doctor is trained based on careful observation and study and not some old wives' tales. She's apparently following in her mother's footsteps. Let me through." He brushed past her, his worry emanating from him as he moved her away from him.

"What do you mean?" Emily swiped at the tears and grimaced as the little boy moaned. "Frank?"

He waved a hand to silence her as he stopped by the young doctor. "How is he?"

Emily leaned against the door frame, unable to leave without hearing the verdict.

"Do you mean, will he live?" Trent continued sponging the little boy as he glanced at Frank, then Emily. "It's hard to say. I will do everything I can, but it's been so long since the bite, the venom has spread throughout his body. If you'd called sooner—" Tommy writhed in his arms and moaned softly when Trent turned him over. "Shh, little one. We must balance your humors by purging you to reduce your fever. You're safe with me."

"What do you need, son?" the elder doctor asked.

"An emetic should serve the purpose," Trent said.

Emily's tears fell more rapidly as the men hovered over Tommy. Safe. With them, but not with her. Elizabeth should not have left her precious one in such clumsy hands. Emily had let her down as she feared she would. Because of Emily's lack of knowledge, her nephew would die. She hiccupped as the extent of her failings seared through her. Clasping a hand to her mouth, she tried to stifle the next hiccup. No one paid her any mind. No one wanted her. They didn't need her except for sewing and overseeing the chores. Nothing more. Unable to bear being in the same room, she grabbed her skirt in one hand, whirled in the doorway, and fled.

Racing into the backyard, she hurried to the winding garden path. Her breaths came quick and shallow, tears in her eyes. She must calm down. She could do no good for anyone in such a state. Her rapid steps carried her through the stark flower beds, dry and brittle stems lying dormant under the pine needles and fallen leaves. She hugged herself against the chill air and the growing coldness within. The barren scene echoed her feelings. She paced the narrow path, wiping the tears from her cheeks as quickly as they fell. Surely she could do something to help. Anything.

She stumbled to a halt. Oh no! She'd forgotten. Selfish, that's what she was. Through and through thinking only of her own wants and needs and feelings. No more.

Water. She needed more water. She'd promised. Running now back up the path, she flew to the water pump at the well and pumped cold water into a bucket. Grabbing the wooden handle, she lifted the pail, water sloshing out and soaking her skirt. Calming her actions though not her agitation, she hauled the heavy load back into the house. The sound of the men's deep voices in low conversation reached her ears as she closed the door and hurried down the hallway.

"There, the emetic has done its job."

"Yes, we should see a change soon."

"Where is that water I asked for?" Trent said as she reached the door.

"Right here, sir." She entered the room and crossed to the young doctor with her load. "I'm sorry for the delay."

"Let me help you." Frank lifted the bucket easily from her weary hands. His eyes did not meet hers when his fingers brushed the palm of her hand as he transferred the handle to his grip.

He did not react to the thrill, a tingling sensation she experienced at his touch. Her heart ached with the loss of their connection. Even though he had coerced her into the feigned courtship, his attentions evoked a sense of expectation and familiarity combined. She found herself eagerly anticipating their time together. She gazed at him momentarily, then glanced at the older doctor watching from the sideboard as Frank added cool water to the bath. Trent kept his eyes fixed on the little boy. Nobody looked at her. She'd become an outcast in her own home. She didn't matter to anyone, except maybe Tommy. And that was questionable. The boy's eyes stayed closed, cheeks flushed as Trent worked over him.

A soft cry erupted from him when the water chilled around him. His eyes opened, and relief flooded through her. Thank God, he lived. She didn't realize she spoke aloud until Frank's surprised look met hers.

"Excuse me." Emily ducked her head and hid her grin. She hadn't killed her nephew after all. Glancing up, she caught Trent's knowing look. "Can I get you anything else, sir?"

Mary slipped into the room, drawing the doctor's gaze away from Emily. The girl carried a stack of towels and placed them on the table within reach of the doctor. With a quick curtsy, she backed away and left the room.

"I think I have what I need for the moment, miss. Now that the towels are here." Trent laid a hand on Tommy's forehead, then his back, and nodded.

Frank stepped closer and felt the boy's arm, his fingers caressing the small limb. "His fever's broken. The purge worked as promised."

Unlike the fleabane salve. Emily smothered an exasperated sigh.

"Fortunately, yes." Trent lifted the child and wrapped him in a towel.

Tommy watched Emily silently as the doctor rubbed him dry. She felt helpless and useless all rolled into one unhappy woman. What more could she do? How could she even begin to make amends for her mistake? Tommy didn't need her, but he surely needed something. Perchance clean clothes to wear after that chilling experience. "I'll fetch his nightclothes."

"He'll need warm things." Frank peered at her. "Can you manage?"

Her cheeks warmed at the slight. She deserved that after her lack of judgment risked the boy's life. Without a word, she nodded and left the room. Would he ever forgive her?

Chapter Twelve

The stars twinkled against the velvet sky, fighting to be seen beside the full harvest moon. Emily braced her hands shoulder-width apart on the porch railing and inhaled slowly. The night stilled, save for the occasional whir of bat wings flashing past or the desultory sound of the night watchman calling out the hour.

Alone. In all things. She sighed, angling her head to examine the sky above. At one time she'd have been grateful for solitude. But not now. She hoped Elizabeth watched her from the heavens. If so, she probably wasn't any happier with Emily than Frank was at the moment. Emily trusted Samantha to know the best way to treat wounds. Samantha always came through for her. Until today. Frank's words echoed in her head, gouging the emotional wound deeper into her soul. What had he meant about Samantha following in her mother's footsteps? Perhaps Amy could answer that question.

It seemed as though her cousin had been away for months. So much had occurred during her absence. Wait until Emily told her about Benjamin's return and his promise to dine with them. Which raised other questions in her mind about the availability of appropriate fare for the festive meal. She must talk with Father upon his return from his short trading voyage to see what stores they could provide or that might be available at the market, and then hope the guests contributed the remainder. Frank likely wouldn't even sit near her, eschew being with her, after her lapse in judgment.

She caught the whiff of Frank's distinctive fragrance mingled with pipe tobacco. Gazing out to sea, she listened for his approach and knew when he saw her by the sudden stillness. Although quiet, his presence charged the atmosphere like a swarm of bees on a summer afternoon, both promising and threatening.

Once, long before the tragedy of Jedediah's death, she had thought Frank had taken a fancy to her. The brothers had joined the Sullivans for meals frequently so Jedediah could visit with Elizabeth. Emily had suspected Jedediah and Elizabeth's visits were more intimate than strict propriety allowed, but once a couple announced their betrothal, people ignored such indiscretions. However, when Elizabeth revealed she was pregnant, the wedding plans were accelerated. Then his death during the fighting at Eutaw Springs in September past left her unwed but with child.

Though Emily didn't have much opportunity to speak privately to Frank during that period of time, she was aware of him at a fundamental level. Each time he entered a room, she detected his presence without him saying a word. His soul searched out hers. Or so she'd thought until she learned he planned to marry. Frank had sacrificed his bachelor status to provide for her sister, a noble act. But an act that quashed any hope of a true relationship between them.

She would never allow herself to experience such pain again. No, better to flirt and move on, nothing serious, nothing permanent. She'd be her own woman, take care of herself. He held no sway over her. She steeled herself to hide the physical reaction his nearness caused, the hive of longing and disquiet buzzing inside.

"Em?"

She inhaled sharply, brought from her reverie with a start. "What do you want? To chastise me further?"

"Not at all."

The floor boards creaked as he moved ever closer. Shutting her eyes briefly, she prayed for strength as her soul hearkened to his call. When his hands rested on her shoulders, her eyes flew open. Before she could think of anything to say, he pivoted her to face him. She fixed her eyes on the cravat hanging loosely around his neck, the shirt unbuttoned to expose light-colored hairs in contrast to his darker throat. He'd obviously responded to the earlier summons regarding Tommy's fever in a state of undress unusual for such a fastidious man. Yet the result was an intimate look at the man beneath the clothing. She swallowed the attraction, denying it to him and herself. She couldn't feel this way. Love and desire didn't fit her plans.

"Look at me." He lifted her chin, applying guiding, gentle pressure with his fingertips until her eyes met his. "I have more experience in these matters than you. The child is my responsibility, not yours."

"I thought you wanted me to care for him. Now I've failed you—and him. For that I'm sorry."

"Please forgive my overreaction." He searched her face. "You panicked and trusted Samantha to know the best remedy, an oversight anyone could make. Do not fret over it anymore, love."

His derogatory comments about her friend delivered in such a patronizing tone irked her. She pressed her back against the railing. The sound of waves slapping the hulls of the ships at anchor created a counterpoint to the night birds calling to each other. Yet his expression revealed his sincerity. "What did you mean about Samantha's mother?"

"I thought you knew." He kissed her hand lightly, his eyes never leaving hers. "Her mother has had her own problems over the years, some whisper she harms more than heals."

The touch of his lips to her hand catapulted her senses toward a dangerous cliff. If kissing her hand could cause such torment, she would never survive another kiss on the mouth. Frank talked to her, formed more words, but Emily didn't hear them as she imagined the feel and taste of his kiss. Brandy and honey blended into nectar, she bet.

The tang of the sea filled the air. Ropes holding the boats fast to the piers creaked with the swell of the waves tugging and pushing them. Moonlight softened the deep shadows. Moistening her lips, she searched his eyes. "Samantha has not had any problems. She said different herbals work differently in people."

"Until now, she's not had anything specific go wrong. She spent many months away and mysteriously reappeared without any real explanation as to where she'd been and what she'd been doing. Word about town implied she'd been up to some questionable activities while away. Given her failing attempt with Tommy, perhaps she returned because she made a grave error like her mother." Frank stepped closer, banishing the cool air from between them with the heat of his body. He brushed a stray hair back into its proper place, his finger lingering against her temple.

"That's absurd." Or was it? Samantha's trip involved visiting her grandmother in Savannah, nothing more. Other than visiting a Cherokee doctor. She shivered, realizing Samantha had never spoken of a grandmother prior to that trip. What had she really been doing?

"I see you don't believe your own words." Frank leaned in and kissed her.

As she predicted, the world stopped with the press of his lips against hers. If she angled her head thus, then his tongue could slip inside and twine with hers. Sizzles of desire rippled through her like the widening rings formed in a small, glassy pond by the splash of a stone. Though the height and depth of the ripple lessened, the reach extended farther and farther until the small pond reflected nothing but the effect of one lone rock. A simple pebble disrupting the calm all around. Reality crashed through her and she pulled back.

"Stop that!" Emily brushed her fingertips across her mouth, unsure if she should savor the taste of his kiss or wipe it away.

Where had his previous anger fled? Why did she no longer care if he kissed her? Her body hummed in response to the desire aimed her way. His eyes drew her in, and she willingly lost herself in their depths.

"Why? You're delicious." Frank kissed her fingertips when she tried to push his mouth away. "I want to taste every bit of you."

She should be shocked. She should, *really*. But the image his words evoked coupled with the anticipated sensations intrigued her. His tongue running across her hot skin. His lips pressing on places only she knew. A thrill pulsed through her when he kissed her again, tenderly at first, then with growing pressure until his tongue sought entrance. She opened her mouth eagerly, her tongue playing with the tip of his, wrapping around it, teasing, tasting sweet brandy. A low moan started deep within her and coursed up and out of her mouth into his. He moaned in response, and his tongue delved into her mouth deeper, more urgently.

Wrapping his arms around her, he pulled her close. His hand wound into her hair hanging down her back. The downward tug he gave raised her mouth more firmly against his and allowed him to explore where he had never ventured. Hot moisture formed between her legs, a wave of pleasure consuming her body. Frank's hand traced down her cheek to her throat, easing her lacy shawl down until it clung to the crook of her arms. The evening breeze caressed her heated flesh now exposed to the moonlight and Frank's attentions.

"You're so lovely, Em," he breathed against her bare shoulder. "I've wanted to do this ever since I met you."

His grip on her hair tightened, further easing her head back and exposing the sensitive flesh of her throat. Her eyes closed when his tongue tickled her collarbone before gliding across her shoulder and trailing down her upper arm. Her legs shook, and his grip around her waist tightened. Without his strength, she would have fallen under the onslaught of sensations enveloping her.

"Frank, please," she whispered. What did she ask for? Her thoughts whirled away, uncatchable in the maelstrom battering her senses.

"Yes, my dear." He kissed her shoulder, her neck, her chin, and finally her lips. "What do you wish?"

She moaned when his tongue resumed exploring her mouth. She couldn't think with him kissing her thus, let alone respond, but she must tell him… What was it again? Down his tongue went, twining with hers, then back out to tease the very inside of her lips. Her legs gave out, and he caught her in his arms, gazing at her with intense eyes.

Part of her longed for him to love her, but when her blood stopped singing in her veins, such a base feeling would pass. The thought calmed the tempest once more and allowed reason to return.

"Frank, put me down." She pushed at his amazingly strong chest using both hands with little effect. "It's not proper. We can't do this."

"If we're careful, we can." He surveyed the surroundings as though not recognizing where they stood.

"You married my sister." Did she say that? Out loud? So be it.

"I did." He pulled back to look at her.

Grasping at wisps of logic, and grateful for the space he'd provided, she took the path of affront to keep some semblance of propriety between them. "Obviously you preferred her to me. I'll not be a consolation prize. Please, stop this sham of caring for me."

"Sham?" He frowned at her even as his grip loosened.

The piazza provided some measure of privacy but only because of the height of the three-story home. Sounds would be readily heard on a quiet evening such as this one. "Put me down. I'm serious."

"As you wish, my love."

She noted the strain in his voice as he eased her away from him and set her back on her feet, keeping one arm around her until she stayed steady.

"I-I need to go." She searched his dark eyes for reproach or anger. Any reaction to help bolster her courage to push him away to a safe distance. Intense desire blazed instead, nearly weakening her newly revitalized resolve. She must go before they took this relationship to places she didn't fathom how to handle. Or at least places where her reactions to this man would spin out of control. Backing away, she bolted from the darkened porch into the glow of lamplight from the house. The sound of Frank's voice made her pause momentarily in the door.

"Sleep well, Em. At least one of us should."

Nobody would be sleeping this night, apparently.

The next afternoon Emily hurried through the market, quickly searching for the last of the ingredients needed to make a special dinner for her father. And Frank. She planned to return home before anyone noticed her absence, but she simply had to prepare a fitting meal for her protectors. She'd brought Solomon with her, and his presence at the edge of the square eased her guilt at hedging the restrictions placed upon her. Solomon was close enough to stand watch but far enough away that she could breathe.

Few people still lingered among the produce and household items. Before long, the vendors would call it a day and pack up their goods and haul them to their homes. Seagulls hopped along, pecking at scraps on the ground. The day had started out dreary, but the sun burned off the morning fog and now warmed the air.

She paused by the pumpkins, debating on which to select. Urgent to return home before either Frank or her father missed her, she skimmed the array of firm-fleshed gourds. Tommy grew heavier in her grasp the longer she stood still. She'd ventured out with him to give Mary and Jasmine a chance to finish the laundry without him underfoot. She shifted him to the other arm and smiled at his happy grin.

"You like being outside, too, don't you? It always lifts my

spirits. Ow!" She gently removed his tiny hand from grasping a long curl gracing her neck. "That hurt. Let's find a nice pumpkin for the soup, shall we?"

Making her selection, she paid the vendor while Solomon carried the heavy gourd away. The remaining few items she purchased fit in the basket dangling on her arm.

"Time to head home, Tommy." She hefted him higher on her hip. "Let's hurry to catch up to Solomon, shall we?"

She shied away from thinking of Frank's reaction as she started after Solomon. The chance to provide a delicious meal to the two men she cared for made her little adventure worthwhile though risky. After the way Frank had kissed her, although beyond decency, she could not discount the fact that she cared about him even if it never developed into more than an intimate friendship.

But then again, she didn't want him to be more than a friend. Did she? Certainly, her father wouldn't object. She shook her head in annoyance at her own inconsistency toward the man. Why couldn't she make up her mind one way or the other?

"Who do we have here?"

The low voice rumbled behind her, sending spikes of dismay through her. Closing her eyes briefly, she faced John as he leered at her. Solomon had reached the far edge of the market square, heading home quickly with his burden as she'd directed. Obviously, that was an error. "Major Bradley."

Ignoring the fact that she held Tommy, the turncoat stepped closer, a hand gripping her elbow. "I've missed you, Emily. We had some good times together."

"A long time ago, before—"

"Before what?" He caressed her arm, twining the long curl lying on her shoulder around one finger.

When Tommy had done the same thing minutes ago, she had not experienced revulsion. She shuddered. Followed swiftly by fear caused by John's lecherous stare. She shouldn't have come after all. Her father had been right yet again. She put herself and Tommy in danger.

What a fool. But she'd protect him now. She straightened her spine, not willing to show this man fear even as it filled her.

"My father expects me home momentarily. If you'll excuse me." She turned to escape his hot breath on her cheek, but he grabbed her arm, sliding his hand down to hold hers. She stared at the muscular fingers gripping her wrist, pulling her toward him.

"What's the hurry, my sweet?" He pressed his lips to the palm of her hand.

A shudder scurried down her back at his presumption. And in a public place. She looked for help, but everyone seemed to have miraculously vanished. Interesting timing. Had he arranged for this encounter? Another kiss replaced the first one, and she glared at the top of the major's head. Tommy's weight multiplied as she tried to hold on to him and her basket on one arm, while the brute captured her free hand.

"You should not presume so." She tried to joggle Tommy higher on her hip.

Without warning, Tommy reached out and grabbed the major's disheveled wig as his head lowered to Emily's hand.

The major yelped in embarrassment as it slid to one side, and he reared his head back like a snake about to strike. John snatched the child from Emily's arms. Crying in protest at the harsh treatment, the infant squirmed in the tight grip of the angry man.

"Leave him be!" Emily grabbed for Tommy, and John snarled at her.

"This brat won't ever do that again." He took hold of one of Tommy's arms and squeezed until Tommy wailed.

Seeing only a red haze of protective anger, Emily attacked. She swung her basket at him and clawed at his arm, but he shoved her away, tightening his hold on the boy. Grabbing hold of his steely arms, she tried to pry them off her charge.

The pain threading through Tommy's cries pierced her soul. Her strength failed to stop the violent man from hurting her nephew. Despite the futility, she continued to pummel him with her fists. Dropping the boy onto the hard-packed sand of the marketplace, he turned on her in a rage.

"You need to learn manners, my dear." Grabbing hold of both her arms, he hauled her to him before slapping her cheek with his full strength.

She gasped at the pain blossoming across her face. Blackness threatened to overcome her senses, but she forced herself back to consciousness. Tommy sobbed at her feet. He needed her to protect him from this madman.

She shook her head to clear the remnants of pain shrouding her mind. Glancing down, she saw Tommy on his back, half-hidden beneath the tables of fresh produce. She must reason with John, make him remember he once cared for her and hope he'd stop this crazy attack. "John, please!"

Another blow to the cheek and she tasted blood. Tommy's cries grew faint as the world spun around her. Brutal hands caught her before she fell, hurting her more. But the fresh pain brought her back to her senses.

She inhaled sharply when a fist suddenly aimed at John's head.

She stumbled when the impact of Sawyer's fist loosened John's grip on her arms. She sat down with a hard *thwump* on the ground and quickly scrambled to gather up Tommy before the two brawling men crushed him. Across the way, Solomon led several men at a run as they raced toward the skirmish, finally returning to help.

Tommy was safe. Thank goodness! Frank's apprentice had knocked John unconscious with one blow.

When Sawyer turned to her, tremors of remorse shook her. She aimed a rueful smile up at him. "He'll never let you forget that."

"Miss Emily, you're safe now." The lad lifted Tommy then helped her up. "Let me get you home."

"Miss Emily, you all right?" Solomon stopped beside her, panting. "That man hurt you?"

"Take me home." Emily took the boy from Sawyer, refusing to cry in front of the men.

She remained silent as he and the black man escorted her back to the imposing house, past her precious pumpkin shattered on the ground, fully aware of the extent of the danger she'd put Tommy in. All for the whimsical desire to have pumpkin soup. She'd promised herself to never be selfish again, but she'd broken that promise and look at the mess as a result. She would do better in future, knowing now that her father and Frank were right to fear for her safety.

As they approached the front steps, Frank rose from a chair positioned to take advantage of the sunshine bathing the porch. Emily's heart sank.

Chapter Thirteen

A few days later, Emily endured Amy's chiding with good humor.

"You'll end up having to marry Frank yet, if you're not more careful than that." Amy had returned as planned, eager as ever to share in her exploits smuggling the goods through the sentry line. "Kissing him is certain to make him want to claim you."

"It's part of our agreement but doesn't really mean anything." Emily shrugged and cut an apple in half, offering a piece to her cousin.

The other part of the courtship agreement she'd ignored but never again. She hadn't told anyone other than Frank, who dragged it from her and Sawyer, about the incident at the market. As far as everyone else was concerned, she had cut her cheek when she tripped in the house. What good would come from sharing what John had done? Obviously, she should not venture out alone. She understood that now with crystal clarity. Frank forbade her adventures, as he called them. He had reminded her of her promise to abide by her father's and his wishes. She'd been stupid to try to circumvent their rules. Telling others of her stupidity served no good, to her mind.

Amy took the apple and examined it before smiling at Emily. "I knew you would have problems with him while I was away.

That's why I thought Samantha planned to visit you more often."

Emily bit into the sweet fruit and wiped the resulting juice from her mouth. "You needn't worry. I'll be fine. Besides, she's been awfully busy trying to help people."

And failing? She wondered if other instances of Samantha's failures had escaped her notice. Samantha had come home from Savannah suddenly, without explanation. Perhaps some incident had occurred there as well. Emily shook off her doubts. She wouldn't let Frank's worries impair her friendship.

"I heard she's been requested by more and more folks over the past few weeks. I hope there isn't an illness spreading."

"I don't believe so." Emily cut another slice of apple and popped it into her mouth. She needed to change the subject to divert Amy's poking into areas she didn't want to discuss. Sweet juices spurted against her teeth as she chewed. "Have you heard? Major Benjamin is back in town."

The pinking of Amy's cheeks as she swallowed her bite of fruit made Emily chuckle.

"So, what does that matter to me?" Amy struggled to appear nonchalant but the flashing glances at Emily gave away her interest.

"He asked about you." Emily winked at her cousin as she took another bite.

"That is neither here nor there." Amy flicked a dismissive wave of her hand. "He is an unfeeling troll and an audacious flirt."

"A flirt, eh?" Emily tilted her head, contemplating the concept. "I found him more egotistical than flirtatious. I guess we'll find out when he comes for the Allhallows Eve dinner."

Amy's blush deepened, and her mouth opened like a daylily receiving the morning sunlight. "You didn't."

Emily nodded, aware of her cousin's discomfiture. "He said he'd be honored and hoped you'd attend as well."

Amy put her head in her hands, covering her face completely for a moment before spreading delicate fingers to peek through them. "I suppose it would be rude to flee to the plantation and not face him, wouldn't it?"

"Cowardly, too." Emily's suspicions regarding her cousin's feelings for Benjamin proved well-founded.

The back door slammed shut, followed by heavy boots on the worn boards. "Emily, where are you?"

Emily's stomach twisted at the heat in her father's tone. She shot a worried glance at Amy. "In the dining room."

The thud of his steps grew louder as he stomped down the hallway and into the room. He nodded grimly at Amy before turning his full attention on Emily. "So, you defied my orders and went into town after all? I'll not have it, I tell you."

"Father, I did—"

He silenced her with a glare. "Frank told me of your little…what did he call it? Oh yes. Your little adventure. And of your meeting with that major." Anger vibrated his bass voice. Fists on hips, he faced her. "From now on you are expressly forbidden to leave this house. Not even a bloody stroll in the garden! No exceptions whatsoever until this bloody war is over. Is that clear?"

Emily's mouth dropped open. Surely she'd misheard what her father said. "Excuse me?" She darted a look at Amy, who also sat in shocked silence.

"I will protect you whether you want me to or not. You're my only daughter now. I will not risk you coming to harm because of my lack of foresight and your lack of discipline. Therefore you're to stay inside until further notice."

"Uncle, you cannot do this," Amy ventured quietly. "It's unheard of."

He turned to her with a glare, his face mottled red and purple. "It is necessary, and I'll thank you to mind your own affairs."

Emily sagged against the table, the forgotten apple lying on the bench beside her where she'd dropped it. He'd finally done it. Made her a prisoner in her own home.

Her soul recoiled. Not even a walk in the garden until the war ended. Who knew how long that might be? Months? If the treaty wasn't signed, how long then? Tears leaked from her closed eyes. Amy's gaze weighed on her but she did not move. She could not.

"But Uncle, surely you jest," Amy pressed. "She must at least be able to work in the garden. You'll permit her that at least."

"It won't be her, especially after recent events." He ran a hand down his smooth jaw and glared at the two women. "She will obey me in this. I know of what I speak."

"Of course, sir, but please be reasonable. She has obligations to this town, the sewing circle and the ladies who rely on her skills. Surely you'll agree she should continue to support the war effort."

Emily peered at her father to gauge his response. He frowned at Amy. A sadness settled on her shoulders at his stubborn expression.

"She's done her part. They'll have to manage from now on without her slaving for them."

"I'm not their slave." Ire bubbled to the surface and forced itself from her. How dare he suggest such a thing? "I give of my time freely."

"No more, you don't. Not after what Frank relayed to me." He crossed his arms over his massive chest and considered her. "I cannot bear to lose you, too. You will stay here. Understood?"

Determination mingled with the underlying fear in his eyes. He'd lost his wife and his daughter, and nearly his grandson. She wiped at the drying trail of tears on her cheeks. She could not be the one to bring more loss, more grief to her father. Despite the difficulty before her—and she could only imagine how to rein in her rebellious nature for the duration—she must be strong for him, as he had been for her throughout her entire life. She had promised to do better and now she must. Sadness darkened her soul, but she would try.

Slowly, she nodded.

"Uncle Joshua, I must protest on Emily's behalf. She must go to church for her own spiritual growth. You must see that, don't you?"

"Church she will attend with the entire family, so permissible. But nothing more."

Amy stood and wiped her hands on the napkin before pacing to where her uncle stood, feet planted firmly as though bracing on a rolling ship's deck during stormy seas. "What if Frank and I both escort her to the sewing circle? Will that reassure you she will be protected?" Amy searched her uncle's dark expression. "Being confined in this house for months will only break her fine, loving spirit."

Emily gazed hopefully on her father's worried countenance. The sadness lightened as he considered Amy's words. He sighed heavily and shook his head.

"I'll agree to this on one condition. Frank must be with her the entire time she goes to the ladies' circle. If he's not available, then you, my darling daughter, will not be going. If you dishonor me by not following my instructions, I'll lock you in your room with a guard at the door until the blasted British have left this town. Understood?" He frowned deeper as Amy clasped her hands together. "Do not push me, young lady."

"Aye, Captain." Amy smiled and kissed him on the cheek. "Thank you, Uncle."

Emily, feeling as though she'd dodged a terrible ordeal, rose from her seat and raced to her father, gripping one of his strong hands. "Thank you, Father. You won't regret this, I promise."

"See that I don't, my dear. I want you to be well and healthy when your brothers finally return."

"You've had word from them?" Emily grasped his arm. No letter had arrived from them in months, and she dreaded their involvement in some bloody battle and subsequent injury. Or worse.

"None. Have faith. They'll come home in one piece, if I know my boys." He turned with a nod and left the room.

But would they come home on horseback or in a box? Emily did not want to voice her fears, for by saying the words it may make them come true. She didn't want to lend the words the power speaking them could yield.

"Emily, we must talk to Frank about Uncle's demands."

Emily wrinkled her nose at the idea. "Yes, I suppose we must. But can't we delay for a day or two?"

"Emily, we promised. We'll inform Frank immediately." Amy laid a cautionary hand on her arm and tugged her into a brief hug. "I know you hate this, but it will make him feel better knowing you're protected. We'll take this one step at a time, and he will soon relent even more. He's worried. He'll ease those restrictions over time."

"I hope you're right, because otherwise I may have to take matters into my own hands. And you know that only leads to trouble."

The final strains of the hymn died away as the rector climbed the stairs to the elevated pulpit to deliver his sermon. The richly carved furniture boasted inlaid woods ranging from pine to oak to mahogany, and was a work of art unbefitting its occupant, to her mind. His position, towering high above the congregation's heads, not only ensured everyone could hear his message, but also forced her to look up at him until her neck hurt. Emily chastised herself for detesting this portion of the service, but to no avail.

She used to love to sing the hymns, her favorite part of church. The organist played the Snetzler organ renowned for its superior quality, its harmonious tones filling the air as the clerk led the "lining" of the psalms, singing the line from the church's lone hymnal which the congregation then echoed back to him.

The grand sound within the high-ceilinged church inspired feelings of piety and peace. Of singing directly to God for his ultimate enjoyment. Perhaps one day the church could afford to buy hymnals for all and everyone could sing together, but for now the price of books soared too high.

Her feelings about attending church had changed for the worse when Reverend Edward Jenkins sailed in from Savannah with the British occupation forces to promote the loyalist sentiments. Perhaps in other times his sermons would be more welcome. But not now. She longed for their kindly, patriotic preacher Reverend Charles Moreau. She feared she may never see him again.

She let her eyes stray to the white plaster ceiling with its intricately carved border known as the Wall of Troy, with its four double roses centered on each of four sides of the rectangle above her. She tried projecting the piety of the other women surrounding her though she only wanted to move, to be outside in the sunshine, to dissipate the energy agitating her.

The nave felt cool in the dim light. The sun shone through the Palladian glass window at the rear of the chancel, situated some twenty feet behind the pulpit, and brightened the dark blue walls as well as the four brown Corinthian pilaster columns. The half dome above was blue to represent the firmament with white clouds floating on it and a "glory" at the peak, a golden sun with radiating beams spreading across the dome.

Two tablets hung on either side of the window containing the words of the Ten Commandments, the Lord's Prayer and the Apostles' Creed in gilt lettering in gilded frames with a golden cherub's head and wings at the top. She appreciated the simple elegance of the chancel, but today she had no patience. *None.*

Emily sat beside Frank on the hard bench in their boxed pew with the half door to her left. Emily's left knee bounced twice before she overruled her impatience and quelled the movement.

Reverend Jenkins droned on with his British pearls of biblical wisdom. She smothered the sigh fighting to escape. She refrained from doing anything that might force a lecture from Frank if she did not maintain the decorum expected during this pious torture.

Frank must have sensed her agitation, for he pressed his leg against hers. She stilled, not because she wanted any less to leave, but because the intimate gesture stirred her latent desires into smoldering embers. His body heat branded her through the layers of fabric, and she shifted away as casually as she could.

How would she explain her restlessness?

Frank's look pressed on her, but she kept her eyes on the rector, praying for calm. Flexing her fingers on her velvet purse, the welcome movement did little to ease the growing tension coiling in the pit of her stomach.

"And peace descended from heaven to answer the prayers of the many who called upon the Lord for help. Amen." Reverend Jenkins closed his Bible and surveyed the congregation.

The rector frowned when he saw Benjamin dozing at the end of the pew in front of Emily. Leave it to men to presume such outrageous disdain for society's expectations and then insist women adhere to a different, more restrictive standard. Emily's agitation quickened. The reverend's pointed glare prompted Frank, who sat behind Benjamin, to tap his head to awaken him.

Benjamin yawned and stretched as he came to, inclining his head in a manner suggesting the rector continue with the service. As if the rector needed his permission, of all things.

Still frowning, the rector said, "Let us pray."

She folded her hands, head bowed, but her eyes refused to close. She stared at the tips of her shoes, praying for the guidance and strength to be the person she wanted instead of what others dictated. Who gave them the right to tell her what she could and could not do with her own life, her destiny? She had thoughts and passions to explore, revel in, and share.

Her fondness for Frank increased the more time she spent with him, but that did not mean she wished to marry him or anyone else. Where did the Bible say Adam and Eve married before they started reproducing? God blessed their union because of the rib Adam shared with Eve without his consent. *Without his consent.* Two people should not be coerced into marrying merely because society demanded such a bondage.

This line of thinking only inflamed her annoyance and verged on sacrilege to boot. Her father might insist on the marriage. She shivered. Could she say no to her father even if she detested the proposed beau? Her father had always provided for her. She owed him everything.

"Amen. God be with you," Reverend Jenkins finally intoned.

"And with you," the congregation responded, minus Emily's voice.

She glanced at Frank. Emily made to leave the pew, but Frank laid a hand on her arm.

"Easy, girl. The rector will think you didn't enjoy the sermon."

"He'd be correct." She pretended to adjust her bonnet.

"Frank, wait." Benjamin stood and reached out to catch Frank's arm.

Emily turned to look up at his striking visage. Frank's fair complexion and golden-blond hair contrasted gloriously with Benjamin's long black hair caught in a queue with a black bow at the end. Another time, perhaps, she might even be attracted to him. Well, if not for his self-assurance verging on arrogance. Besides, Amy would have her hide if she looked at him wrong. She'd been smitten with him since she turned fourteen years old. Perhaps Amy no longer wished to marry because Benjamin had absconded to fight in the war. Without even a note saying good-bye. He'd been gone, goodness, nearly three years now.

He had not changed to the point of being a stranger, but he'd definitely changed. He appeared harder, the boyish glint in his eyes replaced with a cynical light hinting at the horrors he must have witnessed. Her imagination painted images of gashes, gunshots, and blood flowing. She tried to envision what he had experienced but suspected the reality was far beyond anything she could imagine given her relatively safe and secure world.

"Are you in a rush, Benjamin? Mayhap you'd like to walk with us as I escort Miss Emily home?"

"You, an escort?" Benjamin's eyes widened before he laughed. "I thought you'd been promoted to newsman."

Frank glared at him, allowing his stern look to melt into a grin and a wink. "Somebody has to do it. Join us?"

Benjamin assented as he indicated for Emily to precede them down the stone paved aisle and out of the sanctuary. Chivalry obviously had not breathed its last, but she hoped they both understood that just because she walked in front of them it did not mean they could push her in the direction they wanted her to go. She had spent her entire life trying to prove herself to her brothers, let alone her father. Her brothers at least accepted her as their intellectual, if not physical, equal. They'd spent many a night debating the possibilities for the outcome of this blessed war for independence.

The three brothers could not be kept from the battlefield. They fiercely believed in the philosophical attitude that the Continental Congress took when they declared the fledgling country's independence in 1776. She'd been nineteen years old then, six years ago, but the day stood out in her memory. As the three strolled toward the back of the church, Emily reviewed the many events she had witnessed leading up to the impending peace treaty soon to free her town.

The town meeting crier had summoned the residents to the Exchange in the square. The first day of August dragged on, hot and humid, and the townspeople made it clear they did not stand united on independence. Her adored brothers, Ethan, Bill, and Luke, had teased her about her lack of instruction and vowed she'd learn how the various forms of government functioned. Then she'd be capable of understanding why the Americans abhorred King George's taxes.

The announcement that the Continental Congress had declared their independence "as free and independent states" prompted the majority of the audience to cheer. Several men, though, removed themselves from the meeting. Ethan, the gentlest and kindest of her three brothers, explained that the angry men didn't believe in the revolution and vowed to fight on the side of the British dictator.

She had cheered right along with her brothers, rejoicing in the sense of shared purpose and possibilities. Cannons boomed salutes along the Cooper. Little did she foresee the war would take her brothers away for months, now years, at a time with little or no word.

The battle for Sullivan's Island in the summer of 1776 had

sent terror through the town. Many men had sent their wives and children to the country, fearing the British warships crowding Charles Town's harbor meant to take the city. Emily and Elizabeth refused their father's request to leave while their brothers stayed behind to defend the town and the palmetto log fort on Sullivan's Island. Though he was not pleased, they had stood resolute, and he grudgingly accepted their decision.

The slaves throughout the town had been ordered to strip the lead ornaments from buildings to melt into bullets. The fear had eased with the arrival of Major General Charles Lee, the American commander in chief of the Southern Department, and his several hundred Continentals. Fortunately Emily's father successfully argued against the razing of their house along with several other dwellings in order to create a wider angle for the cannon fire.

Then the whole town, collective breaths held, had waited for the imminent attack, which finally erupted on the twenty-eighth day of June. Clouds of smoke hovered over the men defending Sullivan's Island from inside the fort. The sound of the many cannons combined into one continual roar, like a fearsome dragon belching flame and smoke.

Later they learned the men had teetered dangerously low on powder and shot. Only their superior marksmanship allowed them to prevail over the British ships. At nightfall, the cannons had finally stopped. The battle ended with the British ships badly battered and scores of men dead on their decks. General Lee subsequently praised the defenders to George Washington himself.

"Good day, Frank, Benjamin." A man called from in front of the sanctuary, bringing her out of her reverie. "I need a word with both of you, if you don't mind." The tall, lanky man's clothes hung on his frame, his pale eyes fairly glowing in the dim light of the room. His appearance echoed the myriad sacrifices in food and clothing made by the town.

"One moment, sir." Frank turned and smiled at Emily. "I'll catch up with you outside, all right, dear?"

Her heart fluttered at the endearment, but this was not the place to call more attention to the intimate reference. She struggled to control her expression as Benjamin strode past them without a word, his eyes serious. Frank turned his wayward glance back to Emily's smile.

"Leaving me stranded to fight my way out of here, are you?" Emily kidded him. At his surprised look, she laughed. "Go on, I'll manage."

"You're sure?" He glanced over his shoulder to where his friend waited.

Emily waved her hand to shoo Frank away. "Go on."

"Right. See you in a few minutes then." He lightly gripped her upper arms and made her look at him. "I'll be right there with Benjamin if you need anything. Do not leave without me, understood?"

"Yes, sir." She mock saluted him before he turned and walked away.

Emily continued her slower pace to the door, giving Frank time to finish his business with the two men talking quietly with him. She paused to survey the folks remaining inside the building, aware of their gauntness and worried faces even on a glorious Sunday morning.

"I'll wager he's hanged for his troubles." A gruff voice murmured over her shoulder, startling her. She could not see who spoke behind her, but the voice sounded familiar.

"He's sly. He'll manage," another gravelly voice responded.

This one, though, she recognized. Mr. Reynolds had commented on this man and his "troubles." Emily glanced over her shoulder and smiled at the two men. The first man she did not know, his shoulders half turned away as he spoke to Mr. Reynolds. Years of hard work on the plantation and the shipyards led to Mr. Reynolds' muscular arms and body straining his clothing.

"Aye, he's smart, he is. Still, I think the word is out that the good captain is—"

"Quiet," Mr. Reynolds whispered. "Not here. The Reverend approaches."

Emily missed the remainder of their conversation. *Fiddlesticks.* Which captain did they refer to? She knew of only a handful of captains. Some out on a voyage, others who had fled the besieged city.

She stilled, contemplating the threads of overheard conversations and accompanying looks that finally wove into a tapestry in her mind.

Surely not. Not her father. Everyone knew of his honesty and fairness. He'd not be involved in anything illegal, let alone a hanging offense. Why, they'd only hang a man if he killed somebody, an absurdity for a man such as her father.

Or committed treason.

A chill swept through her.

What did the other man say, something about her father possibly privateering? Could it be? Samantha's warning floated in her memory. *No.* She tied her bonnet and resisted shaking her head in disbelief. Her father never lied. *Ever.* He stood as straight as a pillar of righteousness, unshaken by what others wanted him to do for their own ends. There to protect his town, his family. He believed in this country even more than he believed in the sanctity of the church and family.

Her steps faltered, and she raised a hand to her throat to prevent the thoughts from forming into spoken words.

"Emily? Are you all right?" Frank appeared at her side, his hand supporting her elbow in an instant. After a quick, appraising glance, he steered her to a pew reserved for the orphanage children and made her sit down. "What is the matter?"

Her thoughts spun in her head. She forced herself to take deep, slow breaths and not blurt her fears. Not here. Not in this crush of pious townspeople. They did not deserve to learn the man they believed upright and honest actually lived a duplicitous life. She couldn't let them discover the truth. It would ruin him.

A sudden thought formed in her mind, one she quickly acknowledged as the truth.

She was the only person in town who did not know her father ran the blockade and defied the king of England. That he not only stole from a king but did so in a time of war. Her heart stuttered at the recognition of her father's peril. This was the purpose behind the trip he took recently. Obviously, if these two men knew, before long the British would identify him. Then the arrest and ultimate hanging. Mere months after Elizabeth's death. While her brothers fought the same war elsewhere. Was this what John had hinted at that night on the street?

If her father died, she'd have lost both parents as well as her sister.

Panic threatened, ripping her in two like a blade through a tapestry. Her heart raced, shaking the lace edging her cuffs and her neckline. She must pull herself together and not let this overwhelm her. Surely her father wouldn't risk leaving her alone, living in a city besieged by the enemy. She must know for certain before she confronted her father with her suspicions. But how? First she needed the answers she sought, the evidence to prove him innocent.

Or guilty, a little voice nagged.

She straightened her shoulders. Only one place came to mind. His shop.

She needed the ledgers. She knew how much it took to provide for the household, and if the accounts didn't measure up, she'd ask Father for an explanation. That seemed reasonable. She'd go to the office and look at his records. Of course, in order to avoid upsetting him if she was wrong, she'd do so without his knowledge. A quick glimpse at the ledger would settle the matter once and for all. The men may have been wrong, misinformed.

Or correct and her father could die.

"Emily?" Frank's gray eyes centered on hers. "What is ailing you?"

She smiled her biggest smile. "I need a favor."

Chapter Fourteen

J can't believe you want me to sneak you over to your father's shop without his knowledge." Frank sank down onto the pew. He glanced at her, then the few stragglers leaving the church. "I declare, it's beyond me how you managed to convince me. I must have lost my mind."

"Hush now." Emily looked about the room. "Someone may hear you and alert Father so that he'd race home from wherever he went."

Shards of light filtered through the windows, emphasizing the mellow hues of the pine pews and floors. The last strains of the organ died into silence, enabling the sweet music of the birds to waft into the sanctuary.

"I suppose we may as well leave now and be done with this foolish errand." But Frank's legs didn't listen to his brain's insistence to stand. Resolved to put action to his words, he braced his hands on his knees in preparation of standing. "Come, we really must go."

Sighing, Emily rose gracefully, smoothing her hands down her long, plain skirts directly before his face. Beneath her skirts hid the woman he desired more than anyone in his life. He quickly stood. Ignoring the slight tremble resulting from checking the need rushing through him, he reached for her hand and kissed the back of it while keeping his eyes locked with hers.

"What was that for?"

Relief flooded through him at the longing in her voice. He was glad to see desire in her eyes. Though, God forgive him, her father would likely chide him for his weakness, especially risking a kiss within the church walls. But he promised to keep her safe, no matter.

"I'm falling in love with you, my dear," he said slowly. "Is that quite all right with you?"

Her eyes flew open. Not quite the reaction he'd hoped for. He had not expected to see shock.

"Oh, Frank, no."

"No?" Did he hear her right?

"This is unexpected."

"Unexpected?" She couldn't tell that his feelings deepened each moment he spent with her?

She scrutinized him, her eyes softening as he continued to look at her quizzically.

"Not here." She took his hands in hers and squeezed them briefly. "Let's talk after we get home, all right? We'll have more privacy. It will be easier."

"What will be easier?" Was she breaking off their relationship, the one they hadn't even truly begun?

He started to ask, to pursue this enigma, but a hand on his shoulder stopped him. Turning, he came face to face with his nemesis, John Bradley. The man who attacked both Emily and his son. And stole his house. His hands clenched and he moved to shield Emily. A slow smirk grew on the man's face, causing Frank's back to tense and his chin to raise. "Major."

"Captain. Miss Sullivan." John nodded once to acknowledge Emily. "Did you enjoy the sermon?"

"As much as usual," Emily said slowly.

Frank darted a look at her, noting the strain in her expression. "Reverend Edwards provided a thought-provoking message on restraint."

"Yes, of course." John's smirk grew into a grin. "I'm sure he'll miss this quaint church as much as the rest of the town."

"What is your meaning?" A chill spread through Frank at the cold smile on John's face. The British continued to strip the city of everything of value, just like the treasured bells of St. Michael's already on their way to London. Nobody understood exactly why they'd even been taken but efforts were underway to recover them. "Why would any of us miss our church?"

"I'm sorry to be the bearer of tragic news, but I thought you would already know, given your job." John paused, and folded his arms, studying Frank's face. "Are you quite certain you wish for me to tell you both? Or should we step out privately, Captain, man to man?"

"Major, pray share your news." Emily stepped closer to Frank, and rested a hand on the crook of his arm, as though she intended to restrain him from what he desperately wanted to do. "You have my full attention. I must know."

John nodded to her, his smile shifting into a leer. "Why, for you, Miss Sullivan, I'd do nearly anything to make you happy."

Frank wanted to smash a fist into the bastard's grinning mouth. His arm muscle jumped as he flexed his hand, Emily's grasp tightening on his arm at the movement. This was neither the time nor place to seek retribution for his actions. How dare he act so condescending after he'd split her lip and scared Tommy? "Major, please come to the point."

"If you insist. It's just that General Leslie has decided to burn all of Charles Town as we pull our troops out. You may want to gather what you can in the meantime should you wish to salvage anything."

The bastard had the utter audacity to smile as he spoke, laughter in his eyes.

"What utter nonsense!" Frank raised his fist and shook it in the major's face. "The people will not let that happen."

John laughed outright. "Try and stop us." He tipped his hat and walked away.

Emily held onto Frank's arm, preventing him from following the taunting bastard. He frowned down at her, anger blazing through him.

"What will you do?"

"Spread the alarm and prevent such an insane tragedy from occurring." Frank knew what he had to do. "I need to send word to General Greene. Come. We can stop at the printing office on our way to your father's shop."

Sitting on the hard wood chair in front of the mahogany desk at the back of her father's shop, Emily turned the closely written ledger page full of item descriptions, dates of import or export, quantities, and dollar amounts. Out of sight from passersby, she could still see the front of the store, where Frank paced to and fro between the windows flanking the door. It had to be there. She just had to find it.

They'd stopped long enough at the printing office for Frank to instruct Sawyer on a new ad to place in the paper, then he'd walked with her to the export shop. Emily's instincts tingled, alerting her to a change, a portent of misfortune, perhaps. She must hurry.

Over the years she occasionally helped maintain the lists of merchandise passing through the store. Saw the variety of goods and the frequency with which items flowed in and out. The experience formed part of the foundation on which she had hoped to start her own shop after she convinced her father to help her rent the space and acquire the necessary materials.

By proving her abilities with the ledgers, she'd have the tools to persuade him to champion her ambition. In the meantime, the register before her did not balance. She scoured the pages, fingering a bent corner of one sheet while staring at the precise handwriting. Detailed accounts of each item lined several pages.

She glanced up when Frank shifted his posture at the front window. "Relax. Father's gone off on some secret voyage. He won't be back for several days, maybe longer."

Frank scowled at her. "You should not be here yourself. I still cannot believe I let you talk me into this."

"It's not unheard of for me to help with the books." She

turned the page, puzzling over the feeling that whatever bothered her floated like a ghost before her eyes, albeit unseen.

"Perhaps before he restricted you to home, church, and the sewing circle."

She darted a look at him. "You knew?"

"Of course. He told me."

A surge of annoyance flitted through Emily, and she returned her attention to the store's books. "A few more moments, then we'll go."

She paused, skimming the interior of the store, contemplating the sense of a mismatch between what she read and what she saw. Shelves lined the walls, fairly groaning under the weight of the goods they supported. Wooden crates and barrels of all sizes filled the shelves and cluttered the floor. A beautiful set of elaborately carved ivory tusks held pride of place on a high shelf with a wide assortment of colored bottles, statuettes, stuffed animals, and bolts of fabric.

Suddenly it struck her. The list of imported items in the ledger did not reflect the contents of the shelves. When had they arrived? Indeed, many more items occupied the store than were included on the list.

At least legally.

Apprehension settled between her shoulder blades.

The door jerked open, and Sawyer filled its opening, his breath coming quick and harsh. Scowling, he motioned to Frank. "Captain Thomson, you must hurry to the office."

"Sawyer? What are you doing here?" Frank moved quickly toward his apprentice.

"Sir, please, you must come."

"What's the matter, boy? Spit it out." Frank fastened his cape around his shoulders, preparing to follow the boy back to the office.

"The soldiers are nosing about the plates for tomorrow's edition. I didn't know what else to do but come find you."

"You did right, boy. But—" Frank glanced at Emily, an unspoken question in the air.

"I'll be fine." Emily detected concern and uncertainty in his eyes. She shooed him out the door with a wave. "I'll stay put, I promise. Now go."

With a raised brow, he hurried after Sawyer, though he glanced back at her as he passed the display window.

Alone, Emily stared at the book on the polished desk. The sheets contained finely written characters, meticulously executed, as though the writer created a work of art rather than a business accounting ledger with its typical scrawl. Page after page contained details of shipments, their date of arrival, the number of crates or containers included, and their general contents. Here sat proof that her father engaged in privateering.

When the door burst open, she didn't look up, expecting Frank to have returned after handling the intruding soldiers.

"Well, well." A razor-sharp voice sliced the air. "Look who we have."

Fear shot through her, and she raised her eyes to see the turncoat standing in the door, one hand on his pistol. *Fiddlesticks.* Surely John did not think she was dangerous. How ridiculous. Though she definitely had cause to fear him. The memory of him attacking her in the market rose in her mind, the sound of Tommy's cries echoing in her ears. Keeping John calm must take priority if she was to escape this confrontation without further injury.

"Major Bradley." She rose from her seat, staying behind the desk.

He gripped the handle of his firearm. When he moistened his lips with his tongue, she gripped the edge of the desk and watched with growing alarm as his eyes roved her body.

She kept her voice steady with all her self-control. "Is there aught I can do for you?"

"I'm sure, Miss Sullivan." He strode toward her as he spoke, dropping his hand from his weapon in order to grasp her fingers as he reached her side. "However, this is not a social visit."

"I do not understand, sir." She had no choice but to allow him to retain her hand despite the warning bells ringing in her head. She hoped he would not repeat the violence he had inflicted on her previously. She also hoped Frank returned very soon to even the odds.

"Your father permits you to work here?" John's eyes took in the open ledger on the desk. "You handle the books?"

What could she say? Her father had no idea she snooped in his financial records on this day. Further, he would be appalled to find her in this part of town alone, though she adhered to her promise and hadn't ventured out by herself. She'd welcome her father's sudden appearance right about now. And where was Frank?

The soldiers. Perhaps they detained him and now more came to arrest her father. They must suspect him of treason. She must prevent the British from apprehending her father as it appeared he dabbled in activities they deemed illegal. Though she also wanted answers from him, she stood her ground. Her duty was clear: protect her family, as her father protected her. Her father's health and welfare was at stake, and being older he would not fare well in prison.

"I ensure the books are in order for the upcoming week's business." Bravado echoed in her voice. Not a lie, per se, but not the truth either. "Is there a problem?"

John nodded, a lascivious grin spreading across his mouth. "Then you'll need to come with me, my sweet." His grip on her hand tightened painfully.

"I'm afraid that's not possible, as I am expected home." His sweet, indeed! What, did he intend to eat her? She refrained from challenging his claim. But did he feel the tremor racing through her as he gripped her hand? "My father would not be pleased if I keep him waiting."

"Your father is welcome to join you then. I'll send word to him. Where did you say he is?" He pulled her with him as he started for the door.

"Where are we going? What is this about?" She resisted with all her strength but to no avail. She dragged her feet, wishing he would stop.

"Your father works as a privateer, an offense not tolerated by King George." Ice formed in his eyes as he gazed at her. "Nor by me. Taking you to the Provost will surely flush him out." Without another word he hauled her along beside him.

He intended to throw her in the basement dungeon of the Exchange, with its vermin and disease. Terror snaked through her.

"No! Don't do this!" She slapped at his hand with her free one, futilely attempting to loosen the iron grip. "Unhand me!"

For response, he clapped an arm around her waist and dragged her from the store, onto the street, and shoved her at another soldier standing there. The startled man easily subdued her flailing arms and secured her hands behind her with a length of rope. "Don't fight, miss. It only makes the ropes tighter."

"Stop!" She did not have the strength to fight two brawny men as they hurried her down the street. When they turned the corner, she saw the Exchange hunkered at the end of the thoroughfare, its basement windows barred, a pair of stern soldiers standing guard before the steps leading down to the door. "No!"

Frantic at the thought of being locked up in the dark, musty, rat-infested building along the waterfront, she fought against the restraints. As promised, the ropes tightened, searing pain preceding the coppery scent of blood as the rough fibers bit into her tender skin. Still she fought. At one point she managed to twist away from the soldier and turned to flee in the direction from which they'd come. Her mind filled with the thought of Frank. He would help her, save her from this horrific nightmare. What had she done? Her brazen flaunting of the restrictions her father imposed to protect her had landed her in the soup kettle this time.

Looking up Broad Street, she saw Frank stop and stare at her. Unmoving. What was the matter with him? Couldn't he see she'd been arrested? "Frank!"

Strong hands grabbed her from behind, dragging her toward the prison.

The massive door to the Provost banged shut at the far end of the street as Frank raced toward it. Dirk Reynolds stopped midstride when Frank ran past him. Uncaring what anyone thought, Frank kept his eyes on the door and the two men flanking the heavy wood barrier. One guard, seeing Frank's approach, stepped in front of the door, rifle aimed at him as he skidded to a stop. The second guard lowered his gun into position.

"Captain, turn around and walk away." The first guard used his rifle muzzle to suggest Frank change direction while the other guard aimed steadily at Frank's chest.

Right now Emily may be tortured or beaten in that hole. The bloody bastard likely had his hands on her as well.

Feeling ill, Frank took a step, then another. "I must see her."

Two rifles trained on him with each step. He peered at the two men, finally recognizing them.

"Captain, go home."

"David, you know me. I saw them take her in there not two minutes ago." He addressed the first guard, raising his hands in submission. "I must know why."

"Go home, Frank," David kept the gun steady. "You can find out more tomorrow."

"You don't understand. Her father's going to kill me." Frank ran a hand through his hair and grimaced at the guards.

If only he'd been faster, but he'd been so shocked to see his love dragged down the street by two ogres that his brain refused to function. The shock coupled with the damning letters in his pocket, ones he dared not be caught holding, prevented him from reacting swiftly. His loyalist farce teetered on his next actions. He needed a reason before he entered the devil's lair. Now Emily faced the unspeakable terror a woman would experience in such a dreadful place with the man who would harm her if given the chance. The man who abused Frank's home, his son, and his woman.

"If you go in there, someone will do worse than that to me," David said.

"Please, why did they arrest her?" He couldn't fathom what she could be accused of while sitting in her father's store. He'd vowed to keep her safe and failed. His failure fit as comfortably as a horsehair suit.

"The major did not say, sir," the man said. "I have to ask you to leave now or face the same consequences as the lady."

Recognizing arguing with the guard or being arrested did not further his cause, Frank reluctantly turned away. He started walking up the street, heading slowly back to the Sullivan house in defeat.

What in the store had triggered this assault? Had she perchance antagonized Bradley again? Maybe he thought she had something to do with her father's privateering activities. Apprehension raced down his back at the image of witnessing her hanging for her father's treason.

He needed help, and he knew where to find it.

Amy would know who to ask and how to break her out of there without raising suspicion about Frank's involvement. He'd never heard of a woman being held in the Provost as the prisoners tended to be political criminals. Women held no political opinion, so what was Bradley about?

He'd lay ten to one odds that the bastard's commanding officer knew naught of what the major had done. General Leslie would release her post-haste but only if made aware of the situation in a way not involving Frank in the process. He needed Amy's story weaving skills to effect his love's escape from that dark place.

He struck out for the Abernathy home at a run.

Chapter Fifteen

$\mathcal{B}$iting her tongue to refrain from speaking her mind, Emily endured the pushing and pulling down the steps into the Provost. Once used as the Harbor Master's office and for storing the goods being shipped in and out of town, now only pirates and those who defied the king resided within the odoriferous walls. At one time the building had enjoyed the respect of the town. Now it reeked of the pungent odors of urine, spoilage, and decay. She gagged at the overpowering smells assailing her senses.

"Welcome to your home away from home." John paused in the large communal prison.

Dim light leaked through the small windows situated near the ceiling. Several other prisoners stared at them from where they sat on the cold red brick floor or lay on beds made from piles of straw, but kept their distance. The scrabble of claws in the deeper regions of the space skittered chills down her back. John peered at her for a moment, a slow smile creasing his face. His leer frightened her and she shivered.

She stumbled when the soldier pushed her forward, the ropes biting deeper. He tugged at the knot and the rope slipped off her wrists. She rubbed the red skin on each wrist to ease the pain.

"You are dismissed," John said to the soldier, keeping his gaze on Emily. Green eyes cold as a dead fish appraised her while he waited for the other man to heed his order.

Silently the man left, glancing over his shoulder before walking away.

Emily swallowed but maintained eye contact with John. He had a heart once, a deep compassion for animals and people. But, he had hurt her in the market, likely because of the sudden embarrassment when Tommy pulled his wig askew. She raised her chin, portraying a confidence she barely felt.

"First, I must search you for any contraband you might be hiding." His eyes glittered in the dim light. He pushed his sleeves up as he walked toward her. "This won't hurt. You may even enjoy it. Like old times."

"Contraband?" His hands roaming over her? Searching her. *No.* She shuddered as loathing wriggled through her veins. This couldn't be happening. He must not touch her. She must stall him, think of a way to escape.

"Weapons." He took a step toward her, smirking, and she retreated two steps without consciously commanding her body to move.

"I'm unarmed." Her voice shook, and she swallowed. Squelching panic, she met his ogling expression.

"It's required of all new prisoners." His gaze roamed her body, his measured steps closing the distance between them as inevitably as a rising tide. "Especially the women, with those skirts designed for hiding…secrets. My regrets for inconveniencing you, my sweet, but that is why I sent the other soldier out. Given our intimate past, I thought you'd be more comfortable if I performed the task."

A shudder chilled her spine. Years ago, yes, she had longed for his kiss. A long time ago. She'd grown older and oh so much wiser. She no longer found him fascinating or mysterious. Instead, he'd become mean-spirited and violent. And Frank had entered the picture. This man before her, this loyalist turncoat, was completely changed from the kindhearted boy she once knew. He'd matured into a dangerously devious man. No feeling or compassion dared linger within him.

"Shall we begin?" He took another step, then another.

"It's—it's really not necessary, John." She forced herself to use his common name and to remain still though her instincts screamed at her to flee. To where, she did not know. The steps were outside and she'd have to somehow find a way past the guards. She'd never manage to run by them. Right now she needed his trust. Steeling her determination, she swallowed and nodded. "I promise."

"Is that so?" One hand snared a wrist and tugged her closer. The other hand patted down her arm from shoulder to wrist. Her stomach recoiled. He switched hands and repeated the process on the other arm. Bile rose to burn her throat, making it painful to swallow her fear. Turning her around so she faced the wall, he ran both hands down her back. Ten pairs of eyes trained on her mortification, but nobody made a move to intervene. She tried to remain immobile but couldn't and stepped away. She might actually vomit.

He grabbed her by the waist with both hands and squashed her against him, knocking her breath from her chest in a rush. Stunned, she gasped for air, aware of the steely grip digging painfully into her sides. Slowly, he turned her back around to face his seething anger.

Gripping her chin painfully, he glared at her. "Do not move away from me again, or you will regret the consequences. Now, hold still."

Trembling at the venom in his voice coupled with his formidable strength, she forced herself to stand like a sculpture as he slowly relaxed his grip enough to continue plundering her body. Each stroke and pat violated her and left her feeling soiled. Shame washed over her.

This was a mistake, a horrid mistake. Violent tremors racked her composure. *Frank, where are you?*

"It doesn't have to be this way, my sweet." John fingered a wayward curl nestled against her neck.

She recalled the last time he did so and Tommy's tears, which nearly caused her own to start. Did the little boy miss her as much as she missed him? The sudden realization that she may never see him again choked her breath. But her father had not raised her to be a coward.

She shook off his hand with a toss of her head. "What do you mean?" Faint hope bloomed in her heart at the promise of an alternative.

He shrugged. "If you tell me your father's whereabouts, I am sure we can work out a compromise."

"What kind of compromise?"

"You can be mine again, like before." His breath warmed her cheek as he leaned closer, his lips near her ear, his words barely a whisper. "You can be my wife, and then all of this would stop."

Never in a thousand years. "I do not think that is possible since you became a loyalist."

"Of course it is, my dear. Women have no official political opinion but bend to the will of their husband. As you, of course, will." He kissed her cheek, his hands biting into her waist and pulling her against him until her breasts brushed his chest. Panic flared when she felt the hard evidence of his lust against her leg.

"John…" She kept herself rigid, trying to pull away from him, but he held her tight against his hard frame. His suggestion defied logic. Subjugating herself to the will of any man remained out of the question. Never to him.

"Yes?"

"We cannot." Death was more appealing.

His eyes searched her face, widening before narrowing dangerously. "It's him, isn't it? That newsman?"

She remained silent, unsure which answer would anger him more, knowing she did love someone or that she didn't but still refused to be with him. The desperation mingled with lust in his eyes stirred horror within her.

His punishing fingers dug into her again. "Be still." He ran his hands down her hips, squeezing and pinching as he probed through the layers of her clothing.

"Major…" She couldn't say more, didn't know what would help or hurt her situation.

He removed his hands from her skirts and resumed his full height, smirking as he tugged on the strings of her bonnet, slipping it off in one smooth motion. It floated to the floor. "Forgive me, my sweet, but you carry me away with your beauty."

He reached up to search her hair, landing on the hair combs she wore.

"What have we here?" He searched her expression. "I thought you said you had no weapons."

Confused, she shook her head. "I am unarmed. I swear."

His hand reached to her bun and removed one elegant ivory comb, then another, allowing her hair to cascade around her shoulders. He laid the shafts with their engraved tops on his palm in front of her face. The tapered points gleamed accusingly, mirroring the look on his face. "These could definitely hurt someone."

"Hair decorations, nothing more."

The need in his eyes changed to malice as he gazed at the gleaming ivory.

Emily's father had presented the lovely combs to her for her sixteenth birthday. He had ordered them from a friendly merchant he met while on a hunting trip in Africa. The T-shaped combs were hand carved with the silhouette of elephants walking single file, and the long pin tapered from the elephants' feet down to a narrow point. Her heart sank. They could be lethal if used appropriately. Why hadn't she thought of that?

"You're a beautiful deceiver, aren't you?"

"No, I—"

"You lied to me, but we can still make an agreement, if you're willing to bend that stiff spine of yours." He yanked her to him, kissing her full on the mouth, his tongue sliding into the surprised opening. When she bit down on his tongue, he growled in pain and released her. "You wench! You'll pay for that! I believe you're just as guilty of privateering as your father."

"I've done nothing wrong." She stared at him as she realized the severity of the trouble in which she found herself.

"I don't think the general will agree." He snapped the combs in half. "I'll leave you here to contemplate your willingness to assist the crown in stopping your father's treasonous activities."

"But I'm innocent!" She blinked back tears, fear slicing through her when John strode away. Around her the other prisoners, all men in various stages of undress and reeking of sweat and urine, murmured among themselves without making any effort to intervene. "You can't do this."

John laughed as he walked to the door and rapped on it twice. "I already have."

Emily wrapped her arms about her waist to still the tremors racing through her. Whether they started from the dank cold or from the sheer terror of her situation, she couldn't say. But her very bones feared what might happen next. No privy. No chairs or tables. Only cold filthy brick floor and arched walls and ceiling with men she barely recognized as patriot merchants and traders. Still, she was the only female among the group.

After many minutes staring around the dungeon, she found a corner with a mound of musty straw and cautiously poked at it with one shoe before easing down onto the pile. Dear Lord, what was to become of her?

Against one wall a man lay with his back to the room, his nut brown coat dirty but of fine weave. A matching hat covered his head so she couldn't tell anything more about him than that he was male. He didn't move. She studied his back looking for signs he breathed. Nothing. A small gasp escaped before she could contain it. She swallowed the bile rising in her throat. The man lay dead and nobody cared to remove his body? Tears leaked from her disbelieving eyes and flowed hot down her cold cheeks.

Sometime later, the street door opened and late afternoon sunlight illuminated the motionless form. John strode back into the room, paused to peer into the faces staring at him until he spotted her. He crossed the room to stop in front of her, a grim smile upon his lips.

"You will come with me and you will say nothing. Is that clear?"

"But John, that man…" She looked at the still form on the straw mound and said a silent prayer for his salvation. "He's… not moving."

John flicked a glance at the body then snared her arm with a punishing hand. He dragged her to her feet with an iron grip. "Not another word."

Biting back a retort, she hurried to keep up with his long stride. They paused at the top of the steps long enough for John to mention the dead prisoner to the guard, then they were off up the street. They marched up Broad for several long blocks then turned right onto King for several more. His hurried pace tired her quickly, but he kept a firm hold of her arm to prevent her from slowing him down.

Soon she realized where he was taking her. Frank's imposing brick house. Her heart raced. Was Frank inside, waiting? John dragged her up the steps leading to the large white door.

"Keep quiet or you'll regret it." He squeezed her arm until she nodded. He ushered her inside the busy headquarters and across the entrance hall.

He forced her up a sweeping staircase curving from the right side of the entrance hall up to the second floor balcony, steadying her when she tripped on her skirts. He led her to a front bedchamber and rushed her inside.

Dare she speak now? "Why did you bring me here? Let me go home."

"Now, now, don't fret. I've prepared this lovely room for you to stay in."

"No, John. Take me home."

He laughed at her demand then sobered. "You're mine, Emily. That lousy printer will not have you. This is your new home for now."

The furniture included a single bed with a small night table holding a lone unlit candle. A chair waited beside a small table holding an urn and basin. Other than those few items, the room was stripped bare. No drapes at the two boarded up windows, narrow slats of sunlight filtering between the planks. He let go of her hand and gazed at her.

"What is it you want, John?"

"Your love." He half bowed then straightened. "We'll be happy together now that you're mine. Will you marry me?"

"You can't be serious." He'd lost his sanity if he thought she'd ever agree to marry the likes of him.

"Oh, but I most certainly am. If I can't have you, then no one will." He frowned as his eyes darkened to jade and his lips flattened into a hard line. "I'll ask you again tomorrow. Think carefully about your answer."

He spun and slammed the door behind him. Cold terror careened through her when the lock clicked home.

❧

"Major Bradley did what?" Amy's raised voice filled the elegantly decorated parlor. "He put a woman in that hole?"

"I can't believe it either." Frank paced the ornate carpet in Amy's front parlor an hour after witnessing Emily's arrest. He brushed a hand through his hair, resisting the urge to pull the damn bow from his queue. Although her raised voice revealed the extent of her dismay, Amy received the news better than expected. "Dragged her down the main street and into the Provost like some treasonous criminal."

"Poor Em. We have to do something." She rose from the wood chair with embroidered cushion and wandered between the upholstered settee and the cherry buffet, her skirts swirling angrily with each turn. "People die in there."

"That's why I came to you." He tugged off his gloves and slapped them against his hand, the resounding smack loud in the silence following his statement.

"Excuse me?" Amy paused in her circuit of the parlor and stared at him for a long moment. "How is it you think I can help?"

"I cannot approach the commandant. But you have connections with General Leslie." He winked at her. "I think he's smitten with you, like the poor soldier at the town's gate."

"You flatter me." Amy straightened the lacy froth draping from her sleeve and sank back onto the cushioned seat. "I shall think on what you've said. Your news has me rather flustered. Maybe some port to calm ourselves?" She indicated with a graceful hand the decanter of garnet colored wine surrounded by small crystal glasses resting on the low table before her.

At his nod, she deftly opened the decanter and filled two glasses.

"I've seen you in action, my dear." Frank crossed the room to sit beside her on the sofa, taking the proffered glass. "I believe in your distinctive talents."

"Really, Frank, you make it sound as if I lie when all I do is invent entertaining tales." She huffed indignantly, staring into her own glass before glancing at him. "Thank goodness Uncle Joshua won't return for several days. We have time to resolve this ghastly situation before he returns so he won't risk his own imprisonment to save his daughter."

"You know about his missions, then?" Frank studied her for two beats and then drained his glass. He stood and began pacing, the tension in his body too much to handle sitting down.

"I've suspected, but thanks for confirming he has been privateering. I applaud his efforts."

Frank paused in front of the bookcase beside the huge fireplace. A merry fire, orange and red and blue flames, snapped and popped. He stared into the dancing firelight. His Emily held for some fictitious crime in the bowels of hell. The very idea made him ache for what she must be experiencing, feeling, fearing. He turned to face Amy, one hand gripping the mantel. "Might you talk to the general?"

Amy stared at him for a long silent moment, lips parted in thought. Instead of answering, she refilled their glasses. "I warrant I can try, but I make no assurances that my talents, as you call them, will suffice. After all, I do not know why they arrested my poor cousin."

Frank shook his head. "Every avenue was cut off to me."

He prayed the prison guards, as well as the other prisoners, treated his love with care. He'd vowed to her father to protect her. Now look where she sat.

Amy glanced at the mantel clock and sighed. "There's naught to be done this late on a Sunday afternoon. First thing tomorrow, I will pay a visit to the general. We should secure her release as soon as possible before she is harmed one way or another."

"Of course, but between now and then, I'll have no rest. Not with my love in danger." With Bradley overseeing her care, Frank prayed they wouldn't be too late. "If the bastard lays one finger on her, he'll answer to me and my pistol."

Chapter Sixteen

*F*ollow me." Frank tugged her hand, pulling it from its hiding place in her hand muff. Heat coursed up her arm and into her heart. Breathless, she followed him through a side door and into a sun-drenched room.

Frank turned her to face him. His look seared her; his hungry gaze soared across her face, flicked down to her chest. Her heart fluttered in response, making her catch her breath. What would he taste like? How hot would his mouth be? Or would it be cool and enticing? Shivers of fear comingled with anticipation propelled her arms, encouraging her to reach out to him. Draw him closer. He answered her summons by closing the short space separating them.

"Frank." Words failed her. When his lips touched hers, thought melted into sensation.

Curious, she watched him kiss her, his eyes closed as he explored her mouth with his tongue. Thrust and search, thrust and search. Against her will her eyes closed, her body driven by a wave of feeling so intense she floated in his arms. Stars exploded when he deepened the kiss, pressed his lips tighter against hers. Warmth gathered inside her, pooling wetness between her legs. She arched toward him, her body instinctively searching for relief only his body could supply. Her breasts mashed against his chest when his arms gathered her closer to him. Dear God, all this from a mere kiss. She'd found heaven.

Frank paused, then resumed with more restraint until he lightly kissed her mouth, once, twice, his eyes open, gazing at her.

She needed him.

"I love you." Desire burned in his eyes. "I need to be with you."

She waited for the fear to come, as it always did at the thought of being with a man. Touching his face with one finger, she traced his nose, his high cheekbones, sank into the dimple that appeared when he smiled. Still the fear did not come. She raised her eyes from his reddened mouth, searched his steel-gray eyes, for what she knew not.

"Love me." Would he? Did he dare follow through on the suggestion? Longing ripped through her.

"Are you certain?" Frank touched his lips to hers, igniting an unfamiliar wantonness.

Her heart clamored for what Frank offered. His strength, love of learning, desire to travel, and his rock-hard body all spoke to her secret longings. Her fears became petty and meaningless in the bonfire of love and desire shining from his eyes. She chose him.

On a moan she pressed her lips to his, answering his question the only way possible.

Frank's arm braced her back as he bent into the kiss, and she closed her eyes, savoring the onslaught of sensations coursing through her. Liquid fire flowed from her core until his heat engulfed her.

Frank's kisses blazed a path along her throat. Her breathing grew ragged when he explored farther south, fanning the flames of her response. She gasped when his lips warmed the exposed swell of her breast.

"Hush, darling." His breath felt cool against her skin.

She didn't have time to respond before her skirt lifted out of the way, the draft of air creating shivers down her legs. She looked at him when his fingers found her ready and slid inside. He covered her mouth with his, swallowing her cry of pleasure with the thrust of his tongue. Suddenly starving for the taste of him, she devoured his mouth as he explored her inner regions with one hand.

She was falling or soaring, or both simultaneously. She couldn't be sure. Thought eluded her. Only his scent and his touch mattered. Her inner blaze fueled her actions, her needs, her wants.

Her fingernails dug into his coat, pulling him closer. He released one hand to unfasten his breeches. Breaking off the kiss, he looked at her with lust-blinded eyes, breathing quick.

"Emily?"

She kissed him in answer, unable to speak for the furious sensations whirling through her, obliterating all else.

She shifted, searching for a more comfortable position without disrupting the intensity of their embrace. A cool breeze raised bumps along her heated skin.

"Marry me," Frank whispered, tugging on a stray curl, winding it around his finger.

Yes! Yes! Anything you want. I love you, Frank. She reached for his face with both hands to draw him closer for one last kiss.

A loud repeated bumping forced her awake, and she opened her eyes to peer into the darkness of her cell with only the dim glow of moonlight through the slats covering the windows. When the sound came again, she realized the wind had picked up, bumping a tree branch against the side of the house. She got up and lit the lantern, grateful for its light to chase away the remnants of her dream.

She lay back down on the hard bed, utterly alone, with a threadbare blanket to cover her and a flat pillow beneath her head, listening to the sporadic noise amidst the rush of wind. The abrupt shift from her intense dream to this harsh reality made her emotions swim.

Her search for a means to escape had proved futile. John had created her jail with care. But still he had only provided the bare essentials, and two meals a day. Although the main floor hummed with activity, only rarely did anyone venture past her room. John kept the key with him. Even when she pounded on the door, nobody responded. Had he warned the others to steer clear? She'd considered starting a fire to attract attention, but feared she'd die in the blaze. She pulled her fingers through her knotted hair and longed for the brush lying on her dressing table.

So much she needed to tend to, and here she sat. Little Tommy had finally warmed to her, babbling and playing with her. He was crawling faster, getting into mischief at every turn. She also had more food to put up for the winter. Preparations for the annual dinner party needed her guiding hand. Here she was, locked away like her prize peaches in their jars.

Her heart sank at a sudden thought. Her father out of town left no one at home to tend to the running of the household. So much to be handled and no one there to manage the comings and goings of the servants and the household goods.

Did no one, not even Frank, care that she was John's captive? How long would John keep her hidden away in Frank's very house? Did anyone even know where she was?

She rose again and paced the floor, rubbing her hands on her arms to abate the chill seeping into her bones. Her stomach growled, rebelling at being neglected. Anger sizzled through her. How dare he? How dare John do this to the woman he professed to love? She did not deserve to be isolated from her family, for she had done nothing wrong.

Criminy! She stood here alone, waiting, for what she knew not. Where was Frank? Her father? Anyone.

She collapsed back down on the hard bed, sleep a distant concept, and thought about her vivid dream. Warmth flooded through her when she recalled how wantonly she made love to Frank, defying her resolve to be her own person. His loving face appeared in her mind, and she longed to reach out and stroke the shadow of stubble lingering on his cheek. Frank had wiggled his way into her heart, and she had deeper feelings for him than she cared to admit. Simply put, she missed him. Wanted to be with him.

Even if she were to marry, which remained in doubt, she'd still want to have her shop as a matter of principle. To prove women could be successful at business without requiring anyone's assistance.

But then the very foundation of her intent would be undermined by wedding and thus becoming reliant upon a man.

Now what did she do?

Early the next morning, Frank entered the loyalist headquarters in his own house. He had to try to reason with John, one loyalist to another. He found the man in the small parlor. He had waited until the other soldiers and officers had finished their business with him before confronting him about Emily's arrest.

"You cannot possibly believe that." Frank carefully placed both palms on the bloody turncoat's desk.

He fought to stay calm, in control. Acting too upset would only incite Bradley further.

"I have evidence as well as witnesses, all I need to take before the general and prove my case," the major replied.

"You have your imagination more likely." Frank searched his memory for any clues as to what type of evidence the bastard had conjured up. Emily was apprehended in the shop with the account books open. Surely he needed more to convict the girl of treason. Frank swallowed, a painful, dry movement, at the realization that during war anything was possible.

"She's in this with her old man, she admitted as much. She committed treason."

"Treason?" Frank stood upright and glared at the man responsible for this ridiculous farce. Ah, that thought clarified Bradley's intent. "You don't want *her*, though, do you? She's the bait."

Bradley's expression shifted, hinting at a deadly grin. "Why, what do you mean?"

"You want someone else, don't you?" Captain Sullivan's sloop was due soon, but no need to reveal as much if it were the captain Bradley truly sought. "You don't care about Emily."

"There you're wrong, my friend." John stood and walked to the corner of the desk, fingering the wood with one hand. He looked at Frank, his eyebrows arched. "I care very much about dear Emily. We have quite a history, she and I. She means the world to me, and I plan to win her back. If I can resolve two needs with one act, why not?"

No way in hell would Frank allow him to claim his Emily. He stood up straighter and looked down at the shorter, stockier man. No matter the history they shared, they shared no future.

Emily cared for Frank. It may not be love quite yet, but she had slowly warmed to him.

He saw it in her eyes when they laughed over some silly event together. Heard it in her voice when she said his name. Sweat beaded on his brow and he wiped it away. "Major, I believe you're mistaken in your supposition she cares for you."

"You've not been with us the last few days, to see how willingly she comes to me when I visit." He smiled as he drummed his fingers on the desk.

Frank balled his hands into fists at the leer on the bastard's face. Surely he lied. Emily cared for him, not this whoreson. Anger buzzed in his ears. Despite the cool breeze blowing through the open windows, he boiled inside at the audacity of the turncoat.

Footsteps sounded behind him. Frank pivoted to see who approached, and let out a breath when Amy sashayed up to stand beside him.

"Sorry I am so tardy, Frank." She folded her gloved hands in front of her, her drawstring purse dangling. "My conversation with the general took a little longer than anticipated."

"Miss Amy, I'm pleased you arrived." He'd accompanied her to the general's quarters on a second attempt to meet with him, but she'd insisted, to his relief, her conversation with the man be private. Had she succeeded in her quest? His heartbeat pounded in his ears, making it difficult to hear the conversation. "I believe you know the major."

"Yes, though it's been years since I've had the pleasure." Amy crossed to where Bradley stood, hand outstretched. "Pleased to see you again."

The major ignored the proffered greeting and eyed her coldly. "Miss Abernathy."

Amy lowered her hand at the rebuff, her smile fading.

"What did the general say to your pleas?" Frank prayed he'd agreed but Amy's solemn features denied his prayer.

"He did not agree with my plea for Emily's release. I'm sorry."

"I'm afraid her release is quite impossible," Bradley said.

"Your cousin committed treason against the king of England, and it is out of my hands to assign her fate."

"Treason? Emily?" Amy's eyes widened, their green depths sparkling with annoyance. "My dear sir, that is what's impossible."

"Even children hang for treason," Bradley said, his eyes twinkling.

"And you find hangings amusing?" Amy asked, offended. "You must be mistaken if you think my cousin capable of such behavior."

"I know what your lovely cousin is capable of better than you realize." Bradley smirked at them. "In fact, I know her quite well. Intimately, you might say."

Frank clenched his fists tighter at the major's words. Amy's face paled. How intimately had the bastard known his love? A kiss? A fondle? More? Frank's face grew hot as he glared at the man. Not that carnally, surely. The bastard lied. What if he did in some distant past know Emily intimately? That was then. Frank loved Emily. He would forgive her succumbing to flirtations years ago. And despite any protest, protect her from this manipulative and dangerous man. "Careful, Bradley."

"I see." Amy raised a cautionary hand toward Frank and moved closer to the major. "For the sake of her reputation, I assume that tidbit of information will not be shared with anyone else. Am I right?"

Bradley shrugged. "As long as she cooperates with me, yes, I can agree to that."

"Conditions, Major?" Frank opened and closed his fists, flirting with the idea of punching the man. "You would resort to blackmail."

Amy stepped between the two men. She looked up at Bradley. "What happens to Emily if your demands are not met? What is it you want?"

Bradley gazed at her for a long moment before answering. "I made her happy before. I can make her happy again. I want only one thing. She must become my wife."

Frank could not stop the gasp, though he did manage to

mask it as a cough. Emily marry this monster? He started forward, but a look from Amy stopped him. She motioned with her eyes for him to back up and stay quiet. He did so with an effort. He really wanted to pummel this bastard into the floor. How dare he think he could coerce and control Emily's beautiful spirit? To force her to marry anyone, let alone this brute? Gripping the back of a nearby chair, he forced himself to remain still with every irate fiber of his being. Please, let the turncoat say the wrong thing, and he would not be able to stop himself. Amy or no Amy.

"My, my, Major, that is quite a demand. Have you spoken to Emily about your desires?"

"Yes, of course. She's considering my proposal." Bradley looked up at the ceiling with a leer on his lips.

"Ah, so you talked with her?" Amy moved closer to the officer. "She is well?"

Frank gripped the cold wood tighter. So the bastard had seen her. Even offered his hand, but she apparently had not accepted. By God, if he hurt her, he's dead. Pure and simple. But why did he keep glancing up?

"As well and happy as you'd expect." He winked at Frank. "She has been fine under my personal supervision, rest assured."

The wood between Frank's hands splintered.

"There is only one problem with your plan." Amy clasped her hands together. "Believe me when I tell you she will not marry you."

Bradley scowled at her. "How would you know?"

"I cannot tell you, but I do know it for a fact. She will not marry anyone."

Frank's heart plummeted to his feet. Not marry anyone? Surely Amy jested. Of course Emily would marry. All women married at some time in their lives so they could have a home to call their own, children to love and rear. What else did a woman have to strive for, to hope for, if not to love a man and care for him and his hearth? Emily's essays echoed in his mind, their content inflammatory yet suddenly revelatory. Perhaps she did have other dreams she pursued, scandalous and provocative dreams not only for herself but all women. His understanding of her motivations crystalized.

"You lie." Bradley glared at Amy, a rhythmic pulse in the vein on his neck. "You lie!"

Amy shook her head and contemplated the angry man.

"Why will she not marry?"

Amy remained silent, though Frank hoped she'd reveal the mysterious secret behind this observation.

"Tell me." Bradley marched closer and stared at Amy, silently threatening her with his physical nearness.

"It doesn't matter, John." She lifted her shoulders in an apology. "There's nothing more we can do here. Let's go." Amy clutched her purse as she turned to leave.

Frank speared John with stormy eyes. "This isn't over."

"For you, it is. She cannot walk out on me. I know she still cares for me." He gloated at Frank. "She even kissed me. Quite thoroughly, too."

Frank tried but could not squelch the anger clawing inside of him. "You, sir, have gone too far. You dare besmirch my lady's reputation in such a manner?"

"She appeared quite practiced at the art." Bradley stepped closer, puffing up his chest as he closed the space. "I cannot help that she is so easily persuaded to share her favors."

Frank clenched his fist until his nails dug into his palms. He'd had a surfeit of this bastard's innuendo and lies. "I'm calling you out, sir. Tomorrow at dawn be at the dueling alley and we'll settle this."

"You're challenging me to a duel?" Bradley's mouth slowly closed into a hard line.

"Let's settle this." Frank's blood boiled at the brute's outrageous claims. Moreover, if he had actually kissed Emily, had touched her in any way, then the man would die for his presumption. And for falsely arresting her in the first place. He needed to get her out of this mess before her father returned. So, very soon. An idea bloomed in his head as he glared at the major. "If you're man enough, it's to the death."

"You best not miss." Bradley glared at him. "She was mine before; she will be again."

Frank cast a last look at the bastard's frowning countenance. "Pistols at dawn," Frank spat. "Don't be late."

The duel on the morrow kept him awake long after he usually collapsed into bed. He'd checked the pistols and contacted Sawyer to be his second. With nothing to do until dawn, he found himself pacing the street in front of his house. The smell of the burning lamps mingled with the ever-present aroma of salt water. He wanted his home back and in good condition. But more than that, he had a sneaky feeling that Bradley held Emily somewhere inside. He was drawn to the place more because of that niggling certainty than anything else.

The man's obsession with her led him to essentially kidnap her under the guise of an arrest. He had taken her to the Provost, but Frank had learned he'd escorted her elsewhere. David couldn't say to where, but after chatting with Bradley in his office Frank knew. Those repeated glances at the ceiling told him he'd brought her to the house the bastard had claimed for his own use. But where had he secreted her away? He scanned the first floor windows. No light gleamed within. Surely someone remained inside after the lamps were turned down.

He stared up at the front of the house, then glanced up the street as the night watchman turned the corner. He sported a long gray beard and hunched back, carrying a lantern on a long pole. The same man had kept watch for many, many years. Patrolling the streets and checking on nighttime activities, illicit or otherwise. He'd probably continue to do so until the day he died.

The older man's mournful voice periodically called out the time as he stumped down the street. "One o'clock and all is well."

Frank nodded to him as he sauntered past, then turned his

attention back to his house. Surprise swept through him when he spotted light flickering in one of the second floor bedchambers. The light was impeded by boards nailed to the exterior of the window, narrow gaps between them allowing the lamplight to escape. Above Bradley's office. His pulse pounded in his ears the longer he contemplated the possibility. Could it be Emily? He moved to stand closer to the house beneath the window, willing her to give him some sign.

"What are you doing out and about at this time of morning?"

Frank startled at the familiar deep voice and jerked his head to see Benjamin beside him. "Damn, you're a sneaky bastard."

"Answer my question." Benjamin glanced at the house and then back to Frank.

"I could ask you the same thing but it wouldn't do any good, now would it?"

"None at all."

Spying on something or someone apparently. "I may be wrong, but I think Emily is inside." Frank pointed up at the window. "In that room."

"Why would she be in there?"

"Major Bradley claims she's committed treason and arrested her. But the guard told me she'd been removed by Bradley. After talking with him earlier, I believe she must be right there."

"You'd be risking much if you go in at this time of night without orders or a reason for doing so."

Frank shrugged. "I can't help that. She's in danger from him and I won't let him hurt her."

"Very well." Benjamin studied the building, frowning at the glimmer of light flickering from behind the boarded up window for many moments. "It's your house, so is there another entrance that's not quite as obvious?"

Frank thought for a moment and then snapped his fingers. "The servants' stairs from the back hall. Come on."

Benjamin placed a restraining hand on his arm. "Are you sure?"

Frank drew in a long breath and stared up at the window.

"No, but I'm going anyway. I need to know."

"If you release her, then you may be arrested for doing so."

Frank swallowed the rising fear but nodded. "I'll figure that out later. She's innocent."

"I may know someone who can help with proving so should it come to it." Benjamin grinned mischievously. "For now, I've got your back. Let's go."

Pushing aside the curiosity as to which of his friend's many connections he referred to, Frank led the way around the house, down an alley, and into the rear yard. Keeping to the shadows as much as possible, they inched toward the servants' entrance. He tested the door latch but it resisted his gentle tug. He pulled harder but nothing. He looked at Benjamin who moved in front of him and yanked on the pull until it lifted with a squeal. Frank scanned the yard, expecting any moment for some armed guard to charge out of the darkness at him.

"Go on." Benjamin pulled the door open to let Frank slip past him. "I'll wait here."

Frank nodded once and then spun around to soft foot his way down the short hall to the servants' stairs. He lightly ran up the steps, easing into the upstairs passage. Rough snores drifted on the air. The rustle of a straw mattress suggested someone rolling over in bed. A soft thump followed shortly by another, shoes being removed. The house was definitely occupied by loyalist men. He must be quick and quiet. Yet the lamplight gleamed from the chamber at the far end from him. He must know. He couldn't leave without discovering if his love was held prisoner within the walls of his very home.

He hurried toward the light, silently on the balls of his booted feet. When he reached the door, he leaned close to listen for any sound. Soft weeping met his straining ears.

"Emily?" His whisper sounded loud in the quiet of the night.

The weeping stopped abruptly. If it wasn't her, he would soon be in a ton of trouble. But if it was…

"Frank?" Her hoarse whisper sounded cautiously hopeful.

"Is that you?"

"Yes." He tried turning the door knob but it was locked. "I don't have a key."

"John keeps it in his pocket." She'd moved to the other side of the door. "Get me out of here."

"I will." He searched the dim passage, seeking ideas on how to do what he'd promised. Finding none, he braced himself and then spoke through the door in a whisper. "Em, I'll be back. Be ready to leave."

"Don't leave me here…" Her fierce whisper hissed with anxiety.

"Not for long. I promise." He spun on his heel and silently trotted to the stairs, pausing for a moment at the top to ensure he hadn't been heard or seen. Then he descended as quickly and quietly as possible to find Benjamin waiting by the rear door. Despite the stealth Frank had used, his friend faced him, prepared for his appearance. Naturally. "I need your skills."

Without a word, Benjamin nodded and started walking toward him. Frank turned and darted quietly up the stairs, Benjamin close behind and just as silent. Peering into the upstairs passage, Frank determined the coast was clear and eased from the protection of the door frame. Glancing around him, he hurried to Emily's room and halted.

"It's locked and Bradley has the key." Frank pointed at the door knob. "Can you…?"

Benjamin reached into his vest pocket and removed his lock pick. "Step aside."

Frank took a couple of steps away as Benjamin applied the tool to the lock and soon turned the knob. Relief flooded Frank's chest when he saw his Emily rushing toward him, tear stains on her flushed cheeks.

"Frank. I knew you'd come." She trembled where she stopped in front of him, hesitating to finish her flight into his arms with Benjamin as an audience.

He wrapped his arms around her, succumbing to the need to ensure she was indeed safe and his again. "We must away."

Benjamin pulled the door closed without a sound, locking it once again. "Let's get out of here before someone discovers she's missing."

"Too late for that." A sleepy-eyed soldier stood in the passage, blocking their escape with a pistol aimed at them.

Benjamin stepped in front of Frank and started toward the other man. "Now, there's no need for that. We're just escorting this young lady home where she belongs."

"Major Bradley left strict orders she was not to be disturbed." The soldier motioned with the gun for them to go back to the room. "Nor did he say she was permitted to leave."

"He has no authority to restrain this woman against her will." Frank held Emily's trembling body against him. "She's coming with us."

"How'd you open that locked door anyway?" The soldier advanced slowly, a frown on his puzzled face. "Major Bradley said there was only one key and he has it."

"There's more than one way to unlock a door." Benjamin glanced quickly at Frank, sending a silent message with a tilt of his head toward the soldier. He slipped a deadly knife from a hidden place in a fluid motion.

Frank lifted his chin to acknowledge the plan. Frank pushed Emily behind him as Benjamin returned his attention to the soldier and then launched himself at the man. With a gasp of surprise, the soldier dropped in his tracks. Benjamin caught him as he fell and silently lowered him to the floor. Emily sucked in air and Frank turned to hug her to him. She was safe and his.

"Let's get you home." He kissed her briefly, drawing her eyes up to meet his.

"Please." Her whispered plea was laced with terror.

"You alright?" Benjamin joined them, sliding the deadly weapon out of view.

"Once we get out of here, we'll be fine." Frank took one of Emily's hands in his, reluctant to let her out of his sight.

"Righto." With a short nod, Benjamin led the way while

Frank escorted Emily down the stairs and out into the chilly night.

Emily paused outside the house, drew in a slow breath to quell her racing heart after the terror she'd felt at the sight of the soldier with the gun pointed at her man. Benjamin stood to one side, watching her. Such questioning looks Benjamin and Frank wore. They did not understand how she felt right now, but they were about to learn. Now that she was free from John's arbitrary imprisonment, she needed to clear her name. She'd had plenty of time to think about all her grievances, and she wanted answers. Especially from her father.

First, Emily needed to confront her father about this whole episode.

Two long days and nights she had spent in that barren room, dreading the sound of footsteps for fear of John returning to berate her again. Or worse. He stole not only her favorite hair combs but her sense of security, and her dignity as well. Was he daft to think she could love him? And did this really stem from her father's business affairs?

Her father, the man with the highest ethical standards in town, apparently not only engaged in privateering but lied to her about it. It wasn't the act, but the lie that boiled her blood and made her heart ache. How could she trust him? Anger and betrayal drove her steps toward home.

"Wait until I talk to my father," she muttered. "I want the truth of this matter once and for all. He should have told me."

Frank hastened his steps and soon strode at her side. "Are you all right?"

"I will be when I speak to my father."

"But your father is not home right now," Frank said.

She glared at him, then focused on the abandoned street in front of her. "He better be if he knows what's good for him."

Benjamin chuckled. "You're upset. That's to be understood. But you cannot make him appear out of thin air."

"No, I suppose I can't." She sighed deeply and slowed her steps.

"Now that tonight's fun is over, I'll be on my way home, too." Benjamin touched his fingers to his hat. "Good night to you both."

"Thanks for your help, friend." Frank nodded to him as Benjamin walked away.

"I'm glad that so-called fun is over as well." Emily shivered in the chilly night air.

"You're cold. Here." Frank removed his coat and draped it around her shoulders. He tucked her hand into the crook of his arm and covered her fingers with his. "What did they…what did he do to you? Did he harm you?"

Tension radiated from him as he asked his question. Gauging Frank's concern, she divined what he really asked.

"No, he did not hurt me." She squeezed his arm, relishing the rock-hard support it provided.

The feel of his strength beneath her hand recalled her wanton dream, and heat built on her neck and spread to her cheeks. She'd begged him to make love to her then without fear. Would she feel the same way in reality?

He lowered his mouth to hers and kissed her, igniting sparks inside her veins. He lifted his head and whispered, "If he hurt you, I'd have to definitely kill him tomorrow morning. Otherwise, I'd just scare the whoreson."

She didn't have chance to respond before his lips pressed hers again. Emily's senses rioted from the electric effect of Frank's kiss combined with the startling words concerning John.

Frank lifted his head and grinned at Emily. Still reeling, Emily studied Frank's face. "Kill him?"

"Dawn tomorrow." Frank shrugged, eyes serious. "Just him and me."

"A duel?" Emily trembled at the thought. Duels left men injured or maimed, and sometimes dead. If Frank approached the event with the intent to kill, how likely was he to die instead?

"Do not fret, love." Frank kissed her on her forehead. "I'll be home for breakfast."

"You can't be serious." Emily pleaded with her eyes for him to back down from the challenge.

"You're *my* girl, Emily. I'll not have him damaging your reputation." Frank peered into her eyes. He kissed her lips, lightly this time. "I feared you'd hate me for not being there for you. I came for you as soon as I realized where you were."

Thank God. Emily couldn't have stood another day of John's harangue. Frank's love shone in his eyes, and she understood he had done what he needed to free her. She gloried in being his lady now even as a thrill of fear for his safety on the morrow simmered in her veins.

Oddly enough the idea slid into place as easily as her shuttle on the loom. She smiled at him.

Emily hooked arms with Frank, and they strode purposefully down the street. Few others happened to be about as they made their way home. Clouds built in the sky, threatening rain, the scent of it thick in the air.

Emily tugged on Frank's arm to attract his attention. "Tell me, how does one prepare for a duel? What should I do?"

"My dear, women have no place at a duel," Frank said seriously. "Your father would strenuously object."

"I have a more important question." Emily grinned at him, her inner vixen prancing. "What does one wear?"

Frank stopped walking and stared at Emily. "You need not worry your little head about that, since you'll definitely not be going."

Chapter Seventeen

*E*arly the next morning, fog crept along the ground, a low layer swirling with each swish of Emily's skirts as she paced at the end of St. Michael's Alley. What was she doing, acting as the lookout for this unlawful and deadly game? Last night, it seemed such a good idea, to be at her man's side.

The alley, running along the edge of the churchyard, held the honor of being the preferred site for duels. Frank had told her about the alley the night before as he cleaned his dueling pistols, a matched Wogdon and Barton flintlock set he had imported recently through his French connections.

The authorities did not patrol the alley often, making it easy for the challenger to seek and receive satisfaction for ill-timed insults. In this case, the damage to her reputation by John's actions against her.

Low voices emanating from the alley drew her attention. She paused in her pacing and hurried to the side of the street. Frank insisted she keep out of range of the pistols, notorious for their lack of precision. He also demanded she stay far enough away to not be considered a witness if questioned later. She took up her position near a small tree and grabbed the tree trunk, feeling the rough bark dig into her palms.

Sawyer, acting as second, stood near Frank, inspecting the lethal weapon in his hand. John's second, a young lieutenant she'd never seen before, repeatedly rubbed his chin. Dirk Reynolds's voice relaying the ground rules and instructions drifted to her ears. With his reputation for fairness, he was the perfect impartial judge of the duel's satisfactory outcome.

"You'll each take twenty-five paces, then turn." Dirk's quiet voice carried easily across the distance. "This duel will use the traditional English rules. As arranged, John fires first, then Frank, if he can. Understood?"

The two men agreed and raised their pistols to point skyward.

Five men and Emily constituted the only souls about at this time of morning. The cool fog dissuaded the birds from rising to sing and muted the sounds of the waves in the harbor. Silence thundered in her ears. Her clammy palms ached against the bark as she waited. Frank and John stood back to back, pistols ready. From this distance in the dim light she could not tell them apart. Both men possessed the marksmanship skills to hit their intended target.

Such a short distance.

Neither likely to miss.

"One, two, three…" Dirk solemnly counted out the paces, his voice a muffled echo.

Sweat beaded in Emily's hair despite the damp chill of the morning. How could this be happening?

"Turn and fire!" Dirk called.

"Frank!" Emily shouted his name, then covered her mouth with a hand.

Two nearly simultaneous explosions shattered the morning stillness and startled the birds from the bushes. Two puffs of white smoke floated over the scene, obscuring Emily's view of the men. Was either injured? Or dead? Ice formed in the pit of her stomach. She strained to see through the smoke and fog. She finally gave in to the urgent desire to know who had survived and raced into the alley.

A cat's paw of morning breeze flowed around her, dissipating the smoke. The fog stewed about the sprawled figures of the duelists. As she drew nearer, she discerned the loyalist's uniform, the man inside lying unnaturally still. Her breath froze in her chest, but she looked away, sought out the other figure.

"Frank!" Emily gathered her skirts and hurried to where her man lay.

He had landed on his back, arms and legs splayed, eyes closed. The smoking pistol had fallen within easy reach of his open hand. Emily knelt beside him, oblivious to the press of stones through her skirts. *No! He cannot be dead. I love him!*

"Frank?" Placing a hand on his shoulder, she brushed back the hair hanging over one eye. Shaking, she looked at his chest, noted the shallow rise and fall. Something deep within her core uncoiled. She *loved* this man. She couldn't weather the thought of him dying. She gently enclosed one of his hands with her own. "Frank? Can you hear me?"

A low groan escaped his lips as his eyes opened. He stared at her for a moment before sighing, rolling his head slowly side to side. "Emily, I thought I told you to stay away."

She shook her head even as a smile crept onto her lips. He must be okay after all, the darling idiot. "Is that all you can think about?"

Sawyer joined them, dangling the other pistol by its handle.

Frank raised an eyebrow at him. "Bradley?"

Sawyer shook his head. "You're a good shot."

"Damnation." Frank closed his eyes and squeezed Emily's hand.

"Are you hurt?" Emily quickly skimmed his body.

"No, I—" He tried to rise and grunted in pain. He managed to sit up, blinking unbelievingly at the red fluid on his hand. He lifted his arm and looked at the torn sleeve where the bullet had grazed him, leaving an oozing trail of blood. "Maybe I am at that."

"We need to stop the bleeding." Emily tugged the embroidered kerchief from her bodice, pressed it against the wound and hoped he wouldn't notice her hand shaking. Seeing the man she loved with his life essence flowing from him sent her emotions reeling. Frantic, she pressed harder, intent on staunching the escaping blood.

Inhaling sharply, jaw clenched, Frank stayed mute, watching her actions.

"Sorry." Emily eased up on the pressure but kept a firm hand in place.

Dirk approached them, hands on hips. "Why didn't you wait to fire?"

Frank looked at Dirk and shrugged. "I did. I waited until I saw the smoke from his gun. I wanted to take my shot in case he aimed better than I reckoned."

"I see." Dirk frowned. "I must summon the authorities to have his body taken care of. Are you sure you're okay?"

Sawyer inspected the red line when Emily pulled the makeshift bandage away. "He'll live."

"Fine. I'll see to the body." Dirk patted Frank's good shoulder. "Glad the better man survived, friend."

"I think I need a doctor." Frank grimaced.

"I could call for Samantha," Emily suggested.

"I'd rather a man handle this, Em." Frank studied her face, then shook his head. "He'll understand the situation. Nothing personal against your friend."

"If you're certain." Emily smiled weakly at him, torn between loyalty to Samantha and to Frank.

"Dr. Trent is proving to be a better doctor than his father," Dirk said. "And that's saying something."

Enough chitchat. Emily's love might have died, and they all hung around in the fog talking. Emily stood up, avoiding looking at the body nearby. "Sawyer, help me get Frank to his feet and then send for Dr. Trent. Ask him to meet us at my house."

Through both of their efforts, they managed to help Frank stand. Once his wobbly legs steadied, he walked slowly beside Emily down the quiet street toward her home, holding her hand as though it alone kept him on his feet.

"What excuse will you give for your injury?" It seemed unreal to be strolling serenely down the street beside Frank.

Visions of much worse endings to this morning's tale sped through her mind. Fortunately he had survived the duel and received his satisfaction to the challenge. What if Frank had died? A chill raced through her at the thought. Life without him seemed impossible now. Is that what love did to a person? She glanced at him and warmed when he smiled her way.

"Misfire during drills. Happens all the time."

Emily squeezed his hand. "I've not heard of any drills recently. Definitely not for a newsman, either."

He shrugged and continued walking. "I'll think of something; do not fret."

The sun edged out from behind the morning clouds and fog, finally beginning to chase away the misty morning. A pair of bluebirds darted past and disappeared into the bushes beside the road.

"Emily, you must tell me. Did he kiss you?" Frank appraised her reaction. "He wasn't lying, was he? Did you want him to?"

Heart in her throat, Emily swallowed. How much should she reveal? "Many years ago, when we were teens, yes, I wanted him to. But not this time."

"I see." He walked in silence, his steps sluggish. "The man died over a kiss."

"He was not the same person as the boy I knew." She tried to soften the hard reality. The vision of John's face when he searched her in the prison sent tremors coursing down her back. "He meant me harm, one way or another."

"Aye, better he's dead at that." Frank stopped and turned her to face him, lifting her hand to his mouth for a long kiss. "He wouldn't have left you in peace otherwise."

They finished the walk home in silence. As they neared the house, Samantha appeared on the street, hurrying in their direction.

"Emily, Sawyer said Frank had been shot. What happened?"

"An early morning mishap with an imported pistol," Frank said quickly before Emily could form a coherent reply. "Nothing for you to worry about. The doctor is on his way."

"I'm already here. So let's go inside and I'll take a look at it." Samantha herded them through the piazza and into the house. Setting up in the dining area, she indicated a chair for Frank to occupy.

"If you insist." Frank sank onto the chair obediently.

Glad to see him reviving from the shock of the wound, Emily gathered the items needed to properly clean and bandage the gash while Samantha inspected the damage to his upper arm. Emily returned as Samantha finished her examination.

"It's not deep, fortunately." Samantha sat back and gazed at Frank. "Are you sure this was your gun that did this?"

Once more the front door opened, surprising Frank into silence. Dr. Trent strode into the room, a black leather bag in hand. Sawyer hovered in the door behind him until Frank motioned for him to enter as well.

Emily greeted the doctor, who frowned at her before staring at Samantha as though she'd sprouted two heads. Samantha looked up at the intrusion, a flash of resentment in her eyes before she turned back to her work. Nervous for her friend, Emily quickly intervened. "Dr. Trent, thanks for coming, though as you can see Samantha has things in hand."

"Isn't this the healer you summoned to assist with Tommy's injury as well?" Trent asked, critically watching Samantha's ministrations.

How dare he challenge her abilities? Emily regarded the young doctor, wondering how best to respond. After all, Samantha's salve had not helped Tommy as much as the doctor's medicine, but who was to say the two treatments had not worked together? Doubt crept into Emily's mind. She waited to see how her friend responded to the challenge. Samantha turned from where she dried the wound prior to applying a healing herbal salve.

"My methods have worked for years," Samantha said, "and are proven by many other healers before me. But herbals have some variability in effectiveness depending on the type of injury and the position of the celestial bodies. What of your methods, new ways based on what? People in other lands with fancy instruments and books?"

Trent's eyes flashed and his mouth tightened, but he remained calm. "Based on scientific methods and evidence. Not old wives' tales and astrology."

The tension in the room increased to suffocating proportions as the two healers glared at each other.

"You believe in their abilities more than your own." Samantha shrugged, breaking the stare, and resumed her work. "I trust in myself and my abilities."

"I'll not have you attempt to kill another of *my* patients." Trent crossed the room to inspect Frank's arm. "Humph, that will work. Good thing it was a clean shot and didn't leave the lead ball embedded in it. Fortunately it missed anything that would prove fatal."

Frank could have died. The bleak horror of that thought made Emily suddenly dizzy, and she sank onto a nearby chair. Spots formed before her eyes, and she put her head in her hands to steady herself as the room swayed. Dark shadows floated around her. Thoughts whirled in her mind as quickly as the spots came and went. Her breath caught in her lungs at Frank's near miss with death. If John had aimed a little more to the left, the deadly lead ball would have struck his heart instead of his arm.

Pain rippled through her at the thought of losing Frank. His smile. His eyes filled with laughter. And love.

Losing the man she'd grown to love despite all her protestations. Could she endure the eventual pain of loving him and watching him die? She'd survived her sister's death but not without a persistent void in her life.

She groaned aloud, attracting the sudden attention and concern of Samantha. Her friend poured water into a glass and hurried to Emily's side.

"My goodness, you look like you've seen a ghost. Here, drink this."

Emily sipped, glad to have something to fill her mouth so her newfound discovery stayed inside for a bit longer.

She must make a terrible choice, one that sent echoes of fear shooting through her. Stick with her safe path and her vow, or take the risk and follow her heart?

❦

"There, I think that does it." Emily placed the bowl of colorful gourds on the dining room table and stood back to critique the overall effect. "We're decorated for the party tonight. I love the scent of the pinecones and cinnamon, don't you?"

Amy crossed her arms and surveyed the room. "It's lovely. The food is ready, and the guests should arrive shortly."

"I've already ensured dear little Tommy had his supper and is tucked in with Mary upstairs in his room." Emily had given him a kiss on his sweet forehead, happy he'd finally accepted her attentions. "I think he may even like me a bit."

"He'll be calling you mother in no time." Amy hugged Emily and stepped back to look over the room where the feast, such as it was, would take place. "All that remains is to set out the chairs in the upstairs parlor and make sure the fire is stoked."

"I'll see to that, and then we need to dress for the party." Amy crossed to her and squeezed her shoulders before leaving Emily alone to finish in the dining room.

Emily paused to peruse the decorations, then caught herself staring into the fire as thoughts swirled in her head. Her father was expected to return this evening, in time for the festivities. How would she express her disappointment and resulting lack of trust in him? She prayed for courage and strength to say what needed to be said.

Frank entered the room, resplendent in his evening attire. Emily's breath hitched at the sight. He stood tall and handsome in his midnight-blue evening coat and trousers, the dark broadcloth emphasizing the impressive breadth of his shoulders. The bulge of the bandage protecting his shoulder strained the fabric.

That deep-seated emotion she had experienced in her dreams blossomed within her. An ache no salve or herbal could assuage settled inside. She loved him. It was that simple and that complex. What would the future bring?

"My darling, you are enchanting this evening." He sauntered across the room and kissed her. "I could grow accustomed to seeing your smile every day."

"And I yours."

The back door opened, allowing a blast of cold air to rush through the house. "Hallo! I'm back."

Her smile froze before melting into a frown. "Will you accompany me to speak to Father?"

Silently she left the room, Frank following. When he took her hand, her heart skipped, then settled into its normal rhythm.

"Welcome home, Father." She met him in the hall. "Was your voyage successful?"

Something flickered in his eyes as he removed his cloak and hat and handed them to Jasmine. Emily focused on the man in front of her. The man she had trusted all her life.

The man who challenged that trust.

"Very successful, thank you." He glanced at Frank. "The contact I spoke to you about awaits further orders."

What was that about? Emily cleared her throat drawing her father's attention. "I've returned from an adventure of my own." Anger seethed inside at how easily he lied to her. She never suspected until recently, and then to have John throw it in her face, adding insult to injury. "Would you join me in the library for a sherry?"

"I'd like to freshen up first, if you don't mind," her father said warily.

"I do mind, Father. Come, there's not much time before our guests arrive, and we must talk. Now." She ushered him down the hall and into the library, keeping Frank's hand securely in her own until they all crossed the doorsill.

Emily positioned herself in front of the fireplace. Her father stood impatiently in front of her. Frank closed the door behind him. The fire hissed and popped as she stared at her father, silently trying various phrases before she dared to speak them. He gazed back then opened his hands in a questioning gesture.

"What is this about, darling? I must dress for dinner. I'm much later returning than expected due to some rather unexpected complications."

"I'm enthralled and would love to hear about your trip. After you explain why you lied to me." There, she'd said it. Confronting him felt good, to challenge him on his actions.

"Lie? When did I lie to you?"

"Did you think I wouldn't discover the truth? The entire town knows, including the British. That's why I've spent two days held prisoner. All thanks to you."

"You were in the dungeon?" Her father stepped to her and hugged her. "Because of me? Oh God, I didn't know."

"Of course not, you who've been privateering and hoping nobody would catch on. But they did. And they imprisoned me for it."

"Why would they think you were involved?" He set her away from him and gazed at her face.

"I went to your shop to prove your innocence in your own ledgers."

"Tell me you didn't go by yourself?" His grip tightened on her arms. "I warned you to stay home."

"I took her," Frank said. "She didn't venture out alone."

"Major Bradley found me there, where I read through your ledgers and finally understood the deceit you engaged in."

"You should not have gone there. I knew someone in town asked questions, and suspected that Bradley boy. Why else do you think I wanted you to stay home but for your safety?" He peered into her eyes, searching for she knew not what. "I did not want you to be involved in any of this."

"Easy to say now." A tear threatened to show itself, and she swallowed. "Why, Father? Why did you do this?"

"I've done nothing but try to protect you by not revealing everything to you. That way, if they discovered how I supported our government, the British could not implicate you as well." He hugged her to him, and his heart beat against her cheek, strong and even. "You must believe me."

"It's hard to when the father I knew and trusted did not also trust me in return." She pushed away from him. "How am I to trust you?"

He folded his arms across his chest and shook his head. "You have no need to be ashamed of me. What I've done, I'd do again without qualms. I love our new America and will do anything within my power to fight for it and all it stands for. I am an American, not a British subject. I'm working for our government. Would you have me do less than that?"

He had done his duty for their newly formed government, helping turn the tide of the war in their favor. Sometimes a good reason existed for not telling the whole truth. She moved to him, searching his eyes for understanding. "No, but if it weren't for Frank and Benjamin rescuing me, I'd still be locked up."

Her father looked at Frank with relief in his eyes. "Then thank you for stepping up and doing so."

"I also spoke to General Leslie about the incident and all the charges have been dismissed. Seems Major Bradley wasn't following orders after all." He shrugged modestly. "And given his unfortunate demise, the general didn't see any reason to pursue the matter further."

"Demise?" Her father arched his brows at Frank.

"Unfortunately for him, yes." Frank shifted his weight and then cleared his throat. "I did what I had to."

"Frank called him out." Emily grasped Frank's hand and gave it a squeeze. "He defended my honor."

"I see." Her father unexpectedly grinned. "Very good."

"More importantly, Leslie granted me permission to reclaim my house, now that it's no longer needed for Bradley's use."

"Excellent." Her father beamed at Frank.

"That's wonderful news." Emily noted the deep satisfaction evident in Frank's expression at the way things had turned out.

A soft knock on the door echoed in the ensuing silence. Amy's voice quietly called through the door. "Emily, we must dress. Our guests will arrive soon."

"A moment." Emily glanced at Frank, then her father. "I had not understood your reasons. Will you forgive me?"

"There is nothing to forgive, dear." He kissed her forehead and smiled. "You are a true patriot and loving daughter who demonstrates a deep caring for her old father. I love you. Shall we prepare for our guests now?"

Emily smiled at him and took his arm. "Yes, we shall."

"Sir, a word with you?"

"Now? What is it with you two?"

"It will only take a moment." Frank smiled at Emily and motioned with his head for her to excuse them.

Emily withdrew her hand from her father's arm. "Please do not linger long."

She eased the door closed behind her and went with Amy upstairs. But her thoughts stayed in the library. What did Frank need to say to her father in private?

"The sun had faded long ago, hiding behind the ominous clouds sweeping across dead trees. A rattle and clatter echoed through the bare limbs, chilling the three travelers to the bone, but it was only the long claws of the trees scraping against each other in the biting wind."

Emily appreciated the new story Amy had written for her father to read. Apparently the crowd gathered around the fireplace did as well, for they intently listened to each word.

"An enjoyable evening as always." Frank handed her a cup of warm apple cider.

She sipped and smiled. "Thank you, Frank, for everything."

He kissed her hand. "My love, it is entirely my pleasure."

Jasmine appeared in the door of the upstairs parlor and caught Emily's eye as she glanced past Frank's shoulder. Emily nodded at the silent message.

"Only one man survived that horrifying night, and he never spoke of what happened. The end." Her father leaned back in his storytelling throne and smiled at the applause he received at the conclusion of the story.

As the commotion died down, Emily stepped forward and clapped her hands twice. "Dinner is served, everyone. If you'll make your way down to the dining room, we'll eat momentarily."

Samantha appeared at her side, smiling. "That was a wonderful story."

"Be sure to tell Amy," Emily replied. "She has such a gift."

After they took their seats at the expansive table laden with savory meats, vegetables, relishes, and fruits, the sound of laughter and conversation filled the cheery room.

Emily perused the faces around the table, smiling at each in turn. Her father sat at the head of the table, holding court over the proceedings. Emily sat at his right hand, with Frank beside her. Frank's leg casually rested against hers, keeping a constant intimate connection between them. Samantha and Amy sat across from her, with Uncle Richard and Aunt Lucille beside them. She noticed an empty seat beside Frank.

"Who is late for dinner?" she whispered to him. "I cannot think who it is."

"Benjamin will join us shortly." He sliced through the roast duck on his plate. "He is anxious to become reacquainted with Miss Amy."

"How intriguing."

"Isn't it?" Frank chewed with a knowing smile.

"I dare say Amy will not be pleased with such an event." Emily sipped her wine and watched her cousin engage in an animated conversation with the older man beside her.

"I suppose we shall find out, since he has just arrived."

Benjamin moved lithely through the arched opening. Frank stood, drawing his attention, and motioned for Benjamin to join them. Frank remained standing until his friend reached the empty seat.

Amy looked at Emily, dismay haunting her eyes. Amy did not want to reconnect with Benjamin, although Emily only had her suspicions as to why. Now Amy had no escape. Emily shrugged at her cousin and best friend. Amy closed her eyes briefly in resignation, then shrugged as well, though her posture remained rigid.

"Have a seat, my friend." Frank motioned to the empty chair. "You're just in time."

Frank looked at Emily, intently searching her face. He tapped his knife lightly against his flute of wine, holding it aloft as he gazed about the room. The conversation stopped, and everyone watched him expectantly.

When he turned to Emily, her heart skittered at the love shining in his eyes. "I wanted you all as witnesses when I ask this lovely, intelligent woman if she will consent to become my wife. Emily, darling, I love you and want to spend the rest of my life with you. Will you marry me?"

She glanced around the sea of faces, where hopeful expectations reflected back at her.

Amy nodded, wiping at her eyes. Her father waited, one hand braced on the table, the other holding his flute filled with wine hovering above the linen tablecloth. Samantha grinned and inclined her head in encouragement.

Emily looked at Frank, her love for him engulfing her heart. She had her answer.

"Yes."

"You've made me so very happy, my love." He took both her hands and helped her stand beside him. "I love you so. I'll always be at your side to protect you."

He kissed her, a long, lingering touching of their mouths. A joining of their love and lives.

"Now you have to marry him." Benjamin chuckled. "Three cheers to the newly engaged couple."

"Huzza! Huzza! Huzza!" echoed around the room as everyone joined in the celebration.

Darting a look at Benjamin, Amy rose from her chair and

pushed it backward with a scrape. Muttering "excuse me," she fled the room.

Emily watched her friend hurry through the door and noted with a smile when Benjamin also rose and excused himself. Perhaps another romance stood poised to blossom in the near future. Frank cleared his throat, and she returned her gaze to him.

He searched Emily's eyes and smiled. "Would you agree to a traditional wedding on Twelfth Night? Will that give you enough time to prepare?"

"Perfect. Mayhap this war will be over and we'll have even more to celebrate."

"We can hope." He kissed her again, watching her response. "I love you, Em."

"I love you." She kissed him, then smiled into his eyes. "Together we'll form a perfect union."

The End

Thanks so much for reading *Emily's Vow*! I hope you enjoyed Emily and Frank's story. Turn the page for a sneak peek at the next story in the series, *Amy's Choice*!

To find out about new releases and upcoming appearances, please sign up for my newsletter via my website at www.bettybolte.com. I send out a monthly newsletter with book news to share with my readers, upcoming events and signings, and even a few favorite recipes, puzzles, and other doings!

I'd love to hear from you! Feel free to send me an email at betty@bettybolte.com, find me on Facebook at AuthorBettyBolte, follow me on BookBub, or connect with me on Twitter @BettyBolte.

You can always find an updated list of the titles in this series, as well as all of my other books on my website, at www.bettybolte.com/books/.

Thanks again for reading!

$\mathcal{A}$ my glanced at him and then glided to her chair across from his. Defeated, he slowly sat back down and sipped from the cup of coffee. Emily had poured more into the cup while Amy distracted him, and the liquid churned in his empty stomach.

"Benjamin, what brings you out here so early this morning?" Walter slathered yellow butter on yet another slice of bread.

Amy kept her eyes on her plate, but her movements slowed, indicating she listened intently.

"General Leslie made an important announcement last week, one that increases the chance of violent retaliation and looting by the British troops as they prepare to evacuate the city." Benjamin kept his eyes on Walter but watched Amy's actions at the side of his vision.

"Is the war finally over then?" Walter laid down his knife, eyes intent on Benjamin.

"It appears to be, all but the acts of signing the peace treaty and evacuating the king's troops."

"When might that happen?" Emily fisted her napkin and gazed at him with hopeful eyes.

"As soon as conditions allow them to leave the harbor. But between now and then they will scavenge for any items of value they can lay their hands upon." He willed Amy to look at him, and finally she rewarded him by lifting her eyes to meet his. The force of her gaze sent a shock racing through him, stirring a reaction below his belt. Shifting to be more comfortable, he held her stare for a moment.

"But how does that impact us out here?" Amy regarded him, one hand poised above her plate, a bite of ham waiting. "Surely the Britons will not harm us so far from town. They'll be busy preparing to evacuate."

"Clearly you do not fathom the reality of the matter." When Amy merely stared at him, realization dawned as to the extent of the situation before him. He nearly let out a loud breath in annoyance. He checked the reflex. He needed to address the fact that Amy wasn't the only one in danger. Ideas popped into his head and he dismissed several before nodding. A simple solution. "I have come to take the girls back to town where I can keep them safe."

A startled silence followed his pronouncement.

"We are safe here." Samantha strode into the room and made straight for the sideboard.

Benjamin rose to greet her, and she waved him back into his seat. As he resettled himself, he noted Walter had not moved from where he sat crunching on a slice of apple.

"Yes, more so than we'd be in town at any rate." Emily looked from one person to another. "So many soldiers still roam the streets, after all."

"Besides, we cannot move Evelyn." Amy held knife and fork poised to slice through the ham. "I won't leave her here alone. She needs help until the baby arrives, and for a span after."

"She has me." Walter laid his hands flat on the table at either side of his plate. "I can take care of her."

Why did Walter brace himself as he spoke about his wife? Benjamin recognized the defensive nature, an insecurity, exemplified in Walter's behavior.

Amy darted a glance at Walter, then returned her gaze to Benjamin. "That's my fear."

Her mouth formed a stubborn pout as her eyes reflected her concern. What had occurred here to provoke such a statement? Amy glanced at Walter with unease plain in her expression, her distrust of the man evident. Despite himself, Benjamin tensed at the idea of Amy living under the same roof as Walter.

"I know how to defend myself, so I'll stay." Samantha placed her napkin in her lap. "More to the point, Evelyn will deliver any day now, and she'll need me."

Walter looked like he wanted to say something but held his thoughts in check. His brow lowered as he dipped his bread into his coffee. Walter did not act as refined in character as his appearance first suggested. More pieces to the puzzle fell into place, but still some holes remained before Benjamin formed an opinion of him.

"You'll need help with running this place." Emily laid her napkin on the table, her eyes steady on Samantha. "I'm accomplished at that, so I will stay to assist."

Seeing where this was leading, Benjamin made an effort to change the conversation's course. "In the event, Miss Amy stays with me." He spoke with less conviction than earlier as his resolve wilted under the arguments put forth by the women surrounding him. "I can't stay away from town long, not only because Captain Sullivan expects me to ensure the museum collection is not touched, but also because Amy's father requested I bring my betrothed back posthaste."

A feminine gasp drew his eyes to Amy's startled expression. *Damnation.* Too late, he realized his error as, in rhythm with three blinks, her stubborn expression shifted to surprise, then anger.

"Pardon me?" Her eyebrows arched over wide eyes. "You are betrothed? To whom, pray tell?"

The set of her jaw dared him to say what he must in order to tell the truth of the matter. An attack of cotton mouth forced him to try to swallow as he searched for the proper response.

How crass could he be, blurting out his bald intent? His carefully prepared speech blown apart by his own foolish words. Again, words had tripped him up and left him floundering. Yet, his mother would be proud of him for sticking to the facts, even if they created an awkward moment. He heaved a sigh. Nothing for it but the bare truth. "I spoke with your parents a few days ago, and they agreed…"

"Stop." Amy, face red, held up a hand as though warding off a blow. "Pray, don't tell me my parents actually negotiated with you for my hand?"

Betty Bolté is known for authentic and accurately researched American historical fiction with heart and supernatural romance novels. She has published more than 20 books of fiction and nonfiction topics. She earned a Master's Degree in English in 2008, emphasizing the study of literature and storytelling, and has judged numerous writing contests for both fiction and nonfiction.